Deadly

Reigns

A novel

Caleb Alexander

© 2017 by Caleb Alexander

ISBN-13 978-0-9890349-5-1

ISBN-10 0-9890349-5-X

Cover Design: Oddball Designs

Chapter One

The Gulfstream private jet was parked in the middle of a deserted stretched of road in the middle of West Texas. There was nothing but desert, dirt, and oil derricks as far as the eye could see, bobbing up and down and sucking precious black crude oil from the bowels of the earth. And then there were bodies. Nearly a hundred bodies stretched up and down the sides of the highway, lashed to the oil derrick pumps that occupied the both sides of the highway. The stench of death and decay permeated the air.

Damian, Nicanor, and the rest of their men held hand kerchiefs over the lower half of their faces, trying to mitigate the miasmic stench. Flocks of buzzards circled overhead, while many others feasted up and down the highway, on the decaying corpses that provided easy nourishment. Some of Damian's men began to vomit.

"He's lost it," Nicanor told Damian. "Completely, he's completely gone. I fought in every single conflict in Central America in the 80's. I fought with the Contra's, I fought against the Contras. I fought with the Sandinista's, I fought against the Sandinistas. I've witnessed the most barbaric shit anybody could ever imagine, but I've never seen anything like this before."

"Where is he?" Damian asked.

"Somewhere along the Mexican border," Nicanor answered. "Damian, he's gone. His mind is gone."

"Find him," Damian ordered. "Find Dante, and bring him to me."

"Finding him is the easy part," Nicanor explained. "Bringing him back, well, not so much. He's not going to come willingly; he's not going to stop his search for one second."

"He needs help."

Nicanor peered around the scene. "This is beyond help."

"My brother is never beyond help," Damian replied, his voice becoming agitated.

Nicanor turned toward Damian. "All of our political cover is running, all of our police contacts, our politicians, everyone, is running from us. Nobody wants to be associated with this, nobody. He's destroying the family and causing irreparable damage."

"That's why I want him brought in."

"He's not going to come willingly."

"What are you trying to say?"

"Look around you, Damian!" Nicanor shouted. "Look! He's destroying everything that took us years to build. He's killing policemen and politicians like it's free! He needs to be stopped!"

"What the fuck do you think I'm trying to do!"

"You're going to have to wake up to the fact that you may have to choose!"

"Choose?"

"Choose between stopping Dante, or destroying the family." Nicanor told him. "You may have to put him down."

Nicanor's words hit Damian like a ton of bricks. The thought that he would have to harm his brother was beyond imagination. There was no doubt that Dante's actions were destroying the family, and that they would have lasting repercussions, but he could never harm his brother. The alternative would be to go down in flames? To lose the family? To go to federal prison for the rest of his life? To watch the thousands of men who worked for him be picked off and murdered one by one by other organizations sensing his family's imminent downfall? What was the alternative? He could never do anything to hurt Dante, or anyone else in his family. Even when he was beefing with his sister, he couldn't bring himself to kill her.

"Nicanor," Damian said, calling out to his sidekick. "I want you to find Dante, and I want you to bring him to me."

Nicanor shrugged his shoulders. "Sure thing, Boss."

5

"Alive," Damian added, rolling his eyes at his underling.

Nicanor nodded.

Damian turned, and headed back toward his waiting private jet. The pilot began to spool up the engines.

"Get these bodies taken down!" Damian shouted.

"Yes, sir!" Keith, another of his henchmen shouted.

"Keep this road closed until they are all taken down!" Damian told him.

"Sir," Keith asked nervously, stopping at the steps of Damian's jet. "What do we do with all of the bodies?"

Damian walked up the steps of the G659 jet and surveyed the carnage. Crows rested on top of some of the decaying heads, picking out rotting eyeballs and pieces of brain matter. There were men, woman, and in some cases, even children scattered up and down the highway. He knew that his brother had crossed the line.

"Bury them, Keith," Damian told him.

"Do we identify them," Keith asked, swallowing hard. "You know, to notify the families?"

Damian peered at the bodies. "I doubt it if any of them have any family left. Just take them down, burn them, and then bury the ashes."

Damian turned, walked up the remaining steps into the lush cabin of his private jet, leaving his men to perform the gruesome task of cleaning up the results of his brother's rage. The jet's engine came to full throttle, and soon, Damian was once again sky-borne. He peered out of the window at the scene below, thinking of how sick and demented the entire landscape had become. His brother's mind had entered into a dark place, a place where few men ever come back from. He knew that Nicanor was right. When men enter those places, they are no longer men, they become monsters. And he knew in his heart that monsters couldn't be allowed to roam the countryside. He wondered if he would have to order of mercy killing of his baby brother.

*****

Sheriff Mendoza woke to find men in dark suits standing around his bedroom. One of them seated himself on the edge of the bed. Instinctively, Sheriff Mendoza reached for the weapon he kept in a bed holster fastened to his bed.

"It's gone," Dante told him. "And so is the one in your nightstand, the one behind the headboard, your service weapon that you keep on the dresser, they're all gone."

Sheriff Mendoza sat up in bed. His heart was now beating rapidly. Something was wrong. His wife? Where was his wife, he wondered?

"Where..."

"She's safe," Dante told him. "For now."

Sheriff Mendoza's eyes began to focus. He recognized the man sitting at the foot of his bed. That alone told him the reason for this middle-of-the-night visit.

"I had nothing to do with the disappearance of your daughter," Sheriff Mendoza told him. "Nothing! You've got to believe me!"

"I believe you," Dante said calmly. "I know you probably didn't have anything to do with her kidnapping. I just don't think that you've been searching hard enough to find her. I'm wondering, since you're not doing all that you can, then would your replacement do better? I need someone on the team, someone who is going to give it their all. I need someone who will think of my daughter as if their own child was in danger. I need someone who feels my pain."

"Dante, please!" Sheriff Mendoza pleaded. "I'm doing all that I can. I have men on it. I even assigned a detective to the case!"

"I came here tonight, prepared to kill you," Dante told him. "And now, now I'm not so sure. Looking into those big brown eyes of yours I see something. I see a man who understands what it's like to lose his children. A man who understands what's it's like to have his family's life in another man's hands. You know what, Mendoza? I think we've had a breakthrough. I think that we can communicate a lot better now that we're on the same page."

"Dante, I swear to you, on the life of Mi Madre..."

Dante held up his hand, silencing the Sheriff in mid-sentence. "No need for all of that. What I want to know, is what you know. I want to know about strange men checking into local hotels, unknown vehicles coming through your town in the middle of the night, I want to know about traffic cameras and what they picked up the day my daughter was kidnapped. I want to know everything that you know."

Sheriff Mendoza nodded. "You can have the entire file. Everything, you can have it all."

Dante rose from the edge of the bed and slapped the Sheriff across his knee. "That's the spirit. That's the team spirit that I've been looking for. Too bad it took a visit in the middle of the night to get it from you."

"My wife..."

Dante waved his hand dismissing the Sheriff's concerns. "She's fine. Look, you get that file over to me, all of the camera footage that points to that one lone artery out of this one-horse, shit-kicker town, and we'll forget about your previous lack of enthusiasm. Send it over by carrier in the morning, would you?"

The Sheriff swallowed hard and nodded.

Dante started to leave, but stopped and turned back. "I'll be expecting to get word that a packaged arrived from you at 09 A.M. sharp, understand?"

The Sheriff nodded. Sweat poured down his pudgy face as he contemplated the fate of his family.

Dante whistled, and he and his men left the bedroom. The Sheriff could hear them climbing inside of their cars, and then see the headlights as the vehicles pulled away. He rubbed his eyes and climbed out of bed. He feared the horror that awaited him in the other room. He knew that his family was going to be bound and gagged with bullets in their heads. His thoughts were of the worse consequences, when his wife and children ran into his bedroom and hugged him. Sheriff Mendoza broke into tears. His family had been untouched. For now.

Chapter Two

Damian strolled into the living room of the Reign's family's ranch house loosening his tie. He had decided to stay at the family homestead for a few days instead of his mansion in town, because he felt that he needed to unwind. There was so much on his plate right now, with Lucky being kidnapped, his family's political protection running for cover, his new connection in Mexico screaming for the violence to stop. And then there was Princess in Florida, trying to retake and hold on to that state, and then there was California...again. There was always someone in California trying to take over and make moves. The idea that the California drug market was controlled from Texas was unthinkable to a lot of people in that state. California hated Texas in everything from sports, to politics, to even the undercover drug world. Since he took the state, it had been a constant pain in his ass. And then there was Dante.

Damian rubbed his temples trying to lessen the tension that was building in his head. Soon, he would have a full-on migraine if he didn't shut down his thoughts and grab a drink and relax. A nice stiff drink, and then he would climb into bed, close his eyes, and try to get some much-needed rest. He headed for the bar in the family room.

To Damian's surprise there was a guest seated on the couch. Well, not really a guest, but a surprise.

"Aunt Libby?" Damian asked.

His Aunt Libby was married to his Uncle Gideon, his father's twin brother. The two of them had been together since college, long before he and any his siblings had been born. She had always been his aunt. And Gideon had always been his favorite uncle.

"Hey, baby," Libby said, placing her champagne glass down on the coffee table and rising to hug him. She was as beautiful and elegant as ever. She reminded him of a cross between Nancy Wilson and Claire Huxtable. She was sophisticated, poised, polished, educated, and always together. She could throw sophisticated shade with the best of them, or read you your rights with her head shaking and her finger waving if necessary. Even now, she was dressed to the nines. A Louis Vuitton scarf was draped around her neck, hanging stylishly down her Louis Vuitton dress. Her shoes were also Louis, while her diamond and pearl earrings were Cartier. Her Hermes' Kelly bag sat next to her on the couch.

Libby embraced her nephew tight, and then kissed him gently on his cheek. "How are you doing, baby?"

"I'm good," Damian said with a smile. "Why didn't you let me know you were coming? Where's Uncle G?"

Libby sat back down on the couch, and patted the empty space next to her, motioning for Damian to sit. "He's in Atlanta. I came alone."

"Is everything okay?" Damian asked. "Can I get you something? Have you eaten already?"

Libby waved her hand dismissing him. "I'm fine, Suga! I had the driver take me to Ruth Chris as soon as I landed. I had lunch with some of my old girlfriends."

"So, what's been happening? Damian asked, taking the seat next to her. "How have you guys been? And the rest of the fam?"

"Everyone's fine," Libby said with a smile. She took his hand into hers. "Actually, those are the questions that I have for you."

"What do you mean?" Damian asked, lifting an eyebrow.

"How is your brother?" Aunt Libby asked. She paused for a few moments, and then continued. "How is the search going for that sweet baby?"

Damian exhaled and leaned back in his seat. "Not good."

"What do you mean?"

"We can't find her," Damian explained. "It's like she's disappeared off the face of the earth. Every day that passes, the trail grows colder. And..."

He wanted to say that with each body that Dante piled up, the trail also grew colder.

Libby could see the worry in his eyes. "Everything is going to be okay. I've been praying for you, and for Dante, and for that baby! Everything is in God's hands, and we must trust in His wisdom and judgment. Understand?"

Damian nodded. She was telling him to be prepared for Lucky not being found alive. The thought *had* crossed his mind, and with each passing day, he knew that the chances of finding her alive grew slimmer. No one could say that to Dante of course. He had already snapped, and would instantly kill anyone who even suggested such a thing.

Libby caressed Damian's hand and exhaled forcibly. "I want to talk to you about something."

Damian sat up. "What's the matter?"

"Your uncle," Aunt "Libby said, hesitating, as if trying to find the right words.

"Everything's okay?" Damian frowned. "Uncle Gid is okay, isn't he?"

"Absolutely!" Libby said with a half-smile. "In fact, he's better than okay." Libby released Damian's hand and rose from the sofa. She wiped her palms on her dress, lifted her drink and sipped from it. "Your Uncle has been nominated for the United States Court of Appeal for the 11th Circuit."

Damian leaped from the sofa. "Are you serious? That's good!" He hugged her.

"Well, therein lies the problem," Libby continued after their embrace. She straightened her dress and her pearls. "The nomination is a formality. He's been approved before by the Senate, and he has bi-partisan

14

support. They're expecting his nomination to sail through."

"So, what's the problem?" Damian asked.

"The search for Lucky," Aunt Libby said nervously. "Dante is doing a lot of things..."

Damian closed his eyes and nodded slowly, upon realizing what his aunt was saying. It all made sense to him now. He now knew why she was there.

"He's not going to ever stop searching," Damian told her.

"Of course not!" Libby said. "He should never stop! I'm not saying that he should stop. But Damian, he's making a lot of noise. There are a lot of rumors swirling around, even in Atlanta."

Damian nodded. He understood completely. Dante's brutal tactics were making too much noise around the country, and could become an issue with his uncle's nomination as well as with his confirmation. Dante's bullshit was not only affecting his political cover, but now had the potential to damage his uncle's judicial career.

"I've asked some friends to go and get him, and bring him home so that I can talk to him," Damian told her.

"Good," Libby said, nodding. "Damian, you've always been the more sensible one. Talk to your brother. I know he's hurting, and he needs you now more than ever. Be understanding, but get him to see that in the longer term, he's damaging a lot of things, rather than helping. Take him to mass, pray, seek the peace of Christ.   Lucky is in God's hands, and so is her fate."

Damian nodded. He stretched and yawned. "I'm going to hit the sack. Have they made a bed for you?"

"Oh, no!" Libby said, shaking her head emphatically. "I'm staying at the Marriot Resort. I was going to stay here, but you have another guest."

"A guest?" Damian asked, lifting an eyebrow.

"Assata showed up." Libby said with a sly smile.

"Assata!" Damian nearly shouted.

Aunt Libby smirked and nodded. "She's in the shower."

Assata was his mother's baby sister. He and Asatta were only a few years apart in age, and she was a wild one. She got along with Aunt Libby like oil mixes with water.

"Thanks for the heads up," Damian said with a smile.

"Have fun!" Libby told him. She leaned in, and kissed Damian on his forehead. "Goodnight, Sweetie. Sweet dreams. You're going to need some rest."

Chapter Three

Princess stared at the screen on her phone, flipping through her Instagram, checking out all the photos her friends and family had posted. Occasionally she would lift her head and stare out of the window of her Cadillac CT6 limousine. Traffic in West Palm Beach was growing just as bad as in Miami. If it was one thing she hated more than anything, it was wasting her time, and to her, sitting in a traffic jam was the ultimate waste of her super valuable time.

Princess wondered if buying a helicopter would be more practical. It would be better than traffic, but then there would be the issue of finding landing zones close to where she wanted to go. And if it just took her from airfield to airfield, then she would still run into traffic taking a limo from the airfield to where it was she needed to get to. She hated Southern Florida for this reason alone. Too many damn people. Everyone wanted to live in paradise.

Princess lowered the divider separating the passenger compartment from the driver. "Can you re-route us and get us out of this mess?"

"Yes ma'am!" the driver said. He leaned forward, and begin to find an alternate route on the car's navigation system.

"When you find a better route, let the others know," Princess ordered her man riding shotgun next to the driver.

"Yes, ma'am."

The front seat passenger lifted his walkie-talkie. "We're re-routing to get around this traffic, over."

"Roger that." Came back over the walkie-talkie.

"Roger that." Another voice replied.

"Copy that," A third voice said.

Princess's CT6 limo was in the middle of a security convoy that included two long, black, Escalade ESV's to the front, and two more trailing her in back. There was also a second black CT6 chase car about a half mile behind, and another black Escalade about a half mile in front to scout the route. Those cars, would be too far away to matter however.

Princess herself was the first to spot the massive garbage trucks barreling through traffic heading in her direction. They were smashing through cars, knocking them to the side like they were Tonka toys.

"Ambush!" Princess shouted. She pulled out her pistol, and then laughed at the thought. It wouldn't do her any good against the massive metal garbage trucks that were coming her way.

Men ran out of the buildings to her right wearing Barak Obama mask and carrying Ak-47 assault rifles. They opened fire on her convoy.

Out of habit, Princess ducked down. "Fuck! Get us the fuck outta here!"

"Yes, ma'am!" the driver shouted, trying to find a way out of the traffic jam.

The bullets struck the vehicle sending sparks flying everywhere. Her convoy was all armored with the latest in bullet resistant technology. They could withstand a direct hit from a first-generation RPG and not even take a dent.

"Get us the fuck outta here!" Princess shouted again.

She knew that bullet resistant glass was just that... resistant. It would eventually give way. She didn't want to find out how many rounds it could take before it did. At any rate, her armored limo was about to be put to the ultimate test; a masked attacker stepped out of a doorway holding a Russian made rocket propelled grenade launcher.

"RPG!" Princess shouted. She covered her head and ducked down.

Princess' driver hit the gas propelling the big limo forward, ramming the car in front of them, trying to create enough space to maneuver. The attacker squeezed the trigger on his rocket launcher propelling the grenade forward and into the limo's rear tire. The grenade exploded with such a force, that it pushed the extremely heavy limousine twelve feet from its original spot. What remained of the armored tire burned, causing a heavy, black, billowing smoke to permeate the air.

The attack happened so quick that the men in the chase vehicles barely had time to react. Once they realized that their principle was under attack, the security detail bolted into action. They poured out of the two black Escalades and started firing at their attackers. They also had a little surprise in store for the attackers as well. The roof of the second Escalade opened, and out of it, came a remotely controlled mounted mini-gun, that immediately spun into action. The buzz from the minigun tore through the air, while the flames pouring from its six barrels seemed to reach out and cut the attackers in half.

The men in the front Escalade of Princess' caravan also sprang into action. They pulled out their Israeli made Tavor assault rifles and begin to dispatch the attackers with military precision. Perhaps it was because all the men in her security detail were ex-military special forces. While the Reigns family hired foot soldiers from all walks of life, their bodyguards were all ex-military, and all ex-special ops. They didn't' take chances.

Two of the men in the forward Escalade had already spotted the massive yellow garbage trucks barreling toward them. They had seen this move many times in Iraq and Afghanistan during their many deployments. And they were prepared to handle it. They reached inside of the Escalade and pulled out a BOFORS Anti-tank rocket launcher, and a Carl Gustav recoilless rifle. The bodyguard that shouldered the anti-tank missile, aimed, and pulled the trigger. The missile shot out and raced toward the garbage truck, slamming into the cabin and exploding with such devastating force that the garbage truck virtually disintegrated before everyone's eyes. The bodyguard holding the Gustav squeezed his trigger, and sent his explosive round downstream toward the second garbage truck. The round hit lower front section of the cab and exploded, sending the cab of the garbage two hundred feet into the air. Pieces of the truck fell back down to the ground still burning.

"Move, move, move!" the bodyguards began shouting. Two of them raced to Princess' limo, opened the door, yanked her out, and basically carried her to the waiting Escalade in the front. A third bodyguard tossed explosive charges inside of Princess' disabled limo, and then raced and hoped into the back of another Escalade. The remaining detachment of bodyguards climbed inside of the Escalades and the cars pulled away, using the path that the garbage trucks made, as an escape route.

"Back to the Palace!" one of her bodyguards said, over the walkie-talkie.

"Roger!"

*****

Peaches landed in Ohio and walked through the United Terminal toward the exit. She didn't need to hit the baggage claim area, because everything she owned, she carried with her in the gym bag over her shoulder. Her mind drifted to that night at her home, and she could see the fires, hear the gunshots, and almost smell the smoke. She wondered what would be left, if anything of the home she abandoned that night. Very little remained of it, she imagined. The fires, the bodies, the blood; she pictured a scene out of one of those post apocalypse movies where there were bullet casings and blood splatters everywhere. She didn't know how many of her men made it out alive that night, if any. She needed to find Trap and V, and more importantly, she needed to find her brother, Joaquin. She needed to hug them, wrap her arms around them tight, and hold them. Her fears were starting to get the best of her.

Peaches could see the crowd of Black men in black suits just past the security screeners. She was certain they were all heavily armed, and that they weren't going to go anywhere near any of the metal detectors. Thank God she didn't have any luggage and needed any help, or else she have to struggle with it on her own until she got past the metal detectors.

She knew that they were Reigns men because of the way they looked. The Reigns' family's soldiers could be spotted from a mile away. They were always well groomed, and they all had on suits that looked like they cost more than the average person's monthly paycheck. These were no different. They stood out in the Columbus airport like a sore thumb. Forty Black men in dark Armani, Brioni, and Kiton suits, and all wearing dark sunglasses would stand out anywhere.

"Peaches!" Brandon Reigns called out to her and stepped forward from the others. He recognized her from the photo on his cellphone that Darius had sent to him.

Peaches tossed her bag onto the conveyer so that it could go through the x-ray scanner, and hurried through the metal detector. She grabbed her bag and walked briskly to where Brandon was standing. He made her smile, because he looked like a Reigns. They all resembled one another.

"Brandon!" he said, extending his hand.

Peaches clasped his hand and shook it. "Peach."

"Josh," said another one of the suited men, stepping forward. She could tell that he too was a Reigns. "And that ugly individual over there is my cousin, DeMarcus."

Peaches shook Josh's hand, and waved at DeMarcus, who had a cell phone to his ear and was talking intensely. He waved back, and then turned to his cousin.

"Hey, B," DeMarcus called out. "The cars are pulled out front, and the escort says that road is clear. We're ready to roll."

One of the Reigns' hulking, suited men, took the bag from her shoulder and tossed it onto his own. Another waved for them to proceed, while others began talking into their barely visible ear pieces. She was quickly engulfed and surrounded by a sea of well-dressed Black men, with fresh cuts and expensive cologne. To her surprise, when they emerged from the airport, there was a line of 2018 Black Label Lincoln Navigators waiting. But what was even more surprising, was that there were at least a dozen motorcycle cops waiting in the front and the back of the large convoy on luxury SUVs.

Peaches climbed into the back of one, and she was accompanied by DeMarcus, Josh, and Brandon, along with a couple of other men.

"The cops..." Peaches asked, staring out the window.

"They're ours," Brandon said with a smile. "They're off duty right now, so we hire them for escort to get us around town and through the traffic quicker."

The way he said the word *'ours'* sounded weird to her. It was what made her notice that all the motorcycle cops were Black. Brandon twirled his finger, and the convoy pulled off.

"So, we have you set up at the Le Meridien," Josh told her.

"The St. Joseph?" Peaches asked, lifting an eyebrow. "That's in Short North."

Brandon laughed. "You thinking about the Short North Posse? Don't worry about them."

"But..."

Brandon held up his hand. "I know all about Young and Holding, and the beef you have with Short North, and with the Get Money Boyz. The Reigns family got you. You'll have more than enough security to move around safely."

"Yeah, my lil cousin told me to make sure I take care of you," Josh told her. "I can see why."

DeMarcus nudged him. "Cut it out."

"She know she's fine," Josh said winking at Peaches.

"Have you heard anything about my brother?" Peaches asked.

Brandon exhaled and shook his head. "We're searching. I've got people on the force out doing what they can as well. Let us handle that. You focus on putting your organization back together. You need to get strong, and you need to get strong fast. Damian doesn't want Ohio to be a sitting duck for too long. Right now, your state is easy picking for anyone who wants to roll in. The Italians, the Russians, the Serbs, hell, anyone on The Commission."

Peaches nodded.

"You need to recruit, but you need to recruit people you can trust," Brandon continued. "I know it sounds fucked up. We're telling you to hurry, but be careful. It's an oxymoron."

DeMarcus lowered the phone from his ear. "Peaches, my cousin is being nice. The truth is, the situation is fucked up. You don't have much time. We've pulled men from places we can't pull men from, and we need to send them back. Also, Damian doesn't want Ohio to be taken, but Damian doesn't know we're here. He can't find out that we pulled resources and sent them here. Eventually, he probably would have offered you the family's help, but not right now. As you probably know, our family is in a bit of a crises right now."

"Dante has every extra swinging dick we can muster beating the fucking Mexican border," Josh added.

I'm heading to Pennsylvania, and then Maryland," Brandon told her. "DeMarcus will be close by. Josh is staying here in Ohio with you to help out for as long as he can before he's missed. Again, I don't think we have much time."

"Can I go by my house?" Peaches asked.

DeMarcus, Josh, and Brandon all exchanged knowing looks.

"I need to see it," Peaches told them. "Please..."

Brandon rubbed his chin for a moment, and then nodded. His man sitting in the back spoke into his earpiece, and the train of big black Lincoln Navigators changed course.

Chapter Four

Brownsville Texas was known for heat and dust. The streets were barely paved, dust storms were common occurrences, and speaking Spanish was almost a must. It was about as close as one could get to Mexico, without actually *being* in Mexico.

Dante's caravan of big, black Mercedes G Wagon SUV's made its way through the trash hewn streets full of beggars, feral dogs, and impoverished merchants hawking their cheap wares. One of his men pressed his finger against his earpiece so that he could hear more clearly, and then leaned in to Dante.

"He's at Pizza Patron," his bodyguard told him.

"Pizza Patron?" Dante asked, lifting an eyebrow. "What the fuck is that?"

"It's like a Mexican Pizza Hut," the bodyguard replied. "Only nasty as fuck."

Dante laughed.

The caravan pulled into the parking lot of the Mexican pizza restaurant, and his men quickly descended onto the place from all directions. Dante could see the sheriff's patrol car in the parking lot, parked next to a couple of other suspect vehicles. He knew from the looks of them that they were unmarked Fed cars. He had gotten lucky, and caught all his fish in one net.

Dante climbed out of the back of the Black, armored, G-Wagon that he was riding in, fixed his tie, smoothed out his waves, and then headed inside. His men had the entire place on lockdown. The man that he had come to see, was sitting in the front of the restaurant with three other gentlemen.

Sheriff Frederico Pena, Agent Joey Carmona, Agent Richardo Rentenia, and Officer Brian Diaz, what a pleasant surprise to find you all here!" Dante said, approaching the table. "Well, pleasant for me anyway. Maybe not too pleasant for you."

"Don't go too far, Dante," Agent Joey Carmona told him.

"Too far?" Dante asked, pressing his hand against his chest. "You hear that Fat Freddy? Your buddy Agent Fat Joey here, says don't go too far."

Dante slapped DEA Agent Carmona across the back of his head. The agent instinctively reached for his weapon and tried to stand, the sound of Dante's men pulling out their weapons and cocking them, froze the agent in his tracks. He quickly realized, it would be suicide. Dante's men relieved the men sitting at the table of their weapons.

"It's already gone too far, Fat Joey!" Dante told him. "When my daughter was taken from me, it was *too* far!"

"Nobody here has anything to do with that!" Sheriff Pena said forcefully.

"I think everyone here, has something to do with it!" Dante shouted. "Because it looks to me, like instead of you being out there looking for her, you're in here, stuffing your fat greasy faces with disgusting Mexican pizza!"

Dante leaned forward and wrapped his arm around Agent Rentenia, of the U.S. Border Patrol and Customs Agency. "My daughter isn't enjoying a pizza right now, is she? You think she's enjoying a pizza?"

"Look, Dante," Agent Rentenia started. "We're all sorry about what happened to your daughter. We understand how you feel?"

"Oh, you *do*?" Dante asked with a smile. "You understand how I feel? Your daughter is missing?"

Agent Rentenia shook his head. "No."

"Then how the *fuck* can you understand how I feel!" Dante shouted. "Your fat asses are in here gobbling up pizza, and divvying up the cartel's money, while my baby is out there alone and afraid, and wondering why her daddy hasn't rescued her yet. You know how I *feel*?"

"Dante, we have the border on lock down," Border Patrol Commander Officer Brian Diaz chimed in. "No one is getting her out of this country, and across that border."

"Well, that's nice to know," Dante said, shaking his head. "You're finally earning your paycheck. I mean, that is what we're paying you all for, isn't it? You've been eating off my family for years, and your check has never been late, has it? But now, the four of you fat fucks are in here, doing what, planning your next hit? Working out how you gonna get the next shipment across for the cartel? Divvying up the money they're paying you? Doing everything but being loyal to the hand that has fed your fat greasy asses."

"You know I've always been loyal, Dante," Sheriff Pena told him.

"Which family are you fucks in here working for right now?" Dante asked. "Sinaloa? Zacatecas? Juarez? Chihuahua? Sonora? Michoacan, Guadalajara? Jalisco? Don't tell me Tamaulipas because then that will lead me to believe that my daughter is sitting across the border in some cheap fucking motel in Matamoros. Why are the four of you here right now? What are you planning?"

"It's nothing, Dante," Agent Carmona said, shaking his head. "It has nothing to do with your daughter, or the Reigns family."

"Give me a name," Dante told them.

The four men eyeballed one another uneasily, with none wanting to speak.

"Dante, the extra money has been short since the feds shut down the border," Officer Diaz finally explained. "Everyone is strapped for cash. The cartels are at each other's throats across the border, nothing is getting through."

"And?" Dante asked.

"The Mexicali Cartel just needed us to get a few trucks through," Officer Diaz told him. "Nothing long term, just some quick bread in everyone's pockets. We're still loyal to your brother, to your family, to you!"

Dante smiled. "Are you stupid, or are you dumb? The Mexicali boys have been trying to make a play for California for how long? And who owns California now?"

Officer Diaz lowered his head. "You do."

Dante nodded. "That's right! And if they are getting shipments through, even if they are coming in through Texas, they are definitely going back where?"

"Cali," Diaz answered, his voice barely audible.

"And if they have dope in Cali, while we're barely getting it because our suppliers in Mexico are putting pressure on us to stop the war, who will get stronger while we're vulnerable?"

"They will," Diaz answered, his voice barely a whisper.

"Officer Diaz, go to the head of the fucking class!" Dante shouted. "I didn't come here for this, but I'm glad that we're having this little conversation. Initially, this was a motivational trip, to see if I could get you guys to be enthusiastic about finding my daughter. But now, this has turned into a shop keeping trip. I now have to shore up our organization and make sure that we don't end up losing California, because I have a bunch of fat, lazy, double crossing, disloyal cops in the Rio Grande Valley, conspiring to make a buck off of my family's woes. And now, I'm pissed."

"Dante, we're still loyal to your family!" Sheriff Pena told him. "We just needed a little cash. We all

31

have families too. Our people have families that need to be looked after. We're on board."

"Who did Mexicali bring this little idea to?" Dante asked.

"It doesn't matter," Agent Carmona told him.

"It wasn't Fat Freddy, and it wasn't Stupid Brian," Dante said, lifting a finger. "No, it had to be one of you feds. One of you feds took a trip to California, and got approached. And something tells me that it wasn't the fed from Customs, so that leaves the little piggy from the DEA."

"They approached me with the idea, and it was a quick way for us to make some cash until things got back right with your family," Agent Carmona confessed. "Look, like Brian said, it's just temporary. We just need to keep our people's heads above water. Cops have mortgages too. Our kids need braces, health insurance, dresses for prom. It was nothing personal, Dante."

"Then why am I taking personal, Agent Carmona?" Dante asked. "We're supposed to be family. When one part of the family is suffering, then we're all supposed to feel it. You haven't been feeling our family's pain."

Dante nodded at his men. Three of them grabbed the DEA Agent and lifted him out of his seat. They followed Dante around the counter and into the back of the restaurant where the pizza making equipment was. Dante stopped in front of one of the massive pizza ovens, and nodded to his men. They slammed Agent Carmona down onto the counter and held him.

"There is a burning sensation that you feel inside when something is wrong with your child," Dante told him. Your entire body is on fire. You're desperate to get to your child and save them, and there is a heat and anger and frustration that wells up inside when you can't get to them fast enough. That is what our family is feeling. You, as a part of this family, should feel that way too."

Dante's men stuff Agent Carmona into the fiery hot pizza oven head first. The agent's skin quickly began to melt, as did his hair, eyebrows, and eyelashes. He screamed like a wounded animal.

Dante nodded, and his men pulled the agent from the fire. His face was red, blistered, and disfigured. Some of his hair had melted and fused to his forehead, while most of it had burned away. The upper part of the agent's jacket was still on fire. Dante patted the flames putting them out.

"I'll save you," Dante told the agent. He tossed some flour onto the agent's jacket, putting out the smoldering pieces of thread.

Agent Carmona stumbled to the sink, turned on the faucet, and stuck in head beneath the water. Dante grabbed him and pulled him from beneath the water.

"That was rude of you!" Dante told him. "I just saved you from burning, and you didn't even thank me for it."

Agent Carmona peered at Dante through the one eye that he could still open.

"I said, you didn't thank me!" Dante said forcefully.

"Thank you," Agent Carmona said, gasping for air, and still trying to catch his breath.

Dante turned to the others, who had followed them into the kitchen and watched the ghastly show. "If you can't feel like the rest of us feel, then I will *make* you feel it. If I have to stick you in a fire, to light a fire up under you, *I will do it*! I want you *motivated!* I want every fucking stone, every fucking rock, every fucking pebble on the fucking border turned over, until my daughter is found! If I come back to this shit hole, I am going to create a new recipe. I will make real Mexican pizza, with real Mexicans, is that clear?"

That law enforcement officers all nodded. Their eyes were wide with fear. Dante had just reminded them who he really was. It wasn't just about getting checks from the Reigns family, it was also about the obligations that went with that money. Dante reminded them that they had truly made a deal with the devil.

Dante walked past them heading for his vehicle. He stopped at the door. "Tell the Mexicali Cartel that the Reigns family said to go fuck themselves! Bring me their shipment, and don't even think about telling them that it got busted. You tell those motherfuckers that Dante took it. And if they have a problem with that, they can come and see me."

Florida

Princess rolled through the Little Havana section of Miami in her convoy of armored Black Cadillac Escalades. The caravan made a left off of 17th street and turned onto Calle Ocho, where they rolled through the heart of Miami's Cuban community. The community was close knit, and was highly suspicious of outsiders, but a caravan of Black Escalades didn't rouse any particular suspicions. Feds didn't roll in Escalades, only drug lords did, and her caravan appeared to be one with just another 'Jefe' rolling into the community for some authentic Cuban food. No one even thought twice about them.

"We're here," one of her men told her, as they made another turn and pulled to the side of the road. Her men climbed out of the SUVs and slowly made their way into the barber shop.

Princess climbed out of the back of the Escalade, fixed her white pants suit, and her matching white oversized hat which she wore tilted slightly to the side. She strolled into the shop where her target was lying reclined in a barber chair, with his eyes closed while being shaved. Princess walked up to the petrified barber, took the straight razor from his hand, and motioned for him to step to the side. The frightened barber moved away, and Princess carefully began to shave the man who she came to kill.

Princess's men removed the belt from their pants, and carefully made their way to the chair where her target was seated. Two of them wrapped their belts around his wrists, securing his arms to the chair, while two others secured his legs. Another wrapped his belt around the man's waist securing him securely to the seat. He opened his eyes and upon seeing what was happening, began to struggle.

35

"Cardon 'Papito' Reyes," Princess said, continuing to shave the struggling man. "Be very careful, or I could accidently slit your throat."

Reyes thought about the sharp blade sliding up and down his neck and quickly became still.

"You put a hit out on me, Papito," Princess continued. "But you missed."

"I don't know what you're talking about, Puta," Reyes told her.

"Your little garbage pail kid hit team ruined my brand-new Caddy," Princess told him. "And I kinda liked that car."

"No *comprende*," Reyes said, frowning at her.

"Oh, so now you don't speak English?" Princess asked with a smile.

"I don't know what the fuck you're talking about," Reyes answered.

Princess exhaled, and then continued to shave him. "I left Florida, once it was secured, and I went to Texas to repair things with my brothers. I'm in Texas, and things are moving along, and then my precious little niece is kidnapped. And this happens on my wedding day. And instead of me helping to find her, I have to come back to Florida, because I hear that a bunch of you Bay of Pigs rejects, are running around Miami and trying to partner with some Dominicans, and take away my territory."

"No *comprende', Puta!*" Reyes sneered.

"My question is, where are you getting the cocaine?" Princess asked. "That's my first question.

You see, cocaine flowing into Florida, and not coming from me, now that's a problem. Me having to come to Florida and kill all of you, well, that's not really a problem because I enjoy doing that. But, it just takes time, men, and resources away from me helping my brother. Any who, where's the fucking cocaine coming from?"

"*No tres nada, Puta!*" Reyes said, shaking his head.

Princess lifted the razor to his ear, and sliced off his earlobe, sending blood pouring down the side of his face. Reyes screamed.

"*Christo! Chingada Madre!*" Reyes said, cursing her in Spanish. "*Pinche Puta!*"

Princess ran the razor down the side of Reyes' face, slicing it open. Blood poured out of the wound down his neck. Reyes cried out in pain.

"Where is the cocaine coming from?" Princess asked calmly. "How is it getting in to the country, and how is it getting to Miami?"

"Do you know who I am?" Reyes screamed.

"Oh, so now you speak English again?" Princess smiled.

"Do you know who I work for?" Reyes shouted. "She's going to have your fucking head on a spit! *Pinche Perra!*"

Princess lifted the razor and sliced off a piece of Reyes' other ear, causing him to cry out in sheer agony.

"*Mierda!*" Reyes screamed. "I'm going to piss on you when she kills you!"

"She?" Princess asked, lifting an eyebrow. "Who the fuck is *she?*"

"*Mi Carajo! Pinche' Ramera!*" Reyes shouted. He started laughing hysterically. She's going to cut out your liver, and feed the rest of you to the fucking sharks!"

Princess backhanded Reyes, sending blood and saliva flying everywhere. "Who the fuck are you talking about?"

"Your days in Florida are numbered, *Puta!*" Reyes said, spitting at her feet. "She's has an army behind her, and you don't. Miami is gone!"

Princess took the razer, and sliced around Reyes' face, starting at his forehead, and making her way around his entire face. He screamed like a wounded animal.

"What the fuck are you talking about?" Princess shouted, losing her cool. "Who the fuck do you work for?"

"I work for Analiza Arriago Sataenilia, and she's going to cut your heart out," Reyes said, with blood pouring down his face. His voice was becoming slurred and he was losing consciousness from all the blood loss. "You know her as the Black Widow."

Princess pulled out her pistol and put it to Reyes head. She was about to pull the trigger when his head fell forward. She put her pistol away. It would be a waste of a bullet. She turned to her men.

"Pack it up, we're out of here," she told them, while heading for the exit. "Get Damian on a secure line for me once we get to the car. "I'm going to need more men in Florida."

Chapter Five

Damian's white extended wheelbase Rolls Royce Phantom wheeled across the tarmac of the airport toward the private jet section. He could see the White G-650ER Gulfstream jet sitting at the edge of the runway, parked in front of a private hanger and being refueled. His Rolls Royce limo pulled up to the jet near the stairs, and parked. He could see two burly bodyguards standing on each side of the staircase guarding the entrance onto the plane.

Damian climbed out of his Phantom and hurried up the steps and onto the aircraft, MiAsia was seated in the back of the nearly empty plane, with only a stewardess and two more bodyguards aboard. Upon seeing Damian, she waved her hand at her people dismissing them.

"*Qu*," MiAsia said in Mandarin, ordering them to leave. She wanted privacy with Damian.

Her employees walked past Damian and exited the airplane, leaving the two of them alone.

"So, you said you needed to meet with me?" Damian asked, lifting his arms. "What's this about?"

"The last time we met, you offered me *Plata or Plomo*," MiAsia told him.

Damian became slightly uneasy. She wasn't actually crazy enough to fly into Texas and try to pull something, was she, he wondered?

"And?" Damian asked, lifting an eyebrow.

MiAsia rose from her seat.

"I chose *Plata*," she said with a smile.

Damian returned her smile. "And?"

"And so," MiAsia said, walking toward him. "I'm here, to claim my spousal rights."

MiAsia untied the Kimono she was wearing, revealing her nakedness.

"Holy cow!" Damian said, swallowing hard, and taking in her gorgeous figure.

MiAsia wrapped her arms around Damian and stuck her tongue in his mouth. She then yanked off his suit jacket, tossed it onto a seat, and then ripped open his shirt. Her eyes went wide with surprise upon finding out that he was ripped.

"Oh, you've been hiding all of this beneath those expensive bespoke suits?" she asked with a smile. She rubbed her hand over his bulging chest and biceps, and then made her way down to his abs, and then his belt buckle, where she unbuckled his trousers.

Damian's pants fell to the floor. MiAsia pulled her Kimono down from her shoulders, allowing it to fall to the ground. She pushed Damian back onto a chair, and then yanked his boxers down. Her tongue went to work.

Damian leaned back in the expensive crème colored seats of the G 650 and inhaled deeply, as the warmth of MiAsia's mouth surrounded him. She worked him, sliding up and down his rod until it stood as unbendable as a flagpole. She slid her tongue up his abs, and made her way up his chest to his neck, and then climbed on top of him. Carefully, she placed him inside of her, and then hit the button on the side of his chair, reclining the plush leather seat.

Damian could feel every centimeter of her tight, wet flesh wrapped around him. He closed his eyes and clasped her round bottom, as she began to gyrate. MiAsia leaned forward and continued to kiss Damian's neck, suck on his earlobe, and emit soft watery moans of pleasure. Her moans in his ear, the firmness of her large bottom, and the tightness of her canal was driving him crazy. He was doing everything that he could to try to not cum too quick.

Work had gotten in the way of moments like this for Damian. He has been so focused on work, on money, on keeping Bio One afloat, on keeping Energia Oil afloat, on keeping his family's construction company, and entertainment company, and all their other businesses afloat, that he hadn't had time to sit back relax, and enjoy the softness of a woman. And then there was the search for Lucky, him being worried about his brother, his worrying about his political protection, the war with the Mexican Cartels, the supply from the Yucatan Cartels, The Old Ones,

The Columbians, Florida, California, and every Goddammed thing in between. He had so much shit on his plate that he hadn't even realized that he hadn't had sex in a long time. And so now, he was there, getting rode by a gorgeous woman, and about to bust a nut after only five minutes. He would have to tell his brothers, and they would ridicule his ass for the rest of his life. He had to hold it down, the reputation of the Reigns family men was at stake. He wasn't about to go out like a sucker, he told himself.

Damian sat up, lifted MiAsia in the air, and carried her to the wall, where he pinned her up against it. He held her in the air with her legs open, and began thrusting away. She wrapped her arms around his neck and her soft watery moans began to change with each of his thrust. He now knew that he was putting in work.

Damian fucked her until her cries of pleasure became a continuous stream, and once he realized that he had done his job properly, he let loose inside of her. The two of them came together.

MiAsia tapped Damian's shoulder. "Okay, let me down."

"Hold on," Damian told her. He was still coming inside of her, and he couldn't move.

After a few moments of holding her against the wall, they could both feel him stop throbbing inside of her, and they knew that he was done. Exhausted, Damian fell back into one of the sofas on the jet.

"Oh my God!" he said, breathing heavily.

MiAsia smiled. "I have a meeting to go to."

Damian felt as though his soul had been drained from his body.

"I do too," he told her. "Where's your wash room. I need to clean up."

"Clean up what?" MiAsia asked. "The only thing that needs cleaning is this."

MiAsia dropped to her knees in front of Damian, and took his penis into her mouth. She sucked the rest of the cum out of it, and all her juices off of it. Damian leaned back and closed his eyes.

"Oh my god!" Damian exclaimed. "What the fuck are you doing?"

MiAsia rose and smiled at him. "See, now you're all clean."

Damian could only sit back and stare at her. His first thought was, *nasty bitch.* His second thought was, what other tricks did she have up her sleeves if they had the time? His third thought was, he wanted her for himself. He didn't want her to do that to any other man, only him.

MiAsia tossed Damian his pants, his shirt, and his jacket. "Chop, chop! I gotta meeting in St. Louis I gotta get to."

"What?" Damian asked, still breathing heavily.

"I gotta go," MiAsia told him, lifting an eyebrow. "You're not retarded, are you? I have to leave. You know, fly away on the car with wings."

"Are you serious?" Damian asked.

"Damian Reigns," MiAsia said, pointing toward the door. "Get the fuck off my plane, sir."

Damian got dressed, while MiAsia walked into the bathroom. Once dressed, he started for the bathroom door but stopped.

"MiAsia!" he called out to her. "I'm leaving!"

"Okay, see you, Hun!" she shouted from behind the bathroom door. "It's been fun. We'll have to hook up again."

MiAsia opened the door. She had a cell phone to her ear. She waved and blew him a kiss, and then closed the bathroom door back.

Damian walked down the steps of the plane to his waiting Phantom, looking like he had seen a Ghost.

"Everything okay, boss?" one of his men asked.

"Yeah," Damian said, staring back at the plane. MiAsia's people were climbing back on board, and he could hear the generators spooling up to start the engines. "She just took my dick."

"What?"

Damian laughed. "She just fucked me, and threw me off her plane."

His bodyguard laughed.

Damian climbed inside his limo, and his bodyguard followed.

"Boss, I'm going to remind you of what you said to me, the first time you met my fiancé," the bodyguard told him. "You said, a woman like that, you either marry them, or you put a bullet in their head. And you said, after you marry them, you'll probably end up wanting to put a bullet in their head every day for the rest of your life."

Damian laughed. "I remember that. How'd that work out for you?"

"Been married to her ever since," the bodyguard told him. "And most days, I want to kill her, but I love the ground she walks on."

Again, Damian laughed.

"To the Campus," the bodyguard told the driver.

"Wait," Damian said, staring out the window at the plane that was now pulling off. "We're going to the meeting at Bio One. Maybe I need to run by the jewelry store first?"

Again, they laughed.

BIO One Campus

Damian strolled into the conference room of Bio One's shiny new multi-billion-dollar campus on the outskirts of San Antonio, and seated himself at the head of the table. The other attendees were already seated. His attorney, Cherin, leaned over and whispered in his ear.

"You're late," Cherin said with a smile. "Who was she?"

Damian smiled back. "Wouldn't you like to know?"

"Not really," Cherin said, smiling and shaking her head. She turned to the others. "Gentlemen, I believe we're ready to begin."

Dr. Wahlid Hakani, Damian's new chief scientist, rose and walked to a smart board. The lights dimmed slightly, and the smart board came alive. Damian lifted his hand.

"Yes, Mr. Reigns," Dr. Hakani asked.

"Before you even get started, I'm going to say what I say in all these meetings," Damian told him. "Explain everything to me, like I'm a six-year old. Do not throw around any medical, technical, or scientific terms like I went to MIT. Unfortunately, I only went to Harvard."

The others around the table laughed.

Dr. Hakani laughed, and cleared his throat. "Mr. Reigns, of late, we've been experimenting with a variety of breakthroughs. We're attacking cancer in a wide variety of ways. What we, and most others have been doing, was trying to find a cure, a way to destroy the cancerous cells and keep them from spreading and overtaking the good cells. While we're still doing that, we've made breakthroughs in other areas."

Damian nodded. "I'm with you so far, Doc."

Laughter went around the table.

"Let's see," Dr. Hakani paused, trying to find the words to break down the research into layman's terms. "I'll talk a little bit about each approach we're taking.

First, we have found a way to make cancerous cells identifiable to the drugs that we are using to attack them. One of the biggest problems with cancer treatment, is that it carpet-bombs your immune system, destroying everything in an effort to rid the body of the bad cells. This is the problem with chemo and radiation therapy. But, by modifying the cancerous cells, and making them produce a unique marker, we're able to precision bomb only the bad cells. This is less devastating to the good cells and the body's organs, which are not affected by the treatments."

"And how is this done, Doc?" Damian asked.

"By attaching a genomic marker at the cellular level that acts as a beacon, as well as a conduit," Dr. Hakani explained. "It says, here I am, and come on in. It marks the cell, and creates a pathway directly into the cell for treatment."

Damian nodded. "Sounds promising."

"It is," Cherin said with a smile.

"Another avenue we are exploring, is closing the receptors to good cells, so that the bad cells cannot affect them," Dr. Hakani explained. "It's like a vaccine almost. It prevents cancer from spreading, and it allows us to treat what is already there, without worrying about it spreading through the rest of the system."

"Again, Dr. Hakani, I'm impressed," Damian said, nodding.

"Finally, the last new avenue of approach, is utilizing the body's own immune system to attack cancerous cells," Dr. Hakani told him.

"Doesn't the immune system already do that?" Damian asked.

"Yes, and no," Dr. Hakani answered. "Against most disease and infections, the answer is yes. Against cancer, the answer is not effectively. What we're doing is basically weaponizing the body's own white blood cells and using them to attack other cells. Again, it is the aforementioned breakthrough that is helping to make this possible. It is attaching a genetic marker to help identify the damaged cells, so that the good cells can strategically attack them."

Damian leaned forward. "As a business man, I have to ask. Where are we, and at what pace are we moving forward?"

"We are in clinical trials," Cherin told him.

"And we are making advances every week," Dr. Hakani added.

Damian turned toward Bio One's business attorney. "Diane, we had some pretty big offers on the table from Johnson-Johnson, Pfizer, Merck, and a few others for some of our other drugs. What's your take?"

Diane interlaced her fingers and placed them on the table. She shrugged. "I say, sell. We sell some of our other brands, and we use the money to fund the new breakthroughs."

Damian nodded. It was what he wanted to hear. He was in desperate need of cash. Bio One was okay, but his 'other' business was hurting. Dante's search for Lucky had him bleeding money. And it didn't help that oil prices were at historic lows, and continuing to creep lower. His Energia Oil was hurting worse than his illegitimate enterprises. The cash from Bio One was needed to keep his family accounts in the black.

"I'm in agreement," Damian told those gathered around the table. "See what the other companies want, and unload some of our brands. We'll use the cash to push forward on the other stuff."

Damian rose from the table, and the others rose as well.

Cherin clasped his arm. "That was too easy. What do I need to know?"

"Other than what you already know?" Damian asked lifting an eyebrow. "We need the money."

"Bio One is your baby," Cherin told him. "It's always been your dream. And you walk in here and barely ask any questions, listen to a basic ass briefing, and then decide to sell some of the company's prime pharmaceuticals? The last meeting we had, your mind was in outer space, so I guess it's an improvement that you were at least partially aware of what was being said. What the fuck, Damian?"

"Oil prices aren't exactly at an all-time high right now, and Energia is bleeding money and overextended," Damian said leaning in and whispering. "Dante's is blowing through money, and our supply is not exactly reliable right now. We could use the money!"

"You're not selling anything," Cherin told him.

"I thought I was the CEO of this company," Damian told her.

"I've worked just as hard as you have in building this place, and I'm not going to let you throw it away," Cherin shot back. "Tough times don't last, tough people do. Put on your big girl panties, Damian! We *will* get through this! Bio One is going to come out stronger than ever!"

Damian exhaled. He knew that she was right.

"I'm going to hold off on the asset sell," Cherin told him. "We don't need money. What we need is *time*. He'll find her. He'll get her back, and then our expenses will go down. We need time."

"And how much time do you think we have?" Damian asked. "Do we wait until the moving trucks pull up and empty the offices?"

"Boy, who do you think you're talking to?" Cherin asked, placing her hand on her hip. "I'm not just your friend, I'm also your attorney. You don't owe anyone anything! You're not leveraged, let alone over leveraged. All your companies are privately owned, and everything you own has been paid for in cash. There are no investors, stock holders, or anyone else you need to answer to! You just need *time*, Damian."

"Payroll, and expenses, are what's killing me," Damian explained. "Do you any idea how many people we employ? Do you have any idea how many men we've hired, or how much it cost to maintain fleets of cars, jets, boats, and houses? How much it cost to pay off everyone on the planet? Baby, it's the expenses and the payroll that has me bleeding money!"

"Then maybe it's time to cut a deal with one of the big oil companies for Energia Oil," Cherin told him. "Sub lease some of your oil leases. Sell some of your exploration contracts and drilling rights. Transform Energia from an oil company, to a company that focuses on renewables. Cut a deal with China and get into solar energy, invest in hydroelectrical powerplants, wind farms, bio-fuels, hydrogen fuel cells, move away from dirty carbon energy and into the future. Bio One is about the future. Make Energia about the future as well!"

"Energia Oil is the only Black owned oil corporation on the planet!" Damian protested. "It's the only privately-owned oil corporations of its size on the planet!"

"I'm not saying get rid of it, I'm saying transform it," she told him. "It could be so much more. I believed in Bio One, because I knew what it *could* be. I've always believed in you, Damian, because I've always known what you *could* be. And now, I believe in Energia Oil, not because of what it is, but because of what it *could* be. You have always been a dreamer, boy, ever since we were kids. You've always been about tomorrow, about the future, about what *could* be. Where is that Damian gone? Bring him back to me."

Damian leaned forward and kissed her on her forehead. "You've always been there for me, and always been a friend. Sometimes we need old friends to remind us about the good things about ourselves, about the dreamer in all of us."

"Hold on, negroe," Cherin said smiling. "I don't like the *old* friend part. We need to just make sure we clarify that part. I'm an old *friend*, not an *old* friend."

Damian laughed. "And you still crushing, girl. If I didn't know you, I would think you were in your twenties."

"Early, or late?"

"Early."

"Okay, you get a pass," she smiled. "Thanks for lying to me."

Damian laughed. "Thanks for always being there for me."

Cherin hugged him. "We're going to find Lucky, Damian. Believe that. I pray for that baby every night."

"Say a couple for me too, while you're at it," Damian said with an uneasy smile.

Cherin smiled. "I've never stopped. I've never stopped praying for you, for Dante, for Princess, for all of you. I pray for you every night, Damian."

Damian wrapped his arms around her, pulled her close and kissed her forehead again. He rested his face against hers. Her hug meant more to him, than she would ever know.

Chapter Six

Peaches walked through the burned-out rubble of what used to be her old mansion. It was worse than what she thought it was going to be. There was nothing left but charred wood rising out of a concrete foundation. Even her once green lawn was charred black, and it was covered with shiny brass casings, making it appear as if bullets were sprouting out of the landscape.

Peaches stepped carefully through the ruins, trying to see if there was anything that she could salvage. Pictures, obituaries, valuable gifts or trinkets that she had amassed over the years. There was nothing. Josh's men surrounded her property, keeping a lookout as she surveyed the damage. They were close enough to protect her, but far enough away to not catch her wiping away the tears that fell down her face occasionally as she surveyed what remained of her life.

Josh sat inside of the limo browsing his Facebook, Snapchatting, and tweeting. He felt like he was babysitting, and he was bored as hell. He didn't mind looking out for his cousin's girl, if that was what she was supposed to be, but it was still pretty mundane duty to him. He would have rather been in Texas, kicking down doors, torturing mafiosos, and helping in the search for Lucky. Instead, he was in Ohio, babysitting someone who was supposed to be a full fledge *Commission* member, but who had her ass handed to her by who knows. If she was what the Commission was coming to, then the future looked pretty dim for that organization. Back in the old days, the idea of a Commission member getting ran out of their own state, would have been unheard of. It was these new people coming on board, who didn't know shit, or have the muscle, the experience, or the balls to control their own state that was giving the organization a black eye. If he ever got the chance to run his own state, things would be way different. He would put the fear of God in everyone in his state, and make his rule absolute, and his orders undisputed.

"Boss," one of his men, said, getting his attention. He nodded toward an approaching Hyundai Elantra.

All of Josh's men turned in the direction of the approaching vehicle and placed their hands on their weapons which were hidden beneath their suit jackets.

"Peaches, you know who this is?" Josh shouted.

Peaches shook her head. Some of Josh's men stepped in front of her, shielding her from any potential danger. Josh stepped out of the limo, reached back inside, and pulled an FN SCAR assault rifle close. He was going to light the car up if anything looked even the slightest bit suspicious.

The Hyundai pulled through the gates of the estate past where the guardhouse used to be, and approached Reigns vehicles. In parked behind the last vehicle, and the passenger door flew open. Vendetta leaped out of the vehicle, and raced toward Peaches. Peaches shoved the Reigns' men aside, and ran toward her friend. The two of them met in the middle, and crashed into one another's arms crying uncontrollably.

Josh's men took their hands off their weapons and relaxed.

Peaches kissed Vendetta all over her face, and Vendetta did the same to Peaches.

"Oh my God! Oh my God!" Peaches said through her tears. "I love you, I love you!"

"I love you too!" Vendetta said, returning her hugs and kisses. "I was so scared. I was so worried, I didn't know if you made it. Girl, my heart died when I came to, and you weren't with me."

"Me too, girl!" Peaches told her.

"Where's Trap?" Vendetta asked. "Is she here? Have you heard from her?"

Peaches shook her head. "They say she's okay. What about Joaquin? Anybody seen Joaquin or heard from him?"

Vendetta shook her head.

The driver's side door of the Hyundai opened, and out climbed DeMarion with his cell phone to his ear. He started toward Vendetta.

"Ole pretty ass nigga!" Josh shouted from limo.

DeMarion turned and spotted his cousin, and his face lit up. He rushed to where Josh was standing and the two of them embraced.

"What the fuck you doing here?" DeMarion asked.

Josh shrugged. "Babysitting. What are you doing?"

DeMarion smiled. "Pretty much the same."

Peaches and Vendetta walked up.

"Peaches, this is DeMarion," Vendetta said, introducing them. "He is the one who saved me I guess."

"Oh, now you guess?" DeMarion said with a smile. "You get around your homegirl, and now you guess? I ain't shit no more now, huh?"

Vendetta laughed.

Peaches took in the way DeMarion stared at Vendetta, and the way Vendetta was smiling at DeMarion. She also couldn't help but notice DeMarion's looks. She realized that it all meant trouble. Not only was she fucking with Darius, but apparently, V now had a thing for another Reigns. It meant Princess was going to pop a nutty, and maybe even Damian, and then there was the matter of V having a boyfriend that she had been with forever. It was all a train wreck in the making. Worst of all, by his looks, and the way they were smiling and flirting and going back and forth, she knew that they had to have fucked. They were all playing a deadly game, she thought.

"Josh, this is my sister Vendetta," Peaches said, introducing them.

"It's good to meet you," Josh told her, shaking her hand.

"Girl, we've got to catch up," Peaches told Vendetta.

"We've got time, because I'm staying where you're staying," Vendetta told her. "I haven't been to my house yet, and D won't let me because he thinks it's too dangerous."

"He's right," Peaches told her. "I got a room, you can stay with me. I'mma need your help to find Joaquin."

"Girl, you know I got you," Vendetta told her.

Josh nodded toward DeMarion's car. "Nice set of wheels you got there."

"It's a rental, nigga!" DeMarion said with a smile. "I needed to roll incognito."

"Spell it!" Josh said laughing.

"I-n- Fuck you!" DeMarion replied. "I need a whip. A real whip. Some soldiers, some supplies, some straps, a place to stay, the whole thing."

"Why?"

"Because."

"Get your soft ass in the limo," Josh told him. "One of my men will return that piece of shit you're driving. Yo, Peach. We outta here. I'mma get you back to the room, and you and your girlfriend can chop it up and paint each other toe nails, and have a great big sleep over. But right now, we're too exposed out here."

Peaches lifted her middle finger toward Josh, and then climbed inside of the limo. Vendetta nodded toward Josh.

"Is he..."

"Girl, he wished!" Peaches told her. "Not in his wildest fucking dream. "His cousin."

Vendetta frowned. "His cousin?"

"Darius," Peaches answered. "Darius is Damian's younger brother."

"Peaches, are you fucking kidding me!" Vendetta shouted, climbing into the car. "Have you lost your fucking mind?"

"Girl, we'll talk about it," Peaches told her. She shot a side glance toward DeMarion. "Besides, don't look to me like you can be too judgmental."

Vendetta lowered her head and smiled.

Josh climbed into the limo and closed the door. He tapped the driver's window. "And we outta here! Back to the room."

The limo wheeled around, waited for the rest of the caravan to form up, and then headed back to the motel.

Reigns Family Mansion

Damian turned off his computer, rose from his desk, and walked out of his office. He headed into the living room on his way to the kitchen, where he ran into his surprise house guest.

"Assata!" Damian exclaimed.

"Hey, baby!" Assata said, wringing the towel that was wrapped around her long dreadlocks trying to dry her hair. "Come and give your favorite aunt a hug!"

"You know you've always been my favorite," Damian told her.

"You need to say it louder!" Assata shouted. "I'm your favorite auntie! That bitch need to hear it!"

Damian laughed. "Aunt Libby isn't here."

"Oh, well that's good for us then," Assata told him. "Don't nobody want to put up with her stuck-up ass!"

Again, Damian laughed. "So, Assata, what are you doing in town? The last time we talked, you had bought an adobe on the outskirts of Santa Fe, and you were going to grow weed in the desert."

Assata waved him off. "Oh, that was so yesterday!"

"Okay, before that you were living in Trinidad and Tobago, growing weed and selling it to tourist on the beach," Damian told her.

"Damian, that was three years ago!"

"That was the year before last," Damian told her. "And the year before that, you were living in Jamaica with your boyfriend from Ghana, selling t-shirts and weed to tourist from the cruise ships."

Assata laughed and waved him off. "You're talking about Wilson! That bum! He ran off with some little Jamaican tart with my entire stash! If I find either of them..."

"And before that, it was Belize, and before that, you were relocating to Ghana, and before that, Liberia, and before that, you were going to Cuba to study medicine, and before that..."

"Damian, why you keep bringing up old shit!" Assata protested.

Damian smiled. "I'm just wondering, how much your next little adventure is going to cost me."

"I'm not here for money!" Assata said sharply.

"Do you need money?"

"Of course," Assata smiled. "I don't ever turn down money, Sweetie!"

Damian laughed and folded his arms. "So, let's hear it! What's the latest plan involving weed, medicinal herbs, and living on the beach."

"You ain't right!" Assata told him. "That's no way to talk to your favorite aunt."

"You are my favorite aunt," Damian said with a smile. "Always have been, always will be."

"Then why you grilling me?" Assata asked. She sat down on the couch and produced a blunt from the pocket of her t-shirt. "I'm your favorite aunt because I used to sneak your ass candy, and let you follow me to the park and shit. Even gave you your first hit of the sticky icky."

"Really?" Damian asked. "You really gonna blow that in here?"

"Ain't no kids around!" Assata said, lighting up the marijuana filled cigar.

Damian waved the smoked away from his face. "So, what's the deal?"

"You tell me," Assata asked, blowing smoke rings into the air. "How you been, Baby?"

"Better."

"What do you mean?"

Damian exhaled. "I mean, I've been better."

"What's the matter?" Assata asked. She patted the spot on the sofa next to her. "Come, talk to me."

Damian took the seat next to his aunt.

"I miss your momma," Assata said softly.

"Me and you both," Damian told her. "I wish she was here now. I sure could use her help."

"That's what Aunties are for," Assata told him. "Talk to me. Tell me what's wrong."

"Besides trying to keep everything together?" Damian asked. "My biggest concern right now, is Dante."

"How's he doing?" Assata asked.

"Not good," Damian said, shaking his head. "Not good at all."

"Well, what do you expect?" Assata asked. "His baby's been kidnapped. Nobody can go through that and be okay."

"I understand that part," Damian told her. "That's expected, but within boundaries. He's crossed boundaries. I don't know it... Well, I'm worried about his state of mind."

Assata nodded. She now understood what Damian was saying. She scooted in closer.

"Let me tell you something," Assata said, leaning in and lifting his chin up so that his eyes could meet hers. "Ain't nothing like sisters, and ain't nothing like brothers. Brothers have each other's back through thick and thin. They know what one another is thinking, they can feel when the other one is hurting. And the thing about brothers, is that when one is weak, the other is strong. It's like having two of yourself. And just like you would never give up on yourself, you can never give up on your brother. No matter what happens, or what's transpired, you can always fix it. You just have to be there for him, to help him pick up the pieces, and to help him put things back together."

Damian nodded.

"Baby, Dante's mind ain't broke," Assata continued. "Dante is doing what any and every parent would do. Or wished they could do if they had the money and the resources. He's turning over every rock, every stone, moving every mountain, and going after everybody who could have had anything to do with taking his baby. He's a father, and he's *acting* like a father. Child, my Daddy would have done the same thing. Did your momma ever tell you how Daddy took out all his guns when your daddy came to pick up my sister for prom. Child, Daddy laid out all his guns like he was cleaning them, and questioned your daddy down. He wanted to know exactly what time he was going to be brining your momma back after the dance, and told him not to be a minute late!"

Damian laughed. He could see his grandfather doing exactly that.

"You've always been the strong one, Baby," Assata told him. "You always been the most mature, and the most stable and level headed one out of your brothers and sisters and your cousins on both sides. They all looked to you for strength, and direction. If you crumble, then this whole family crumbles."

Damian nodded. "I just don't know what to do. I don't know how to bring him back, reel him in a little. I know what he's going through, but he's got to reel it in. He's making too many waves, I got people running for cover, I saw some of the things he's done."

"Bring him home," Assata told him. "Bring him home, let him get some rest, talk to him. Ain't no sense in burning down the whole house to get rid of a few termites. Somethings got to be left afterwards."

"That's what I'm trying to make him see, but he ain't listening," Damian told her. "All he can see, is that his baby needs him."

Assata nodded. "She needs him *alive.* She needs this family strong. Ain't no sense in finding her and getting her back, if the entire family is broke and gonna get killed off a week later anyway."

Damian smiled. Assata had a way of breaking things down like the small-town country girl she was deep down inside. She reminded him so much of his mother.

Assata wrapped her arms around Damian and pulled his head to her chest. "You bring him back here, and I'll talk to him. He always listened to me.

"That's 'cause he knew that you would get a belt and whip his ass," Damian said with a smile. "He's too old for whippings now."

"Bullshit!" Assata smiled. "You ain't never too old for a whipping!"

"My momma used to say that to us," Damian said. He could feel a tear welling up in one of his eyes.

"I know, Baby," Assata told him. "Our Momma used to say it to us. I know you miss your Momma. I do to. I can't replace my sister, but I want you to know that I'm always here for you if you need me. Always!"

Damian nodded. "I know."

"I should have been a better Aunt," Assata said softly. "I'm running around trying to grow the best hydro, and my babies here in Texas need me. Maybe I could hang around..."

"No!" Damian said, lifting his head quickly. "Hell no!"

"Fuck you!" Assata told him.

Damian laughed. "You know I would love nothing more than having you here, Girl!"

"Uh-huh!" Assata said pursing her lips. She held out her hand. "Gimme me some."

"Didn't I just tell your ass I was going broke!"

"*Going* and *being* is two different things!" Assata told him. She waved her fingers. "Hand it over."

Damian pulled out his wallet. Assata snatched it. She pulled out three twenties and tossed his wallet back to him.

"That's it!" Damian asked surprised.

"I'm going to the grocery store," Assata told him. "I'm cooking for you from now on. No more restaurants, no more fast food, no more bad shit. You gotta eat to live."

"I'm not eating no vegetarian diet shit!" Damian protested. "I'm a carnivore."

"I'll make some jerk chicken, some peas and rice, some plantains, some sweet potatoes, some carrots, all drizzled with natural honey."

"I don't eat goat!" Damian told her.

"Rabbit, fish, chicken, fresh fruits and veggies, I don't mess with no pig, no catfish, no scavengers!" Assata told him.

Damian nodded. "Deal."

Assata rose and headed to her bedroom to put on some more clothes.

"Assata!" Damian called out to her.

"Yeah?"

"I really am glad to have you around," Damian told her.

Assata nodded, tossed her dreadlocks back over her shoulders, and headed to her bedroom.

Chapter Seven

The convoy of black Yukon Denali XL's pulled up to the gates of the hardened compound and were met by armed guards holding Colt M4 assault rifles. There were re-enforced armored plates behind rows of fencing and concertina wire in front of the steel walls. Guard towers were set at every two hundred yards, and the guard house itself was basically a concrete bunker with steel plates and concertina wire surrounding it. It was a massive complex, well-fortified, and well lit. The U.S. Army would have had hell trying to mount a direct assault on it.

Dajon Reigns powered down his window as the guard approached the rear of the armored SUV.

"I'm here, on the orders of my brother Damian," Dajon told him. "Nicanor called ahead."

The guard nodded, lifted his hand and twirled his finger in the air. The guard controlling the barricade moved it, while another man inside of the bunker pressed a button lowering the tired spikes, and opening the massive steel door leading inside. The caravan of Denalis motored past the guards and into what had come to be known as Little Guantanamo.

Dajon had heard about the place, but even then, he was still unprepared. He was wholly unprepared for the stench of death that permeated the air. He and his men quickly produced handkerchiefs and covered their mouths and noses.

Dajon made his way to the middle of the compound, where he whistled loudly to get everyone's attention. The men who worked at the compound were already eyeing him with suspicion.

"Can I have everybody's attention!" Dajon shouted. "I need everyone to gather around, I have an announcement to make. Tell those guys on the outside to get in here. My guys will take watch. Get those guys down from the guard towers. I want everyone right here in front of me!"

The men working the compound slowly gathered in the center of the yard and formed a semi-circle around Dajon. They were all highly suspicious, and extremely curious as to what he was about to say. Dajon turned to Marquis, the man who Dante had placed in charge of his torture facility.

"Is that everyone?" Dajon asked.

Marquis peered over the crowd of assembled men and then nodded.

"Okay, listen up!" Dajon shouted. "What I'm about to talk to you about, is door number two. This is the door that Damian has *chosen* for you, because of your loyalty to the Reigns family. Door number two, is that all of you are going to be re-assigned. This place is now closed for business. No more intakes, no more torture, no more nothing. Now, before I tell you more about door number two and how wonderful it is, I need to tell you about door number one."

As if on cue, dozens of men dressed in all black combat gear walked into the facility carrying assault rifles. Their faces were covered with black mask, and they were even wearing black combat boots, black gloves, black combat gear, and black tactical helmets. They surrounded the men who worked the compound. Black masked men appeared in the guard towers, as well. After a few moments of frightening silence, men dressed in white or yellow bio hazard suits started flooding into the compound. Some carried clipboards, others held machines that were used for sniffing out decay, others held the leashes of German Shepherds who were also trained to sniff out dead bodies, and others were pushing dollies that held giant barrels. Some of the barrels were empty, while others held various chemicals. All the men in bio hazard suits had mask over their faces. They looked like they were ready for a biological, nuclear, or chemical cleanup.

"Door number one, is that all of you are executed so that there are no witnesses as to what happened here," Dajon told them. "But like I said, Damian chose door number two for you. All of you, are going to be re-assigned. You will be sent to new duty stations in Houston, Dallas, Maryland, Florida, California, or Pennsylvania. None of you will be sent to the border, and none of you will have to be involved in the search anymore. Damian is giving all of you a month off before reporting to your new job, and he is ordering all of you to take a vacation. He doesn't care where, just go. Go sit on a beach, relax, unwind, and get your mind away from this place."

Dajon's men opened back packs, and began to pull out bands of hundred dollars bills. Each of the men were handed two of the ten-thousand-dollar stacks.

"Take your wives, your children, your girlfriends, whoever, and get out of here and relax," Dajon told them. "Go to Corpus or Galveston, charter a fishing boat, go fishing. Do whatever you need to do to clear your mind, your nose, your bodies, from the stench of this place. The family is also making available psychologist for you. These mental health professionals work for the family, they are cleared, and you are cleared to talk to them about your experiences or about anything else on your mind. They will keep what you tell them confidential, even from the family. But make sure, that they are the *only* ones you ever tell about this place. Other than them, don't ever mention this place again, for the rest of your lives."

"Hey, Dog," Marquis told him. "All my people are straight. Ain't none of these cats new hires, they've all been with the family for years."

"I know that," Dajon told him. "That's why they're still alive." He turned back to the men. "I want to make something very clear. Door number two, is a door that *all* of you have to accept. If any one of you snitch, then *all* of you die. We will not only kill the family of the person who snitches, but we will hunt them down to the ends of the earth and kill them as well. And don't think that protective custody can save you, or your wife, and your children. We find people in protective custody, trust me. Another thing, is that to us, family isn't just your wife and your kids, it's also your mother, your father, your brothers, your sisters, your cousins, your aunts, your uncles, your

71

grandmothers, your grandfathers, it's your childhood best friends. We will wipe your entire family off the map. And then we will kill you."

"That's not necessary," Marquis told him.

"And like I said," Dajon continued. "It's a deal that *all* of you take as one. If one of you snitches, then all of you will die. So, if there is anyone among you who you think is going to snitch, you better tell us. Your lives, is in each other's hands. Trust me, door number two is a much sweeter deal."

"All of our shit is wound up tight, right?" Marquis asked his men.

"Right!" many of the men replied in unison.

"I told you, Dog," Marquis said to Dajon. "We straight. Ain't no snitches here."

"Good!" Dajon told them. "Now, the men you see here, are the clean-up crew. Before you take off and head home, or to the local airport, or wherever you're going, I need for you to let them know where all bodies are buried. We need to know where each and every single body is buried, not just the mass graves. Twenty years from now, I don't want some kid stumbling upon a pair of teeth, and then some cold case detective does a record search, and finds out who owned this land at the time. We're here to make everything about this place, vanish into thin air. This place was never here. I need to know everything. I don't care if you think you burned the bodies really well, I don't care if you ground them up in a grist mill and then fed them to some hogs. If that's the case, then I want the fucking hogs! My job, is to make this place disappear. I need everything, and then you guys can go."

72

Marquis clapped his hands. "Let's get to work. Show 'em everything."

Marquis started to walk away but Dajon clasped his arm.

"One moment," Dajon told him. "I need to speak to you."

Marquis peered at Dajon's hand and then up at Dajon. "What now?"

Dajon's men stepped closer and surrounded Marquis.

"Damian came down and checked this place out," Dajon told him. "You had some pretty sharp words for him. You said that this was *his* doing, that he empowered our brother and that his acquiescence allowed this to happen."

Marquis swallowed nervously. He nodded.

"If it's one thing that Damian doesn't like, it's yes men," Dajon told him. "You stood up to him, and you told him some hard truths. Damian wants you in San Antonio working for him *personally*. You ran this place, kept things together, demonstrated leadership and organizational skills. You're being promoted."

"What?" Marquis asked. He was taken aback. He thought he was about to get a bullet to the back of his head.

"I said, you're being promoted," Dajon told him. "You're working directly for Damian now. I don't know whether to give you my congratulations or my condolences."

"What's that supposed to mean?" Marquis asked.

"When you impress the boss and he has his eye on you, that could mean either one of two things," Dajon explained. "Either you continue to rise, or you disappoint him so bad that you end up in a shallow grave somewhere. And if you continue to impress him, then the jobs you get only get tougher and tougher, and the decisions you have to make only get shittier and shittier. Your soul ends up being the price you pay for heights to which you rise. Me? I would have rather stayed anonymous, collected my check, washed the blood off at the end of the day, and continued to go home to my family. But that's just me. Congratulations."

Dajon turned, and headed off to the supervise the closing and the destruction of the torture compound known as Little Guantanamo.

*****

Reigns Family Ranch

Damian pulled back the reigns on his Arabian bringing him to a halt.

"Whoah, boy!" Damian said, gently rubbing the side of his black steed.

Stacia rode up next to him, halting her horse as well. The two of them peered back over the landscape of the Reigns family ranch, taking in the beauty of the scenery, not wanting the day to end.

"I had the best time," Stacia told him. "This was my favorite part of visiting your parents ranch when I was younger. I loved going on horseback rides."

"I thought I was the favorite part of your visit," Damian said with a smile. He dismounted his horse.

Stacia laughed, as she dismounted as well. "Uh, that was later, once I was into boys. Before that, you came in second."

"Close second, or a distant second?" Damian asked.

Stacia pulled an apple out of her saddle bag and fed it to her horse. "Probably a distant second."

Damian laughed. "At least you're honest!"

"Always," Stacia told him. "I'll always be honest with you."

Damian lifted an eyebrow.

"Okay, I'll be honest with you most of the time," Stacia corrected. "I am sorry that my kids, our kids, aren't going to have this growing up."

"Why is that?" Damian asked.

"I'm leaving," Stacia told him. "For good."

Silence engulfed their conversation as Damian tried to digest what she was saying.

"I'm taking a new position," Stacia continued. "It's in Washington. It's a big promotion."

"Congratulations!" Damian told her.

Stacia nodded. "I'm moving over to Homeland."

"Doing what, exactly?"

Stacia turned toward him. "It's not in narcotics enforcement or interdiction or anything like that."

"But you don't want to tell me?" Damian asked.

Stacia shrugged. "It's not like I've not violated every single security clearance I've ever gotten because of you already."

They both laughed.

"Don't tell me," Damian told her. "If you're not supposed to tell me, then don't. Do this one the right way."

"Thank you," Stacia told him. She fed her horse another apple, and rubbed his muscular body.

"Sometimes in life, you just want to do things the right way," Damian told her. "Get tired of shortcuts, get tired of cheating, and conniving, cajoling, and all of the underhanded deals, and the back handed deals, and all of the bullshit. You just want to be legit."

"I know," Stacia said, pulling Damian close. "You've always wanted that. You've always wanted to be legit, to leave the business. Don't give up on that. I think, that if you ever gave up on that, you would die."

Damian laughed.

"I'm serious!" Stacia told him. "I think it would poison you from the inside. You have a goodness inside of you, Damian. You try and try and try to do the right things and to move your family to doing the right things, and then life keeps dealing you shitty hands. But don't give up. Promise me that you'll never give up. That goodness, that desire to *be* good, to do good, that's what makes you who you are."

Damian smiled and nodded. "I promise." He lifted his finger and crossed his heart. "Scouts honor."

"My father got promoted too," Stacia told him.

"Nathan?" Damian laughed. "What the hell is Nathan doing now?"

"My Dad, well, pending Senate confirmation, is going to be the next Deputy Attorney General of the United States."

"Holy shit!" Damian whistled. "I'm in trouble now!"

Stacia laughed. "Boy, he ain't even worried about you."

"Anymore?" Damian asked, correcting her.

"It's all about terrorism nowadays," Stacia told him. "Almost every single agency has re-oriented itself to combat terrorism. That's how you get budget dollars. Congress isn't allocating money for cocaine or marijuana anymore. You want funding for your agency, you have to justify it by showing Congress how integral you are in stopping terrorist or fighting terrorism. You want promotions, get on a terrorism task force. Besides Meth, nobody gives a shit about drugs anymore."

"I can't tell," Damian told her. "They are still squeezing the hell outta the border."

"Yeah, those programs are still intact, but they claim they are more worried about terrorist getting across, or getting a dirty bomb across," Stacia told him. "But, you are making people pay attention again. Dante, is making people worry about drug violence on the border again."

Damian nodded. "I know, I know. It's got to stop."

"Fast."

"We can't cut it off until we find Lucky."

Stacia nodded. "Understood. But you're going to end up paying a heavy price in political protection, and in business. They are going to have to eventually send in a lot of agents to stop the violence. He's killing police like its free. Politicians love your money, but the one thing they love more than your money, is getting re-elected. And unless they do something about the violence..."

Again, Damian nodded. "Message received, loud and clear.

"Your girlfriend hasn't told you this?"

"My girlfriend?"

"Your little FBI tart!" Stacia said with a smile.

Damian laughed. "You mean Grace?"

"Whatever that hooker's name is!" Stacia told him. "You know she's getting promoted?"

"Really?" Damian asked, lifting an eyebrow.

"You little baby momma is moving up big time," Stacia told him. "She's going from being Special Agent in Charge of the Houston field office, to being director of a multi-state regional task force. She applied for a spot with the U.S. Attorney's office, and was about to get it, and then the Bureau gave her this promo."

"Okay, so what does this regional task force do?"

"Drugs, baby," Stacia told him. "She's coordinating the federal government's anti-drug operations for Texas, Oklahoma, Arkansas, and Louisiana."

"I thought you just said that the government wasn't interested in drugs anymore?" Damian asked.

"They are, but not like they used to be!" Stacia told him. They still have a drug policy, and still conduct anti-narcotics operations. Look, she going to be in charge of customs, homeland, DEA, FBI, ATF, Border Patrol, Coast Guard in her area. She'll raid some meth labs, close some illegal grow operations, they'll put her on the news to show that they're doing something, and that's about the extent of it. Trust me, the feds are throwing most of their money into stopping terrorist."

"So, where does all of this leave us?" Damian asked.

"Where we've always been," Stacia told him. She exhaled. "Mike is in D.C."

"Ahhh," Damian said nodding. "Is that the reason for the new job?"

Stacia shook her head. "The reason for the new job is because I'm an ambitious bitch, I love power, and the job pays more. Mike being in D.C. just means that the kids will get to see the man who they've known as their father for all their life. He wants to work it out, Damian."

"And what do you want to do?"

"I want to be happy," Stacia said, shrugging. "Can't wait on you all my life."

"That's not fair!"

"I'm kidding, Damian!" Stacia said, bumping her shoulder against his. "We ain't getting married. I ain't getting any younger. My kids love their father. Why not?"

"Yeah, why not?" Damian told her. "You've thrown a lot at me. And now, I'm going to come off as an asshole. I don't know if this is the moment when I'm supposed to beg you to stay, or tell you that I'll marry you, or what? I'm fucking lost right now. And that in itself probably makes me seem like an asshole!"

Stacia laughed. "No, this is not that moment. Damian, you know how we are. You know our history. It ain't for us. We would probably end up hating each other, and I never want to feel that way about you. I love you too much to ever want to even take the chance of going there."

Damian nodded. "Thanks for that."

"For what?"

"For letting me off easy."

Stacia smiled. "Do you love me, Damian?"

"More than words could express. Always have, always will."

Stacia leaned over and kissed him on his cheek. "Then that's good enough for me. That's always been good enough for me."

"You never wanted more from me?"

"You gave me a shit load of kids!"

The two of them laughed.

Stacia shook her head. "It crosses my mind from time to time, and then I regain my sanity. I have your love. I can come to you and get anything that I want. I look at my kids, and I see you. I have enough."

"And waking up..."

"I don't have to wake up next to you to know that you love me, or that I love you. Plenty of people waking up next to warm bodies that they don't love and aren't loved by."

Damian nodded.

"C'mon, let's get them back in their stalls and grab something to eat," Stacia told him. "I'm fucking starving."

*****

Laredo, Texas

Dante rounded the corner holding his black Sig Sauer pistol with the large silencer attached to the end of it. He found the person he was looking for, relaxing poolside. A sawed-off shotgun sat resting in his lap.

"I've been expecting you, muthafucka!" Oso Torres-Rivera told Dante. He gripped his sawed-off shotgun. "I knew, that eventually you would make the mistake of coming my way."

"I heard you cut a deal with Galindo, fat boy!" Dante told him. "That's a no-no! You work for my family. Imagine if all of our people started cutting their own deals, and buying coke from whoever they wanted to? What kind of fucked up, disorganized world would we live in?"

Oso puffed on the fat Cohiba Siglo VI cigar he held in his mouth, and then blew rings of smoke into the air. "I ain't no pussy ass Sheriff, or some punk ass DEA agent. I do what I want to do. If you ain't got the dope to supply my people, then I go and get it from wherever the fuck I like."

"Wrong answer, Fat boy!" Dante told him. "Disloyalty, is punishable by death."

"Not this time, Ese!" Oso told him. Oso placed his fingers in his mouth and whistled. "You fucked up this time, boy!"

Oso's men poured from out of his mansion and nearby pool house. They were heavily armed with assault rifles and shotguns. Dante and his men were quickly surrounded.

Dante slowly clapped his hands. "That's why I always liked you. I used to tell Damian all the time, that you were the smart one, and that you were the one to keep an eye on. Boy, was I right."

"You're smiling, like you're not going to die today," Oso told him.

Dante shook his head. "If only you were as loyal, as you were ruthless. You could have gone far in my organization, Oso. Probably ran the entire border region for us."

"How about this?" Oso said, sitting up. "How about I kill you, I kill your men, and then I get your punk ass brother, and then I fuck your sister and make her suck my dick, before I kill her too!"

"You want to *fuck* my sister?" Dante said, shaking his head. "And, you want to make her suck on that tiny little burrito you have between your legs? Wait a minute, I have to tell her this. I just have too."

Dante pulled out his phone, and dialed up Princess.

"Hello?" Princess answered.

"Hey, sis, you'll never guess where I am!" Dante told her. "I'm at Oso's, and he has something that he wants to tell you. Hold on, I'll put it on speaker." Dante placed the call on speaker, and then held the phone up toward Oso.

Oso rolled his eyes and shook his head.

"Well, apparently the cat's got his tongue now," Dante said. "Did you know he had the hots for you?

83

He said that he wanted to fuck you, and make you suck his dick."

"Ewwww, no thank you!" Princess said on the line.

"Fuck this shit!" Oso said, he lifted his sawed-off shotgun, pumped it, pointed it at Dante and pulled the trigger. The gun clicked.

"Hold on, hold on!" Dante said excitedly. I'm going to turn on the camera, I want you to see the look on his face." Dante turned on his camera and turned the phone toward Oso.

Oso pumped his shotgun again, and again pointed it at Dante and squeezed the trigger.

"You see the look on his face, Sis?" Dante asked. "That's the look of a dumb muthafucka, who just realized how fucked he is. Look, I going to count down now..."

Oso turned toward Lizard, his right-hand man. He pumped the shotgun again, and then squeezed the trigger again.

"There it is!" Dante said excitedly. "There's the look of a man who just realized, that he's been betrayed by his own men."

Dante broke into laughter, and so did Princess.

"I'll pump it again," Princess said, acting like she was pumping a shotgun. "No, wait a minute, it has to work this time..."

Dante and Princess shared a good laugh.

"Hey, Dante," Princess told him. "I gotta go, but do me a favor."

"What's that, Sis?"

"Bring me that teeny-tiny dick, that he wanted me to suck," Princess told him. "I'll put it in teeny-tiny test tube, and keep it as a memento of his love for me."

"You got that, Sis," Dante told her. "Love you!"

"Love you!" Princess said, ending the call.

Dante turned to Lizard. "You now run Laredo for the Reigns family. Thank you, for your loyalty."

"And this piece of shit?" Lizard asked, nodding toward his former boss.

"You heard Princess," Dante told him. "Cut off his dick. The rest of his body, I don't care what you do with it." Dante peered into the sky. "Hell, even the buzzards gotta eat, right?"

Lizard smiled and nodded. Two of his men grabbed Oso and lifted him off the lounge chair and carried him away. Dante twirled his finger in the air, telling his men to mount up, their business was done. It was time to get back on the search for his baby girl.

Chapter Eight

Nicanor landed in the Grand Cayman aboard one of the Reigns family's private jets. The jet taxied to the end of the runway and then turned onto an adjacent strip and made its way to private waiting away near the rear of the airport. There was a second jet waiting for him.

The stairs came down and Nicanor jogged down the steps and up to a waiting limo. The door to the limo opened.

"Nicanor!" Johnny Talamantez exclaimed, opening his arms wide. Nicanor and Johnny embraced warmly. *"Como esta', mi amigo."*

"Muy Bien, Gracias!" Nicanor told him. *"Como estas usted?"*

"Good!" Johnny told him. "C'mon, the boss is waiting."

Nicanor climbed into the limo and the driver pulled off to make the short trip out of the airport to the shopping area just outside of it.

"How is Damian?" Johnny asked.

"He's well," Nicanor told him. "How's the family?"

"They are good. My daughter, she's growing up. Too fast, as a matter of fact. She became a young lady last week. Scared the shit out of her."

Nicanor and Johnny laughed.

"I remember those days," Nicanor told him. "When my daughter got hers, she screamed like she had seen a ghost."

"Children!" Johnny said, shaking his head.

"Especially daughters," Nicanor told him. "They have us wrapped around their little fingers."

"Isn't that the truth?" Johnny told him.

"How is Don Yanez?"

"He's good," Johnny told him.

The limo pulled up to the Rolex store, and several suited men standing outside opened the limo doors for Nicanor and Johnny. One of them waved for them to go inside.

Inside of the store, Don Benito Yanez was trying on various diamond studded Rolex watches. The salesgirls had several laid out on the counter for his comparison, while he had two of the watches on his wrist holding them up so that the sunlight can illuminate the diamonds.

"Nicanor, come in," Don Yanez said, without turning around. "You are here just in time. My mood has changed for the better. Shopping always puts me in a better mood." He turned to the salesgirls. "I'll take them all."

"All, *Senor?*" the salesgirl asked.

Don Yanez nodded. "All of them." He snapped his fingers and one of his men pulled out his Black American Express Centurion Card and handed it to the salesgirl.

"If shopping puts you in a good mood, then I am grateful," Nicanor replied with a slight smile.

"You should be," Don Yanez snapped. He turned and faced Nicanor. "Why did Dante kill Don Torres-Rivera?"

"Excuse me?" Nicanor asked, taken aback.

"I said, why did that fucking *animal,* kill Don Torres-Rivera?" Don Yanez shouted. "Oso Rivera and I were God brothers! I was God father to his oldest daughter! We go back since grade school, and this morning, that *pinche mayate* murdered him in his home while he was swimming! In his own home!"

"Don Yanez, I know nothing about this," Nicanor told him. "I've been on a plane since yesterday. I've made several stops on the way here, and I've not communicated with anyone back home. Please, allow me to see what has transpired."

"No need!" Don Yanez said, waving his hand and dismissing Nicanor's pleas. "We told you to stop the violence, to end the war with the northern cartels, to stop the search, the killings, all of the noise. We don't like noise! We don't like attention! We like to do things quietly in Yucatan. We love it when tourist come and spend their dollars in our peaceful corner of

Mexico. But your family is drawing too much attention to itself, and some of that attention could bring attention to us. And that is unacceptable."

"Senor Yanez, please allow me to talk to Damian," Nicanor told him.

"You can talk to Damian," Don Yanez told him. "And when you do, you tell him that our arrangement is off! Until the Reigns family gets its house in order, and all of the violence ends, there will be no more product from us."

"Senor Yanez, there cannot be any attention drawn to your organization," Nicanor told him. "You're completely insulated. Your ships deliver the product to our oil rigs off shore, and those oil rigs send the product into the states via an underwater pipeline. It's completely safe and secure. No one will ever discover nor suspect our methods of transferring the goods."

"The water has been turned off," Don Yanez said, matter-of-factly. "You're cut off for now. Stop the violence, and we can discuss terms for turning the spigot back on."

Don Yanez nodded to his men, and they opened the door to the jewelry store, motioning for Nicanor to get back into the limo for his ride back to the airport. Nicanor stormed out of the jewelry store and climbed into the back of the limo. He pulled out his cell and called up Damian.

"Hello?" Damian answered.

"City Public Service," Nicanor told him. "That house we have. Well, there's a problem with the plumbing."

Damian exhaled. "How much is the plumber going to charge to fix it?"

"Says that it can't be fixed," Nicanor told him. "Needs a completely overhaul. They're going to have to shut off the water until everything gets fixed."

"Dammit!" Damian shouted. "Get home! Get home now!"

"On the way," Nicanor told him, disconnecting the call. He stared out the window as the limo wheeled into the airport. It was going to be a long flight home.

*****

Ohio

DeMarion climbed out of the shower, removed a towel from the nearby towel bar, and wrapped it around his waist. "Hold on! I'm coming!"

He walked into the bedroom and to the motel door where he peered through the peep hole. To his surprise, it was Vendetta standing at his door. He opened it.

"What a pleasant surprise," he told her. "To what do I owe the pleasure?"

"What are talking about?" Vendetta asked.

"You've hardly said two words to me since I got you back to Ohio in one piece," DeMarion told her.

"You want a cookie?" Vendetta asked. "I thanked you for saving me. I thank you again. I thank you a million times! Are you happy?"

"What can I do for you?" DeMarion asked coldly.

"Can I come in?" Vendetta asked.

DeMarion stepped to the side and allowed her into his hotel room. "A message from the boss, I presume?"

"Which one?" Vendetta asked. "Mine or yours?"

"I was just joking," DeMarion told her. "I don't have a boss. I have a big mouth cousin who *thinks* he's the boss. Did they send you here? Are we going back out again?"

Vendetta shook her head. "No, they didn't send me here. And yeah, we're probably hitting the streets again today. We need men, we need to recruit, Peaches needs to find her brother. A lot of shit needs to be done in a short period of time."

DeMarion exhaled. "I guess you're right. Good luck to you guys."

"What do you mean?"

"I'm flying out."

"What do you mean, you're flying out?"

"Look, I took care of you, I kept you safe, I got you back home, my job is done."

"Your *job*?" Vendetta asked. "That's what I was to you? A *job*?"

"What more were you supposed to be?" DeMarion asked. "You have a man, don't you?"

"Well, yeah, I guess," Vendetta said stuttering.

"You guess?" DeMarion asked, lifting an eyebrow.

"I mean, I did," Vendetta told him. "Hell, I don't even know if he's still alive! I don't know who's alive? You can't leave!"

"Why not?" DeMarion asked. "Tell me why I need to be here?"

"Because, Peaches needs you! Your cousin needs you here!"

DeMarion tilted his head to the side.

"I need you here," Vendetta said softly.

"For what?" DeMarion asked. "Josh has enough men here to keep you safe. You recruited some soldiers. Everyday you're getting stronger. You don't need me anymore."

"Yes, I do!" Vendetta said forcefully.

"For what?"

Vendetta rushed to where he was standing, placed her hands on his face and kissed him passionately. Slowly, DeMarion's hand found its way around her waist. Vendetta placed her hand on his tucked towel and pulled it loose, causing it to fall to the floor. She pushed DeMarion back onto the bed, kissed his navel, and glided her tongue down to his flesh pole. The more she licked around it, the more it grew, and before she knew it, she had stopped kissing and licking and was just staring at it in amazement.

"What's up?" DeMarion asked, noticing that she had stopped.

Vendetta could not believe what she was seeing. She had never, even while watching porn, saw a piece like the one DeMarion was packing. He had a trunk like a baby elephant.

Vendetta clasped his penis with both her hands, and opened her mouth as wide as she could, trying to suck on the head. Trying to be a sexy little freak and swallowing it was out of the question. She had one hand on the base, and her other hand was next to that hand, and he still had at least another eight inches of dick rising up past her hands. And it was *thick!*

She tried as best she could to slide her mouth up and down on his massive pole, but found that it was stretching her mouth out so much that her jaws were beginning to cramp. She abandoned the idea of showing DeMarion her immaculate head game, and decided that it was time to try and tame the beast that stood before her.

Vendetta pulled off her pants, panties, and shirt, and then climbed onto the bed. She thought that she could mount him like she normally did her boyfriend, but his rod was way too long. She had to lift one leg and rise up off the bed, and then lower herself back down onto his flesh piece. And once she did, she immediately began to wonder what she had been thinking.

93

Vendetta slid down onto DeMarion carefully, stopping once she felt like he had hit rock bottom. She was scared to lower herself onto him any further, so she held herself up with her hands and leaned forward. They kissed passionately.

DeMarion wasn't aware of her fear, or hesitation, or the fact that she thought he couldn't go into her any further. He clasped her plump ass, and thrust upwards sending four more inches of penis into her cavity. Vendetta jumped and cried out in pain. No one had ever been inside of her this deep before.

DeMarion was touching places inside of Vendetta that had never been touched. He was deep inside of her, and could feel a tightness around the upper part of his dick that he recognized from quite a few girls that he had dealt with. He realized that she hadn't been dug out this deeply before. To the first four inches of his dick, she was still a virgin.

Vendetta felt like DeMarion was deep inside of her stomach. He was opening up places that had never been spread apart before, and touching walls that had never been rubbed up against. Every time he thrusted up into her, she wanted to scream. He was stretching her out, filling her up, sliding in and out and rubbing up against places that had never been rubbed. She could feel every vein, every contour of him inside of her, and it all felt good.

DeMarion stared at Vendetta's face. Her eyes were closed, and her mouth was open and twisted. She would bite her lip, cry out, and scowl with each of his thrusts. They had just started, and yet beads of sweat were already forming on her forehead. She was trying to balance and stop him from sliding inside too deep, but it wasn't working. And then, the muscles in her ass started contracting and her legs started shaking.

Vendetta didn't know what the hell was happening to her body. Somewhere from deep inside of her, it felt as if something broke, some kind of floodgate opened up. She felt as if water were pouring from her stomach down her vagina. Her legs began shaking uncontrollably. She tried to stop them from shaking, but couldn't. It was almost embarrassing to her. She was coming. And doing so uncontrollably. She didn't know what the fuck was going on.

Vendetta knew that she had orgasmed before from intercourse. Mostly, she got her nut when her boyfriend gave her head. She thought she was orgasming when they had sex as well. But it never felt like this. This one was a deep orgasm, like it was coming from somewhere deep inside of her. Other times, it felt more clitoral, sometime even vaginal, but this! This was something she had never experienced before, and she had never lost control of her body before. She didn't know what or how this was happening.

DeMarion felt her become extra wet. He felt her legs shaking, he could see goose bumps forming on her shoulders, and he could see her eyes roll back and her lips trembling. He knew that she was orgasming. He also knew that she wasn't really allowing him to get to her like he wanted to. He pulled her body close to his, and rolled over on top of her. Vendetta cried out so loudly that it was nearly a full-blown scream. She gasped, clasped his arms, and tried to scoot up and get some dick out of her. Every time she scooted up, he scooted up. She continued to try to back up and alleviate her couchie from the amount of dick that he was putting inside of her. Eventually, she ran out of bed. DeMarion had her where he wanted her, the headboard blocked any further retreat. In fact, she had put herself into an even more difficult position, because DeMarion scooted up once more, causing her legs to be lifted into the air, placing him firmly between them. He lowered the boom and slid all the way inside of her.

Vendetta screamed. She clasped his arms, wrapped her arms around his back, then pounded the headboard, and then squeezed the covers. She didn't know what to do with her hands. She was trapped, and she was taking something the likes of which she had never taken before. DeMarion had twelve inches of thick dick churning deep inside of her, and he was opening places that had never been opened up before. She tried to regulate her breathing to deal with the amount of meat that was going inside of her.

DeMarion kissed her face and neck, and slowly built into a rhythm with his stroke. He was busting her out, and she was wondering what the hell she had gotten herself into. Vendetta's moans continued to build until they became a constant cry in his ear. Not knowing what to do with her hands she simply wrapped them around his neck and held on for dear life. She was hoping that it was going to be over soon, but DeMarion was showing no signs of letting up. All she could do is lie there and take the punishment that he was dishing out.

Vendetta's orgasms were coming back to back. She had completely lost control of her body. Now, it wasn't just her legs that were shaking, but her entire body. She banged her fist against his shoulder subconsciously tapping out, but he paid no attention to it. He was delivering a master stroke.

Vendetta could feel DeMarion beginning to go harder. His strokes were getting faster, harder, deeper; she couldn't take it anymore. She could feel her voice getting hoarse from all her screaming and moaning, and it even felt like his penis had somehow managed to grow even larger. It was as hard as steel, and wider than a fat ass cucumber, and it was sliding in and out of her like a piston in an engine. Just when she was about to scream for him to stop, she found relief. She felt him shoot deep up inside of her. His orgasm felt like a shotgun blast to her insides. His hot cum exploded deep up into her body, causing her to scream.

"You okay?" he asked, smiling at her.

She was breathing too hard and heavy to answer right away.

"I'm good," she said softly. She could still feel his meat throbbing inside of her. "You finished?"

DeMarion kissed her on her lips and nodded. He pulled out of her, and his pull out caused her to gasp. "I'mma hit the shower again real quick."

"Me too," she told him.

"C'mon, we can take one together," he said.

Vendetta quickly shook her head. She didn't want to chance him getting horny again.

"Na, I gotta get back to the room," she told him.

DeMarion leaned forward and kissed her once again.

Vendetta climbed out of the bed, grabbed her clothes, and began to dress. Her legs were sore, as was her uterus. DeMarion owed her some new walls, she thought to herself. If nothing else, after today, she knew what she *didn't* want, and that was DeMarion as her everyday man. He would be good to hook up with once a month, or once every two months, but no woman could deal with that thing between his legs every day. She felt like she now knew why his ass was single.

Chapter Nine

Nicanor strolled through Damian's mansion, going from room to room, searching for his boss. He checked the office, the family room, and the kitchen, and Damian wasn't in any of those places. He had called Damian on the way from the airport, and Damian promised him that he would be home. Nicanor's concerns came to an end when he rounded the corner and saw Damian inside of his home gym, lying on his bench press working out. Nicanor opened the glass door to the gym and stepped inside.

Damian racked the weights he was lifting and sat up on the bench. "How bad is it?"

"We're completely cut off," Nicanor told him. "They're pissed off about Dante killing Oso, and worried that all the violence will bring them unwanted attention."

"Fucking cowards!" Damian shouted. He grabbed a crisp white towel from a nearby work bench and wiped the sweat from his face. "A fucking cartel worried about violence? What the fuck is the world coming to?"

Nicanor laughed. "I tried to tell him that our operation is rock solid. There is no way they could be implicated in anything."

Damian nodded. "Well, that means we have now left shit creek, and drifted into shit ocean without a paddle."

Nicanor seated himself on a nearby bench. "We have a few months' worth of supply left."

Damian shook his head. "Not nearly enough. And I never replaced what we took out of the reserves from the last drought. So, the reserves are not full either."

Nicanor whistled. "So, what's the plan?"

Damian shook his head. "I don't know. We need supply."

"Bolivia?" Nicanor asked. "Good product, but tough route. And we don't have any high-ranking Bolivian officials on payroll. There is Peru. Even better product, but again, tough to get here, and nobody on our payroll. We'd have to build up an entire infrastructure from scratch."

"And by the time we did that, we'd have *been* out of supply," Damian said nodding. "We need to be able to use the same supply lines, the same infrastructure, the same politicians. We have to get it from Mexico."

"Make peace with the border cartels?" Nicanor asked. "They'll still have the same demands. And Dante would never go for it!"

"I know," Damian snapped, growing frustrated. "We have to find another supplier."

"Not the border cartels, not the Yucatan cartels, then who?"

Damian peered up at Nicanor. "We could reach out to Chiapas."

"Chiapas?" Nicanor said, growing animated. "Are you fucking kidding me? Tell me that was a joke!"

"What else is there?" Damian asked. "Who else is there?"

"The Chiapas cartels are lunatics!" Nicanor protested. "Damian, they are a bunch of sadistic, whacked out madmen, who snort just as much cocaine as they sell. They cut people's heads off, and wear the skulls like hats, and the victim's ears around their necks as necklaces!"

"If you have a better idea, I'm listening."

"Damian, listen to me," Nicanor told him. "Forget about Chiapas. I know these men. I fought with them in Central America. I fought against them. These are former members of the Honduran death squads, former Nicaraguan counter insurgency special forces guys, former Contra rebels, former El Salvadoran death squad soldiers, they are all former paramilitary, and ex-military special ops, and anti-communist guerillas. They are fucking hard core. Even the Mexican military doesn't fuck with these guys. Forget about dealing with them."

"Okay, then who?" Damian asked. "Michoacan? Jalisco? Zacatecas? Sinaloa?"

Nicanor crossed his legs. "We all know about the product from Michoacan. Unless they improve their quality, that's a non-starter. Same thing with

Zacatecas. Jalisco is okay, but they won't fuck with us, and you know Sinaloa won't fuck with us."

Damian exhaled. "Okay, so the problem with Bolivia and Peru is no network, right? Okay, so the cartels in those countries already have the right people on payroll. Our problem is getting it from there, to here."

"That's a big fucking problem!" Nicanor said with a slight laugh. "We're not talking hundreds of kilos, we're talking tens of thousands of keys a week. We supply the entire fucking Commission, plus all our states. And oil tankers originating from Peru, pulling up to our oil rigs in the Gulf, ain't gonna fly. Even a blind man can see that's bullshit."

"Could we load cargo ships in Peru, and then transfer the product at sea to an oil tanker?" Damian asked, thinking out loud. He shook his head. "That wouldn't work. Why would an oil tanker go out to sea, meet another ship, and then go to an oil rig? Satellites would pick that shit up quick. And the ships from Peru never making it to the U.S., but just meeting up with another ship in the middle of the ocean, and then turning around? That wouldn't fly. We need those ships to come straight from fucking Peru and be able to offload at a U.S. Port."

"Which means satellites, Coast Guard inspections, Homeland Security, Customs, Agriculture, and all the rest," Nicanor told him.

"We need to get around the Coast Guard," Damian told him. "We need to avoid their ships, and all of their little *safety* inspections."

"We need schedules."

"Can we get schedules?"

Nicanor nodded. "We can pay somebody and get the schedules. But what happens if the ships get diverted? We need to keep that from happening. We need to make sure that the Coast Guard minds its own business. Same thing with Homeland and Customs."

"So, we need Homeland to be cooperative?" Damian asked with a smile.

"Are you thinking..."

"Why the fuck not?" Damian asked, lifting an eyebrow.

"And Coast Guard?" Nicanor asked. "They fall under the jurisdiction of Homeland and DOD. You're not going to get anyone at the Pentagon onboard. They have a certain moral code that's hard as fuck to crack. Especially at that rank. Remember, they're politicians in uniform, and they're more interested in covering their ass to insure the next promotion."

"We can use that against them," Damian told him. "And we don't have to get anyone at the Pentagon, or even at Coast Guard. We just need Homeland, and the general in charge of the U.S. Northern Command. We get those two, we can open up the sea lanes into this country, and bring in pure Peruvian flake."

"And getting that shit through the Panama Canal?" Nicanor reminded him. "You haven't forgotten about that, have you?"

"Not a problem," Damian told him. "Princess will handle Homeland, and I'll handle Northern Command personally."

"And who's going to handle Panama?" Nicanor asked.

Damian smiled at him.

"Fuck, Damian!" Nicanor protested. "I just got off a got damned plane!"

"See you when you get back," Damian told him. "Fly out, and brief Princess in Florida for me, would you?"

"Asshole!" Nicanor said, rising from the bench. "I need a raise! A big fucking raise!"

"Nick!"

"What?"

"We just need the canal administrator to get on board," Damian told him. "We probably don't have to kill anyone on this one."

"And if he doesn't get onboard?"

Damian shrugged. "Then his replacement will."

Nicanor got the message loud and clear. If he didn't get on board, he was a dead man. Nicanor nodded, turned, and stormed out of the gym to fly out to Florida and brief Princess on Damian's plan.

Damian lifted his cellphone and dial a number.

"Hello?"

"Stacia, my sweet, honey, baby, darling," Damian said, laughing.

"What the fuck you want?" Stacia asked playfully.

"Everything you got on Homeland, and Northern Command. Especially the dirt."

"Are you serious?"

"I'm flying out as soon as I get out the shower," Damian told her. "I need it ASAP. And you can get what you have on Homeland over to Princess."

Stacia exhaled. "Okay, done. Anything else?"

"I love you."

"Fuck you, and I love you too... sometimes..."

Stacia disconnected the call, and Damian laughed. He rose from the bench and headed to the shower.

*****

Florida

Princess waved at Nicanor as he boarded the Reigns family's private jet to head off to Panama. She turned and continued to flip through the file that Stacia had faxed her. She knew what she was going to use to get to Homeland Secretary. She also understood why Damian had her meet Nicanor at Reagan International Airport in Washington D.C., and she also understood the urgency of the situation.

Princess walked to her waiting limousine and climbed inside.

"Where to, ma'am?" the driver asked.

"We're going to hook up with the Secretary of Homeland Security," she told the driver. She handed him her cellphone. "That's the address."

*****

Matamoros, Mexico

Dante was the first one inside of the restaurant. He didn't wait for his men to step inside first and clear the room. Dante lifted his silenced pistol and put a bullet through the eye of the security guard at the door. The guard dropped instantly, and was dead before he hit the floor. Dante shifted his weapon and placed a bullet into the skull of the second guard at the door, dropping him as well. He and his men walked into the restaurant with their silenced weapons, killing everyone inside. This was not a capture mission, but a kill mission. He wasn't here for information on Lucky, no, this wasn't even about Lucky, this was about the family's war with the Northern Cartels, and this restaurant was one of their meeting places. Everyone inside was a target, and so, everyone inside had to die.

Dante shifted his weapon and took down two more cartel members who were sitting at a nearby table, causing them to fall backwards out of their chairs. He then took out a man running from the kitchen, sending a bullet through his mouth, and

106

causing brain and blood to splatter against the walls just to the rear. Dante wheeled, and took out another man stepping out of the restroom, sending him flying back into the bathroom door. His body rested on the floor propping open the door like a human doorstop. The Reigns family men went through the restaurant taking out targets like a precision military special ops team. When they were done, there we only two people alive. One was crawling on the floor to a younger man, who bore a great resemblance to him. They deduced that it was the man's now dead son. The second survivor was lying on his back clutching his head. The bullet had passed through the rear of his head and exited without damaging his brain. His second wound was a gut shot, and blood covered his shirt making it appear as though someone had doused him with a bucket of dark red paint.

Dante walked up to the man crawling to his son, and watched as the man pulled his son into his arm, and tried to wipe away the blood that was coming from his mouth. He cried as caressed his son's face, and hair, and kissed his forehead.

"A father should die before his son," Dante told him. "I'm sorry for that."

The man rolled over and peered at Dante with a hatred that was palpable.

"Do you have other sons?" Dante asked.

The man nodded.

"They will try to come for me," Dante told him. "They will try to avenge you, and they will die too. At least you will die before them."

"You search for your daughter?" the man asked in broken English.

It immediately captured Dante's full attention. "Yes. Do you know where she is?"

The man coughed, sending blood flying out of his mouth. "We no have your daughter. At first, I want to say, that I hope she die in your arms. *Pero*, now I don't say that. I hope you find her, I hope that she *sees* you. I hope she *knows* you. I hope she sees the truth about you, and you have to live with her eyes seeing your soul for a long time."

Dante frowned, and turned toward the other man. He lifted his weapon and put a bullet in the other man's head. "Mother fucker!" He turned back to the last man. "Do you know where she is? Do you know where my daughter is?"

The man shook his head, and caressed his son's face. "If I knew, I would give her to you. I want you to carry her with your bloody hands. My son, he knew me. He knew my job. And he still look to his *padre con amore.* Will your daughter love you, when she finds out who you really are? Children fear the monster under the bed. The monster in your house is not under the bed."

Dante lifted his weapon and pointed it at the man. He started to squeeze the trigger and then stopped. "I hope you survive. I hope you survive and have to go back and tell the boy's mother that her son is dead. What eyes will she look at you with?"

Dante turned and headed for the door, twirling his finger in the air, telling his men that they were out of there.

Chapter Ten

Admiral Jon Paul Kidd was eighth generation navy. His forefathers served in the Continental Navy at the birth of the nation, and every generation since had dedicated their life to protecting the American nation's interest at sea. He was the son, grandson, great grandson, and great great grandson of admirals. His family's name was legendary within the naval community. He was destined to follow in his forefather's footsteps, and rise to the nation's highest naval billet; Chief of Naval Operations.

Admiral Kidd's current job was Commander of the United States Fleet Forces Command, which meant that he was in charge of all the naval personnel based in and around the continental United States, including the Caribbean and the Gulf of Mexico. He was the man who could move ships, change schedules, re-routed naval task forces, he was the man that Damian had come to see.

The admiral was in command of nearly 200 ships, more than 120,000 navy and Marine Corp personnel, and more than 1,300 aircraft. He carried upon his shoulder immense power, and immense responsibility. Today, he carried something else on his shoulder as well, his grandson.

Admiral Kidd held his inquisitive grandson's hand, as the two of them toured the U.S.S. Wisconsin, a former battleship that now served as a museum and tourist attraction in Norfolk, Virginia. The Admiral had been aboard the battleship as a young ensign before it was retired, and had been aboard it as a child when his father commanded it. It was also a ship that his grandfather had commanded during World War II. His family credited that ship with bringing his grandfather home safely. Today, he was passing down the stories, and the family legacy, to his grandson.

Damian walked passed the Admiral and bumped into him.

"Excuse me, sir," Damian told him.

"Not a problem," Admiral Kidd said, continuing to point things out to his grandson.

Damian stopped and lifted a large iPad. "You seem very knowledgeable about this ship. Perhaps you could help me."

"Sure," Admiral Kidd said. "What do you need?"

Damian pulled something up on the iPad, stood next to the admiral, and showed him what was on the screen. The admiral's face turned ashen.

"Who the fuck are you?" Admiral Kidd asked, forgetting that his young grandson was present.

"Someone who has a lot of connections with the press, and with several representatives on the Armed Services Committees, both in the House and the

Senate," Damian answered. He flipped through the iPad, changing the display from letters, to pictures. Pictures of the Admiral with a woman who was not his wife. "The military frowns on this sort of thing. It ended General Petraeus' career. Conduct unbecoming, fraternization, a whole bunch of other charges. Navy is not going to look too kindly upon this. But let's set aside the navy, what about Mrs. Kidd? She's going to cut it off when she finds out."

The admiral leaned down and kissed his grandson. "Jon, run over there and look at the display while I talk to the man for a minute."

The boy ran off, and the Admiral turned back to Damian. "Okay, cut the bullshit. Who the fuck are you, and what the hell do you want? Where did you get that? Did she give those to you?"

Damian held up his hand. "First off, no she didn't. I had her computer hacked, and my people pulled the pictures and your emails off her computer. She knows nothing. But what I know about her, is that she's not all that she's cracked up to be. She has a handler."

"Bullshit!" the admiral shouted. "I know her better than that!"

"She not Swedish, she's actually Finish, and her people are long term communist," Damian told him. "You're fucking a Russian operative. Not only are you cheating on your wife, you've compromised national security. They are not just going to retire you, they are going to make an example out of you. And even if they do allow you to retire quietly because of this, they won't be so inclined to do it once they find out about the no bid contract that you slid to your buddy. They will fuck over you good for that one."

"Who are you?" Admiral Kidd demanded. "Who do you work for?"

"I work for me," Damian told him.

"You do know that I can have a team of hitters in your home by midnight?" Admiral Kidd asked. "Battle hardened vets from Afghanistan and Iraq."

"I can have a hit team in yours," Damian replied. "But even worse, I can walk away, and text everything that I have to the fucking Washington Post and the New York Times, and have your ass in a military prison by midnight tonight. We can get into a pissing contest if you want to. I guarantee you, I will win. And what's more, it won't just be your career ending, but your family's legacy."

Admiral Kidd stepped toward Damian. "You touch my family, you're a dead man."

"I won't touch them, the military will," Damian told him. He flipped through his iPad and showed the Admiral more pictures. "You see, Admiral, the apple doesn't fall far from the tree. Your son is also sticking his dick where it doesn't belong. He's cheating on his wife too. And even worse, it's with an enlisted woman under his command. His career, like yours, will be over with."

Damian could see the resistance bleed from the Admiral. He was defeated. Like most warriors, he would fight until the end, as long as it was *his* life at risk, but like most warriors, his weakness was his family.

"You have me at a disadvantage, Mr…"

"Names aren't important," Damian told him. "What matters right now, is that I have your attention. Do I have your attention?"

"I will never betray my country, if that's what you're after," Admiral Kidd told him.

"I wouldn't ask you to," Damian told him.

"What do you want?"

"Simple," Damian told him. "I need schedules."

"Schedules?"

"I'm a drug dealer, Admiral. I need to ship my cocaine into the country. I need the Navy to stay the fuck out of the way."

Admiral Kidd laughed. "You're a two-bit cocaine peddler, and you went through all of this trouble, because you think that I can give you a schedule? Sorry to inform you, but the Navy has more important things to worry about than drug shipments coming in from South America. You should have tried the Coast Guard."

Damian smiled and nodded. "I'll worry about the Coast Guard. But I know that the Navy patrols the Gulf as well. Not only by ship, but by air."

"We're looking for Russian submarines!" Admiral Kidd sneered.

"You also participate in interdiction operations with the Coast Guard, the DEA, Customs, and Homeland," Damian told him. "You participate in anti-narcotics task forces in the Gulf as well. I just want to get my shit through, you can bust everyone else's. Hence, I need schedules, and maybe even some re-routing in case of an emergency."

"You're really asking me to do this?" Admiral Kidd asked.

"You are the Commander of the United States Fleet Forces Command," Damian told him. "You still have plenty of good years left to serve. You could be the next Commander of NATO, the next commander of the U.S. Pacific Command, the next commander of Northern Command, or even Southern Command, or Central Command, and you're on your way to being Chief of Naval Operations, and even Chairman of the Joint Chiefs. It's what you and your wife have been working toward for thirty years. Are you going to throw away your marriage, your career, your son's career and marriage, and ruin your family's legacy, as well as ruin future command for future generations because of a schedule? Cocaine will get into this country anyway. It will come through the ports, it will come up from Mexico on trucks, through the tunnels, across the Rio Grande by mule. It's coming anyway. Continue to serve your nation, Admiral. It's just a schedule."

"Grandpa, guess what I learned?" the Admiral's grandson shouted, running up to him.

"Stay free for him," Damian said, nodding at the boy. "Don't ruin his family, don't ruin the way he looks at you. You've done worse things that just pass along a schedule."

Admiral Kidd leaned down and embraced his grandson tight. He peered up at Damian and nodded.

"Good decision," Damian told him. "I'll be in touch."

"Hey, am I ever going to get this off me?" Admiral Kidd asked.

Damian nodded. "It' temporary. Just until the border opens back up. And just so you know. I want out too."

"Then why are you doing this?"

Damian peered down at the boy. "For my family. All the decisions that I've made, I made them for my family. To keep them safe."

The Admiral locked eyes with Damian for several moments, taking his measure. The two of them nodded at one another, before Damian turned and walked away, disappearing into the crowd of tourist.

*****

Washington D.C.

Secretary of Homeland Security Isaac Duncan stepped out of his Washington D.C. townhome and made his way toward his waiting black Chevy Suburban. He immediately noticed something was off.

"Where's my normal driver?" Secretary Duncan asked, climbing into the back of the Suburban. He was shocked to find a woman sitting in the back seat.

"Who are you?" He peered around. "Where are my regular security guys?"

Princess pointed at a black Cadillac parked just in front of the Suburban. "They're in the trunk."

"Who the hell are you?" Secretary Duncan asked. He tried to open the door to the Suburban, but the two bodyguards standing outside, slammed it shut and then stood with their backs leaning against it. "What the hell is going on here? Do you know who I am?"

"If I didn't, do you think I would be here?" Princess asked, lifting an eyebrow.

"I'm the Secretary of Homeland Security!" Duncan shouted. "I will have you thrown *under* the prison! You will *wish* that you were at the Colorado Maximum Security Prison!"

"Are you finished with your hissy fit?" Princess asked.

"What do you want?" Duncan demanded. "Wait a minute. I know you! I know who you are! You're the sister! If this is what I think it is, you've made a *big* mistake, Sweetheart! I will crucify you, and your entire filthy organization!"

"Let me know when you're finished," Princess told him. She lifted a glass and sipped some wine.

"*Let me out of here!*" Secretary Duncan shouted. Once again, he tried to open the door, but could not. "Kidnapping is going to get you the death penalty!"

"Actually, it won't," Princess smiled. "And actually, I'm not kidnapping you. You're here, because

116

you want to one day be President of the United States. You're here for damage control. Now, would you like to get out, and I send what I have to MSNBC, so that Chris Matthews, Rachel Maddow, and Lawrence O'Donnell can crucify your ass on the evening news, or would you like to hear what I have to say?"

"I don't have much of a choice, do I?" Duncan asked.

"You always have a choice, Isaac. Whether you make the right one, is up to you. Would you like to step back inside and talk to me now?"

Secretary Duncan peered at his front door. "In my home? My wife...."

"Is out of town," Princess said, finishing his sentence. "Are we going to start this conversation off by lying to one another?"

Princess opened her door, and her bodyguards opened the door so that the Secretary could exit the vehicle. He walked back to his home, followed by Princess and her men. He didn't notice the second black Suburban pulling up behind the one he was just inside of.

Secretary Duncan walked into his living room and tossed his jacket over a nearby arm chair. He loosened his tie, and then walked to his bar, where he started fixing himself a drink. Princess walked to the Secretary's refrigerator where she opened the door, pulled open his fruits and vegetable drawer, and found an apple. She walked to the sink, rinsed the apple off, and took a bite.

"Help yourself," Secretary Duncan said sarcastically. He drank from his glass of Scotch. "I'm all ears."

Princess took another bite from her apple. "Graduated from Harvard, magna cum laude. Worked your way through college, scholarships helped, but weren't enough. Graduated pretty heavy in debt. Went to work for Morgan Stanley, then Goldman Sachs. Met your wife, and instantly fell in love. Of course, the pretty nice trust fund that she inherited from her grandparents helped you fall in love quicker than normal. That, and the fact that her daddy was loaded, and connected, well, I imagine it was love at first sight."

Duncan smiled and let out a slight snicker. "Okay, is that what we're here to discuss? My marriage? Who doesn't marry for money? Women do it all the time."

"You were the perfect couple," Princess continued. "You were broke as hell, and she was rich as fuck. Paid off your loans, invested in Goldman stocks, a little inside knowledge helped you along. You were ambitious, she was a socialite, you parlayed that into a run for city council, and a landslide victory. Then came the mayor's office, and finally Congress. You were one of the youngest members of the House of Representatives when you were elected. Everything was rolling right along. Only thing is, you were still obligated to the Army because of your partial ROTC scholarship. September 11th happens, your reserve unit gets called up, and you, as a member of Congress could have been excused from deploying. But no, you calculating son-of-a-bitch. You go to Afghanistan with your unit, then into Iraq, and you ended up doing a total of four tours in Iraq and Afghanistan. A real, live, decorated hero."

Secretary Duncan smiled and nodded at Princess. "I see you've done your homework."

Princess took another bite, and slowly walked from around the counter. "As a battalion commander, and a military man, you were able to get on all the right committees. Homeland, Armed Services, House Intel, Foreign Affairs, Ways and Means, hell, even Appropriations. This gave you your foreign policy chops, and that book you wrote about the Korengal Valley, and about your combat action in Fallujah, made you look like an expert on terrorism, counter insurgency, and defense policy matters. And that's what led to your nomination to be the Secretary of Homeland Security."

Secretary Duncan clapped his hands sarcastically. "Wow, I'm impressed. That recap is almost better than the movie is going to be."

Princess smiled and shook her head. "People will still want to go and see the movie. They're drawn to movies about sex scandals."

"Sex scandals?" Duncan sneered. "Try again, Sweetie. I'm as clean as a baby's bottom."

"You do know about bottoms," Princess said with a smile. She nodded at her men. Other men, whom the Secretary was unaware of, led a figure into the room. The man had a black canvass bag covering his head and shoulders.

"What the hell is this?" Duncan asked.

Princess walked to the masked man, and pulled the bag from off his head. Secretary Duncan's face turned pale white, as the color bled from it.

"Steve?" Secretary Duncan asked. "What the fuck is this?"

"I started my story with you graduating from college," Princess told him. "Now, let's go back to those wild and crazy college years."

"You bitch!" Secretary Duncan shouted. He turned to Steve. "What the fuck is going on?"

"Not Steve's fault," Princess said, biting her apple. "Steve just can't stand the thought of being tortured. I mean, I lit my hand-held blow torch, and he started crying and telling shit from the moment his head popped out of his mother's couchie. He told about the priest who tickled his asshole when he was eight, all the way up to three days ago when he stole his co-worker's chocolate milk out the office fridge. I mean, I couldn't get this mother fucker to shut up."

"What did you tell them?" Secretary Duncan asked.

"He told us that you were a booty bandit, a rump ranger, that you couldn't stay out of his asshole the entire time you guys were college roommates," Princess told him

Steve put his head down.

"How the fuck could you do that?" Secretary Duncan shouted. "How could you betray me like that?"

"Like I said, Steve does not like torture," Princess interjected. "I mean, I've have old ladies who held out longer. So, the question is, what am I going to do with this information, Mr. Future President?"

Secretary Duncan lowered his head.

"Fox is going to crucify you," Princess told him. "Rush and the rest of the conservatives are going to tie your ass to a spit and roast you. You wife, well, she'll probably cut it off. And your father in law, well, he's going to fly down here on his private jet with one of those really expensive shotguns that he has in his gun cabinet, and he's going to invite you to go skeet hunting, and he's going to accidentally blow your face off. Your career is over, you'll be humiliated so bad, that you'll think about suicide. But you're not going to go that route. The reason that you're not going to kill yourself, is because you'll leave your kids behind to face all the bullshit that you weren't man enough to face. Elementary school kids can be cruel as fuck. Your Daddy's a peter puffer. Your Daddy's this, your Daddy's that. I mean, those little snot nosed bastards go hard in this day and age."

"What do you want?" Secretary Duncan asked. "Money?"

Princess bit from her apple. "I have enough money. In fact, I have so much money, that I'm going to take old Steve here, and I'm going to send him all over the world with some of my men as bodyguards to protect him. Steve says that he wants to travel. So, in order to keep Steve safe, and away from you, I'm sending him to France, Italy, Spain, Germany, Greece, and everywhere in between. He's going to live a fabulous life traveling abroad, until I need to wheel his ass out in front of the camera's to tell the world that Congressman GI Joe, the real American hero, loves to give reach arounds while he's getting shit on his dick. That's one option. I may never need him. Am I ever going to need him, Isaac?"

"What do you want?"

"Something so small, so tiny, so trivial, that you won't even believe that I bothered with all of this just to get it."

"What is that?" Secretary Duncan asked.

"I need Coast Guard schedules," Princess told him.

"Coast Guard schedules?"

"For the Gulf!" Princess said, snapping her fingers. "Don't be slow, follow along. I need to get my shit into the States."

"You've never had a problem getting it in before."

"Well, that was too much work," Princess said, tossing her apple into the trash. "I don't want to work that hard anymore. I want it easy. As a matter of fact, I want it so easy, that I could drive my specially marked eighteen wheelers through the border checkpoints, and not get searched. Get me?"

"How can I control that?" Secretary Duncan asked. "The Coast Guard schedules, I understand. But I can't control which trucks get searched and which don't. That's random. And then you have the dogs to contend with."

Princess nodded at her men, and they took Steve out the room.

"How about if my trucks, had the same markings as the CIA's trucks?" Princess asked. "You people know which trucks to search, and which ones not to. I can paint those bitches with the exact same markings, and roll them through right along with Langley's fucking trucks."

"You really want to play with the CIA?" Secretary Duncan asked.

"I'm not playing with them, or their shipments," Princess told him. "I'm just trying to sneak mine through. What they don't know..."

"Are you trying to get us both killed?" Secretary Duncan asked.

"They won't know," Princess told him. "Do you think they have someone sitting at the border seeing if other trucks look like theirs?"

Secretary Duncan exhaled, and then nodded.

"You've made a wise choice, Mr. President," Princess told him. "I am curious though. What kind of trucks are they using. Don't tell me, Monsanto Trucks? Dow Chemical? BSAF? Knight?"

"You just guarantee me, that no one else is going to find out about this!" Secretary Duncan told her. "And you make sure that his ass doesn't talk to anyone else about this. Ever!"

"You have my word, Isaac," Princess said smiling, and fixing the Secretary's tie. "Steve does not like torture. And for some unknown reason, he's scared to death of sweet little old me."

Secretary Duncan took a long drink from his glass. "*No*, you don't say!"

Princess shrugged and smiled. "Your men are going to be sleep for quite some time. I hit their asses with enough tranquilizers to put a horse out. You need a ride to work?"

Duncan shook his head. "You know, I think I want to take the day off today."

Princess stopped. "No suicide."

Again, Duncan shook his head. "I'm not checking out. I'm just mentally exhausted. I'm taking an Uber to the park. I'm going to walk around the pond, feed the fucking ducks, and think about how much my life is fucked up."

"Your life is still golden," Princess told him. "You can still have the White House."

"At what cost?" Duncan asked. "I just made a deal with the devil. What more are you going to want?"

"I think I want to be drug Czar!" Princess said laughing. "I'll lead this nation's war on drugs."

"Strangely, I think you'd be good at it," Duncan told her.

"Nothing else, Isaac," Princess told him. "I want nothing else. I just want to get my shit in. You can bust everyone else's."

"You going to throw me some busts?" Duncan asked. "You know, quid pro quo. Make me look good."

"Sorry, Boo!" Princess shrugged and smiled. "Not a snitch."

Princess headed for the door, and stopped short. "Isaac."

"Yeah?"

"For what it's worth, Steve told me about your relationship," Princess told him. "He loved you. I think he still loves you. He kept your secret all these years. I think he loved you enough to let you go and live this life, while he lives his. I saw some letters between the two of you. And I know that you were still sneaking off and hooking up with him up until a few years ago. I also know that you're still in touch with him. It's okay. I know what's it's like to love someone of the same sex. I had a husband at one time, and I was still in love with another woman. Society is changing. Maybe not fast enough for us, but its changing."

"Why are you telling me this?" Secretary Duncan asked.

"Because this trip was not all business," Princess told him. "Deep down somewhere inside of me, there's a teeny tiny part of me that's still human."

Chapter Eleven

`Peaches turned the handle on the shower to the off position once she heard the banging on her hotel room door. The knock was hard, pounding, and rapid, like a police SWAT Team was about to kick in her door.

"Hold the fuck up!" she shouted. She reached out of the shower and grabbed a towel, wrapped it around her waist, and then grabbed another and wrapped it around her breast. She stormed to the motel room door. "Who the fuck is it?"

The person banged on the door again. Peaches peered through the peep hole, only to see that the person was covering it with their hand. She walked to the bed and lifted a pistol and pulled back the slide to make sure that a round was in the chamber. She walked back to the door.

"You got three seconds to uncover that muthafucking peep hole, before I start shooting!" Peaches shouted.

"Open up the door, old scary ass muthafucka!" the person shouted.

Peaches recognized the voice, even though the person was trying to disguise it by making it deeper. She removed the chain, unlocked the bolt and threw the door open.

"What the fuck are you doing here?" she asked.

"Is that how you greet the love of your life?" Darius asked. He stepped forward and tried to wrap his hands around her, but she stepped back.

"I'm serious, what the hell are you doing here?" Peaches asked. She peered out into the hallway to see if anyone else was out there. "Get your ass in here!"

Darius walked into the room, and Peaches locked the door behind him. "I thought you had to stay in San Antonio? Why are you in Ohio? I thought we agreed that it was too dangerous for you to come here?"

"You agreed," Darius said with a smile. "I didn't. Do I look worried about these niggaz?"

Peaches exhaled and shook her head. "You just don't understand. You are a target! You ain't from up here. These niggaz will *bury* you. And then your peeps will blame my ass."

"I'm a grown ass man," Darius told her. "It's not your responsibility to protect me!"

"Your ass is hard headed, just like all these other niggaz!" Peaches shot back. "Men! All of you think your asses are invincible! At least until you're laying up in the emergency room, or laying on a cold metal table in the morgue!"

127

Darius pulled her close. "You care about me, huh?"

"I don't know why!" Peaches said, folding her arms.

"You know why," Darius said with a sly grin. He pulled her towel loose, causing it to fall to the floor.

"I don't even think so!" Peaches said, grabbing for her towel.

"Body slam!" Darius said, scooping her up and tossing her onto the bed.

"Boy, stop!" Peaches shouted.

Darius dove onto the bed with her, with his head landing between her legs. Peaches closed her legs, tightening her thighs around his head. His tongue was still free to maneuver. Darius licked around the outside of her vagina, and then parted her lips with his tongue. The warmth of his tongue lapping against her labia was enough to get her going. She opened her legs giving him full access to her treasure.

Darius licked her clitoris, and then pulled it into her mouth and began to suck gently on it, applying a gentle suction. Peaches arched her back and moaned. That was her spot. Darius released her pearl tongue, and flicked his tongue licking rapidly for several moments, before engulfing it into his mouth and sucking on it once more. It drove her crazy.

"Oh, my God!" Peaches cried out. She clasped the back of his head, and began to gyrate as he sucked.

Darius sucked her clit, and slid two fingers inside of her, gently caressing her G-spot. It was an overload of pleasure for her. The more he sucked, the more she gyrated, and the tighter she gripped the back of his head. The tighter she gripped, the more rapidly he sucked on her. It built, until she screamed a continuous cry of pleasure.

"I'm cumming!" Peaches shouted. "Ooooh, please stop! Please stop! "

Darius continued to suck. Peaches continued to cum. Finally, she shoved his head away from her vagina.

Darius laughed, and then kissed around her privates, working his way up to her navel, and then up to her breast, where he took her nipple into his mouth. Peaches was still breathing heavily. She clasped the back of his neck and he sucked gently upon her breast. Darius worked his way up to her neck where he licked and sucked, and then engulfed her earlobe and sucked on it as well.

Peaches took Darius's manhood into her hand, placed it on her vagina, and then lifted her ass so that he could slide inside. Despite her wetness, she still gasped as he penetrated her. It had been a while, and it felt so good to her. She needed everything that he was giving to her at that moment, she needed to cum, to relax, to ease all the tension and worry in her body, and he was doing just that.

Darius slid in and out of Peaches rapidly, pounding deeply, causing her to cry out each time he plunged deep inside of her. She clasped his back, and then dug her nails deep into *his* flesh each time he dug deep into *her* flesh. She opened her legs wider, trying to ease the pleasurable pain that she was experiencing with each of his deep strokes. She could feel the muscles in his back working overtime. Rubbing her hands over his sweaty, bulging muscles, while feeling him sliding in and out of her caused her to cum once again. She bit down upon his shoulders and cried out.

"I'm cumming! I'm cumming! Right there! Right there! Keep going! Ooooh!"

Darius didn't let up. He kept digging deep. He worked his magic wand like he was churning butter. Peaches gripped his muscular ass and held on. She was orgasming non-stop now.

Darius slowly built up to a punishing climax and found himself pounding her. Peaches cries were now non-stop. She clenched her teeth and grabbed the bed sheets and twisted them into a ball. She could feel his rod growing stiffer, longer, and then she felt his warm fluid shoot deep up into her. They had both came this time, and neither could move. They laid stiff, with him throbbing inside of her releasing his life into her, while she laid breathing heavily excreting her own juices. Finally, they were both able to relax and their exhausted bodies went limp. Peaches' cell phone rang.

"Hello?" Peaches said, lifting her phone and sliding the answer bar to the side. Her eyes flew open wide. "Girl, where you at? I'm on my way!" Peaches jumped out of the bed and ran into the bathroom to clean up.

"What's going on?" Darius asked.

"Hurry up!" Peaches shouted from the bathroom. "We gotta go! That was Trap! She's here!"

Darius climbed out of bed, and walked into the bathroom to get cleaned up.

*****

Starbucks

Peaches and Darius pulled up in Darius' rented Mustang GT Convertible. Trap was standing outside with Chi-Chi. Darius was barely able to stop his Mustang before Peaches jumped out and rushed to Trap. The two of them embraced tightly, and tears flowed.

"Girl! I thought you were dead!" Trap said crying.

"I was so worried about you!" Peaches said crying. "Oh, my God! Thank you! Thank you, Sweet Jesus! Thank you!"

Peaches hugged Chi-Chi. "Girl, I didn't know if anyone was alive!"

"You know I wasn't going out like that!" Chi-Chi said, hugging her. "Them muthafucka's tried, but Cheech was ready for they ass!"

Peaches laughed through her tears. She turned and hugged Trap once again.

The driver's side door of a black Mercedes S Class opened, and out climbed One-eyed Omar. He was talking on a cellphone. Peaches raced to him and leaped into his arms. The two of them embraced.

131

Darius threw his car in park and climbed out, joining her.

"Omar!" Peaches cried out hugging him. She kissed him. "Oh, my God! Oh my God! It's good to see you. God answered my prayers!"

"Ain't a muthafucka alive, that can kill Omar!" he said, in his deep raspy baritone voice.

"What happened?" Peaches asked, wiping away her tears.

"We all got hit," Omar told her.

"Everybody?" Peaches asked. Her heart fluttered. That meant her brother got hit as well. "Has anybody seen Joaquin?"

"He's hiding out," Omar told her. "I got the nigga staying with some of my peeps out in Cincinnati."

Peaches burst into tears and wrapped her arms around Omar once again. She began crying uncontrollably.

"Hey, cut that out!" Omar told her. "You know I got you, Baby girl! I got you!"

Darius took Omar's measure. He liked him. He could tell that Omar was dangerous, not just from the scar running down the side of his face, but by the look in his eyes and the way he carried himself. He could also tell that Omar was real. And loyal. He got hit, handled his business, and then went to save the rest of his peeps. Darius decided that he liked Omar a lot.

"We got hit by somebody with a lot of juice!" Chi-Chi said. "My first thought was that bitch ass nigga

Hassan. But after checking around, I found out that it wasn't him. His soldiers were in Detroit that night. Besides, even Hassan couldn't put together that much muscle."

"How did you find him?" Peaches asked Omar. "Where was he? Is he okay?"

Omar nodded. "He's fine, Sis. I got to him right after I got Trap out the hospital. I got Trap, then went and scooped him. Cheech went to your spot to grab you. His young ass was in the hood shooting dice and shit. He's alright. If you don't count the money that nigga lost shooting craps that night."

Peaches couldn't help herself, she hugged Omar again. "Thank you! Thank you!" She turned to Chi-Chi and hugged her.

"Sorry, I got there too late," Chi-Chi told her.

Peaches shook her head. "Girl, don't you even think that! I'm just so happy that you made it. And you got to Trap in time!"

"Yeah, this Black ass motherfucka woke me up outta my sleep, talking about we gotta go." Trap said, with a smile.

Peaches laughed. She clasped Trap's hand. "V is safe too. She's made it. She's safe. I don't know where that bitch is right now, but she's in good hands."

Trap smiled and nodded. "I called her too. We all made it." Trap clasped Chi-Chi's hand.

"And now comes the hard part," Chi-Chi told them. "We gotta survive. We gotta find out who did this, and we gotta rebuild."

"I got one of them alive," Omar told them. "Before he met his demise, I got outta him who he worked for."

"Oh really?" Chi-Chi asked, surprised. "Why didn't you tell me?"

"This the first time I talked to you since that night," Omar answered. "Hell, we was so busy trying to get to Peach, and V, and Trap, and everybody, I didn't have time."

"Okay, so who sent the muthafuckas?" Peaches asked.

"He worked for Kharee," Omar told them.

"Kharee ain't got that kinda muscle!" Trap told them. "Bullshit!"

Omar nodded. "He was one of Kharee's niggas."

Peaches shook her head. "Them wasn't none of Kharee's people that hit my crib. They was *too* on point."

"Then what that tell you, Baby Girl?" Omar asked with a smile.

Peaches thought for a few moments. "That Kharee brought in some out of town hitters? Some professionals?"

Omar clapped his hands. "You may go to the front of the class."

"Kharee ain't got that kinda juice!" Trap said shaking her head. She still wasn't convinced. "He don't have the money to pull that kinda move. Let alone the balls!"

"Not by himself," Omar told them. "Which means he has somebody backing him. Somebody pretty heavy."

"And the soldiers sent to my crib were Black," Peaches said, thinking out loud. She turned toward Darius. "Mutherfucka!"

The others turned toward Darius.

"I know you don't think..." Darius started to speak, but Peaches cut him off.

"Of course not, nigga!" she told him. "But I fucking have an idea. I'll bet you them mutherfucka's was from Alabama!"

"Baby Doc," Darius said nodding. "That son-of-a-bitch!"

"He wanted Kharee on The Commission," Peaches told them.

"Then how did you get on there?" Omar asked, eyeing Darius suspiciously. "No disrespect Lil Sis, but you don't control all of Ohio. So why were you chosen? Sounds to me, like this whole shit is being manipulated from some spots far away from Columbus. Sound to me like we're all pawns in a proxy war of some kind."

Omar's stare at Darius turned ice cold.

"Let's think this shit through," Peaches told them.

135

"Yeah, we need to get V, and all of us get together and think this shit through," Trap told them. She stared at Darius. "Alone."

Darius smiled. Peaches had warned him. They didn't trust outsiders.

A car rolled by basing, and hit its brakes. They watched as it busted a U-turn in the middle of the road. All of them reached for their pistols. Chesarae pulled up and hoped out of the car and hurried to where Peaches was standing. He scooped her into his arms and kissed her.

"Where the fuck you been, Peach?" Chesarae asked. He kissed her face in rapid succession. "Damn, you had me fucking worried! What the fuck happened!"

Peaches pulled away. "Where the fuck you been?"

"Looking for you!" Chesarae told her. "Trying to find out what the fuck happened that night!"

"Well, you sure in the fuck ain't do a good job!" Peaches shouted.

"What's that supposed to mean?" Chesarae shouted back. "I hear about what happened, I race back to Columbus, get to your crib, and everything is fucking destroyed! I'm checking the morgue, the jails, calling everybody! Nobody knows nothing!"

"Did you call Omar?" Peaches asked.

Chesarae shook his head. "I didn't know whether O was dead or alive! Ashaad hadn't heard from Trap, V was missing. Everybody else was dead!"

"Well, I'm okay, Ches!" Peaches said nodding. "You can rest your little head. I'm A fucking okay."

"Why the fucking attitude?" Chesarae asked. "You giving me attitude, when you should be checking ya mothafuckin soldiers!" He pointed at Darius. "These scrub ass niggaz you hire as bodyguards are the ones you should be mad at! This nigga *look* like he'll fold just like the rest of them niggaz you had guarding your crib that night!"

"Scrub?" Darius said, stepping forward.

Omar jumped between Darius and Chesarae.

"Oh, you wanna have some nuts now, huh?" Chesarae asked Darius. "Where was them nuts at when my woman's crib was getting run up in?"

"I ain't her bodyguard," Darius said smiling. "Although, I have been keeping her body close to me."

"Oh, really?" Chesarae asked. He turned to Peaches. "Is that what's been happening? You been fucking with the help? Is that why you been tripping with me?"

Peaches pushed Chesarae back to his car. "Just leave, Ches! Get the fuck outta here!"

"Naw, you gonna talk to me!" Chesarae shouted. "Who the fuck is this old punk ass nigga? You fucking around on me, Peach?"

"Ches, we ain't together!" Peaches shouted. "You can't just show up at my door one day and think everything is back to normal!"

"You wasn't saying that when you was visiting me on the weekends!" Chesarae told her. He stared at Darius. "Every weekend!"

Peaches shoved Chesarae into his car. "Get out of here!"

Chesarae started up his car and roared the engine. "I got you! This is how you repay a nigga?" he said, nodding. He shifted his gaze to Darius. "I got you too, Off Brand!"

Chesarae raced away, and Peaches turned back toward Darius. Darius lifted his hand silencing her before she could speak.

"Don't!" Darius said. "I see why you didn't want me to come to Ohio."

Darius walked to his car, climbed inside, and left.

Peaches turned toward Trap and threw up her hands.

"Bitch, you always managing to get yourself into some love triangle bullshit!" Trap said, shaking her head and smiling.

"You don't have time for this shit," Chi-Chi told Peaches. "We have a Kharee problem. You can get Ayanla to fix your life later. Right now, we have to make sure you stay alive."

Peaches exhaled. "We also have a Hassan problem."

"How so?" Omar asked.

"The Commission wants to give Hassan Michigan," Peaches told them. "If Hassan is allowed to consolidate all of Michigan, you know what that means."

"He'll come for us," Omar answered. "He ain't gonna leave Ohio alone, no matter what he says."

"Exactly," Peaches said, nodding. "Hassan can't be allowed to take all of Detroit, let alone all of Michigan. And, we have to take Kharee off the table."

"He'll be ready for us," Omar said.

"And, he's had time to recruit and get big," Trap added. "I'm sure, since he's wiped out our entire organization, his people have taken over all of our territories."

"Then that means we have to keep recruiting, and start taking them back," Peaches declared.

"What do you mean, keep recruiting?" Omar asked, lifting an eyebrow.

"I haven't been sitting on my ass since I've been back," Peaches smiled. "I've managed to put together a few soldiers."

"Me too," Chi-Chi said with a smile.

"I got some niggaz," Omar added, with a crooked smile.

"Then let's get to work!" Trap told them.

Chapter Twelve

Julian Jones stepped off his private jet onto the tarmac and straightened his tie, as he peered around the private airfield. Although he absolutely loved Atlanta, he hated the hot summers. His days at Morehouse were some of the best days of his life. Back then, Atlanta was popping. He had a million stories to tell from all the years he attended Freaknik, and even more stories to tell about sneaking into the dorms over at Spelman. Those were the days, he thought, as he smoothed out his waves, and climbed into the back of the waiting Rolls Royce Phantom.

Julian was in town for a special meeting with his arch nemesis Emil, to talk peace, and squash any lingering beef between the two of them. Emil said that they needed to get along to help Princess in Florida, and Damian in Texas. But he knew that it was really just an attempt keep him from putting that dick to his wife. It was only a matter of time before he put that pipe to Princess, and Emil would be done with. His fuck game was like Lays Potato Chips, no woman could stop at just one fuck. No, Julian smiled, they came back for more and more. Princess wouldn't be any different.

The Phantom motored through traffic until it pulled beneath the awning at the Four Seasons Hotel in Atlanta. There, a doorman pulled open the enormous suicide doors and waved for Julian to step out. Another doorman held open the entrance to the grand hotel, welcoming him to come inside. Julian's men were already there securing the area. He climbed out, nodded at his men, and made his way inside for the quick trip to the conference room that had been reserved for the meeting.

Emil and his men were already inside. Emil was seated at the opposite end of the conference table, and he was loosely surrounded by twenty of his men. He motioned for Julian to take the seat at the opposite end of the conference table.

Julian unbuttoned his suit jacket and seated himself at the table. He nodded at his men, who left the room. Emil turned and nodded at his own men, who also left the room. He turned back to Julian.

"Appreciate you agreeing to this meeting," Emil told him.

"Of course, why not?" Julian told him. "Old friends should be able to sit down and talk."

"Are we, Julian?"

"Are we what?"

"Friends?"

"Why would you suspect differently?" Julian asked.

"Friends don't try to fuck their friend's wives," Emil shot back.

Julian leaned back in his chair. "I figured that's what this meeting going to be about. Sure, you disguised it as a meeting to get along, to clear up any misunderstandings, to bring our organizations together to support Princess in Florida. And right off the muthafucking bat, you start with that shit. I'm not trying to fuck your girl, Emil!"

"My wife!"

"If I remember, the wedding didn't happen because of a certain kidnapping," Julian said, lifting an eyebrow.

"You seem happy about that."

"Jesus Christ, Emil!" Julian shouted, sitting up. "Happy that a little girl got kidnapped? Are you really going to go there, Bruh? Are you? Cause if you are, let me let you in on something, I don't need no kidnapping to go down, in order stop your wedding. That's for one. And two, ain't no wedding gonna stop no woman from giving her pussy to who she wants to give it to, when she wants to give it to them!"

"You're a snide little son-of-a-bitch!" Emil shouted. "You fuck with my wife, that's your ass!"

"Hey, don't check me, check yo girl!" Julian shot back. "You going out like a bitch! You don't never come at the player because your game ain't strong enough to keep your woman in check!"

"Player?" Emil snorted. "You're a two-bit punk! An over aged frat boy who's dick in going to get him killed!"

"By who?" Julian laughed. "By your woman? She's the only one in your relationship with balls!"

"Fuck you!" Emil shouted. "You wanna try me? You wanna see what I'm capable of?"

Julian laughed and slowly clapped his hands. "I see that bitch done made you tough, Roscoe!" Julian leaned forward. "As much as you want to be, and try to be, and pretend to be, you ain't Damian Reigns. And you damn sure ain't Dante. Ain't nobody worried about you, Emil. You ain't gonna bust a grape. The only reason ain't nobody took Georgia away from your soft ass yet, is because we know you got Damian's dick all the way down your throat. Does he at least give you a reach around?"

Emil lifted his cell phone from off the table to threw it at Julian, who managed to dodge it. He jumped up and charged after him. Julian's men and Emil's men heard the commotion and rushed into the conference room to pull their bosses apart.

"You're dead, mother fucker!" Emil shouted. "Dead! You hear me? You're dead!"

Julian straightened his suit, and smoothed out his waves. "It's been nice. I'm off to Florida to meet this hot ass Black chic from Texas who's been dying to give me the pussy."

Emil tried to go after Julian again, but his men held him down and forced him back into his chair. Julian's men opened the conference room door for him to leave. He headed out the door but stopped short and turned back to Emil.

"Too bad it has to be like this, I liked Damian," Julian told him. "He's going to be pissed off at me for a while for having to kill his bitch. But maybe once I marry his sister, he'll get over it."

143

Julian turned and walked out.

"Get off me!" Emil shouted to his men.

Emil's men released him. He rose from the conference chair, straightened out his suit. He picked his cellphone up off the ground and turned on the camera feature, and checked his lip to see if it was bleeding.

"That mother fucker is a walking dead man," Emil told his men. "He just doesn't know it. Damian is not going to be able to stop me from killing him, and neither is The Commission. I'm just going to have to deal with the consequences later. But that smug, slick, Rico Suave looking mother fucker is dead!"

One of Emil's men stuck his head in the conference room. "The car is around front, boss."

Emil nodded, straightened his suit once again, and headed out of the conference room, down the hall, and through the main lobby area. Walking through the lobby, Emil could sense something was a bit off. What was usually a luxurious lobby full of hotel guest was nearly barren. Only two clerks working the desk, and a bell boy pushing a luggage cart were there. The bell hop stopped the luggage cart near the hotels exit and walked into the room behind the front desk. That piqued Emil's curiosity even more so. The Four Seasons was one of the top hotels in Atlanta, and it's unthinkable that a luggage cart would be left unattended near the front door for all the guest see. Emil looked to the concierge desk, only to see both clerks duck down behind it. He quickly turned back toward the exit, but there was no one there. His eyes shifted to the luggage cart.

"Get down!" Emil shouted to his men, as he dove for the floor.

The explosion from the baggage ripped through the hotel lobby sending shrapnel flying everywhere. Most of his men were torn apart instantly by the speeding nails, ball bearings, and shards of razor sharp metal that had been placed inside of the suitcases. The few who were left were laying on the floor clutching their heavily bleeding wounds and crying out for help. The flammable gel that had been added to the explosive had the hotel lobby and most of his men on fire. The hotel's sprinkle system came alive.

Emil, bloody, and now wet, tried to stand, but found that he too had been wounded. He pulled a long, thin, sabot out of his knee, crying out in pain with each centimeter of its extraction. When finished, he tossed the bloody metal shard onto the ground, braced himself against the remains of an arm chair and rose. Limping, he made his way to the shattered glass doors of the hotel's entrance and peered out.

Help was running inside to treat the living. Someone grabbed him, and lowered his bloodied and blackened body to the ground. Emil couldn't help but to laugh. He laughed because he couldn't believe that Julian would try to kill him on his own turf. He laughed because he didn't see it coming. Most of all, he laughed because he was still alive.

"Julian!" Emil shouted into the sky. "I'm going to kill you, Julian! I'm going to fuckin kill you!"

He laughed the laughed of the demented, as the ambulances began to arrive on the scene. He was still laughing as he was placed on a gurney, and lifted into the back on the emergency vehicle. Everyone around thought that the trauma had made his mind go mad. Emil was laughing, because he was in shock, disbelief, and because he life had once again been spared.

*****

New York

    1110 Park Avenue was located on Manhattan's Upper East Side. It was one of the most desirable addresses in all of New York, nestled right across from the Guggenheim Museum, with water views of Central Park's Jacqueline Kennedy Onassis Reservoir. Despite it being down the street from the Central Park Zoo, and all of New York's greatest museums, high end boutiques, and toniest restaurants, today's meeting location had actually been chosen for its discretion. No one, would suspect that heads of the East Coast oldest and most powerful families, would set foot in such a chic, modern, and distinctly extravagant place. Don Biaggio's daughter had allowed them the use of her twenty million-dollar condominium while she was in Paris on a shopping trip. The Old Ones sat gathered in her living room waiting for their guest to arrive.

    Malcom 'Baby Doc' Mueller made his way through the glitzy lobby with its turn of the century decor, where Biaggio's men escorted him to the waiting elevator. He hated having to come to New York almost as much as he hated New Yorkers. He was a Southern gentleman at heart, and found the fast pace, the congestion, and the rudeness distasteful, not to mention the horrible weather. He also despised Italians, or Sicilians, or whatever the fuck they referred to themselves as being. They all reeked of olive oil, he thought. Spaghetti, cheese, cheap wine, and tomato sauce, combined with too much cheap cologne. Even the Old Ones didn't seem to know when to put down the cologne bottle after two sprays. They seemed to douse themselves in it. Well, that, and olive oil.

The elevator stopped at the penthouse, where Biaggio's men escorted him into the penthouse, where the old dons were waiting.

"Malcom!" Don Biaggio said, rising. "Welcome, welcome. We were just talking about you."

"I'll bet," Baby Doc said, walking to where Biaggio was standing, and embracing him Sicilian style. He wondered how many times they had used the word *nigger* before he stepped into the room. Probably more than a concert full of rappers at a summer jam festival.

"Please, sit down," Don Biaggio said, waving toward a nearby seat.

Baby Doc seated himself in a chair that seemed to be arranged so that it was the designated hot seat. He quickly noticed how the old don's seating arrangements were aligned to form a semi-circle around his. He felt like he was in court.

"Well, no sense in beating around the bush," Don Guiseppi De Luca said, leaning in. "We invited you here, to talk about Columbus."

"Yes, what happened in Columbus?" Don Amedeo Esposito asked.

Baby Doc turned to Don Biaggio. "I must admit, that I'm a little confused about this meeting, Don Biaggio. It was my understanding that our arrangements were considered confidential. But I see that you have included your associates in our activities."

Don Biaggio waved his wrinkled hand through the air, dismissing Baby Doc's concerns. "Malcom, I'm an old man. My time in this world is limited. I thought it best that my associates have a complete understanding of what we are trying to accomplish together. I was under the impression that we were working together to limit the Reigns family's power and influence across the board. In exchange, we would take care of your supply issues."

"And we are doing just that!" Baby Doc told them. "My move in Columbus, was to prevent another Reigns family stooge from taking a seat on The Commission. If she was taken out, then someone friendlier, someone who would even share our goals, would then take her place. It was a move beneficial to everyone."

"A girl?" Don De Luca lifted an eyebrow.

"You attacked a woman?" Don Tito Bonafacio asked, clearly demonstrating his disgust, and uneasiness with the idea.

"A ruthless, young, brash, individual," Baby Doc explained. "The amount of people she has killed to get to where she is, means that she does not warrant your sympathies. It was business, and necessary."

"I don't see how Ohio is necessary to our plans," De Luca told him. "We wanted the Reigns family out of Jersey. In exchange for Jersey, you would get to eat of off our supply."

"You want Jersey," Baby Doc told them, growing frustrated. "The bigger plan is to first keep them from getting stronger. Taking Ohio out of their camp does that."

"Ohio is a side show!" Don Lombardi declared. "It puts everybody's necks at risk, for no reason. We don't give a shit about Ohio, we want Jersey, and if possible, Philly! Attacking some girl in Ohio, how does that help us? That doesn't sound like business, that sounds personal."

"Right now, the Reigns family is scrambling for men," Baby Doc told them. "They are bleeding money, and every available soldier they have, is spread throughout Texas and Mexico. Jersey is weak, Philly is weak, California is weak, Florida is weak. Take away Ohio, and they can't get men from there. I'm putting California in play as well. They'll have to decide whether they want to pull men from the search and send them to California, which Damian will want to do, but Dante will not, or lose California. I'm putting Florida in play. They can't keep California, and Florida. Princess will want to hold on to Florida, while Dante will not want to give up a single man to help her keep it. In the end, it is my goal to make them lose Florida *and* California, as well as New

149

Jersey, *and* Philly. They will be too weak to try to re-take any of them, and if they do, they'll concentrate on one of the big states, not Jersey."

De Luca exhaled forcibly. "I see your plan, but it's dangerous. A lot of moving parts. Too many moving parts. The best plans, are always the simple ones. And what if Damian pulls troops away from searching for that little girl and sends them to California, or Florida, or even Jersey. Then what? We get in a war with The Commission?"

"That's why we have to do it my way," Baby Doc told them. "No fingerprints on the operation. We allow others to do the dirty work, we just supply the money, the political cover, the police protection, the strategy..."

"And the muscle?" Don Esposito said, interrupting him. "You sent men into Columbus. You didn't leave just fingerprints, but giant muddy footprints."

"They won't trace anything back to me," Baby Doc said, leaning back in his seat and smiling. "The girl lied. She doesn't control the state. She still has rivals in it, plenty of them. It looks like a local war between rivals. If she keeps it up, The Commission will cut her loose anyway. They don't like attention."

"They don't like attention?" Don Lombardi said sarcastically. The Don's around the room snickered. "Those fucking Reigns are tearing up the earth down there. They got every news organization in the world talking about the bloodshed in South Texas and Mexico. They think it's a cartel war between the

Mexicans. Pretty soon, the politicians are going to have to do something."

"That's good for us, right?" Baby Doc asked.

Don De Luca shook his head. "I've never used the feds to get rid of an enemy. I won't start now. This is *our* thing. We keep the police out of it. Are we clear on that?"

"Of course," Don Biaggio said, stepping back in to gain control of the meeting. "Malcom, perhaps we should concentrate more on our original plan."

"Our original plan was to deal a blow to the Reigns family, am I right?" Baby Doc asked. "We're supposed to be working together. You get New Jersey, I get dope from your Colombian connect, and the Reigns family gets what it deserves."

"Focus on Jersey!" Don Lombardi told him.

"I agree," Don Esposito chimed in. "We need a smaller plan, much more focused, more limited. We need deniability."

Baby Doc stared at Don Esposito and thought him a coward. All of the old men, were cowards. They lacked vision, as well as the understanding of the broader strategy.

"Malcom, perhaps it would be better if you forgot about this Ohio adventure," Don Biaggio told him. "Now, what of our shipment?"

"My men are ready," Baby Doc announced. "Make sure your people are ready and make sure it's going to be delivered on time."

"The ship will be arriving in Mobile next week," Don De Luca told him.

"My men will help offload it, and then we'll transport it by truck to one of my warehouses in Birmingham," Baby Doc told them. "From there, your people can collect your shipment, and get it where it needs to be."

"Wonderful to have a new partner and a new friend," Don Biaggio said with a smile. He lifted his glass in toast.

"Especially a friend with a port," Baby Doc said, lifting his glass. He knew that the Old Ones needed his port, just as much as he needed the cocaine that the new El Jeffe was sending them from Columbia. While the rest of The Commission was depending on the Reigns family to get the shipments through from Mexico, he was going to ensure his supply. And if the Reigns family couldn't supply The Commission, he would be ready to step in. The power on The Commission would shift dramatically. He would be the man calling the shots. And if they somehow managed to keep California, he would make them give it up in exchange for his supply. He was about to bring their asses back down to earth, and maybe even get lucky enough to put a few of them beneath it.

Chapter Thirteen

HEB was the largest grocery chain in the State of Texas, and the fifth largest grocery and supermarket chain in the country. It's HEB Plus stores were the size of Super Walmart's, and carried everything from groceries to large screen smart televisions. It was inside of one of these super-sized grocery stores that Leo Limon, the Sheriff of Maverick County, was purchasing a few honey-do items on his way home from a long day's work. It was also in this Eagle Pass, Texas HEB where Dante had followed him to.

Sheriff Limon placed his small, red, carrying basket onto the store floor as he examined shelf after shelf of toilet paper. Some packs listed at twelve hundred square yards, while other brands listed themselves as containing six hundred and twenty-six. For a man who ran a vast department of deputies spread over thousands and square miles, something so simple as picking the right toilet paper should have come easy, he thought.

"Don't squeeze the Charmin," Dante said, standing behind the Sheriff, twisting the long silencer onto his barrel.

Sheriff Limon turned quickly, and upon seeing Dante, could feel gas escaping his stomach. He lifted his hand. Everyone on the planet had heard about the deaths of all the law enforcement officials in Texas and Mexico. He knew Dante, and he knew why he was there. The silenced weapon in his hand served as confirmation.

"I have a daughter!" Sheriff Limon, pleaded.

"Me too," Dante said with a smile.

"Please, I had nothing to do with your daughter's kidnapping," Sheriff Limon said, pleading. "I did everything I could after the Amber Alert went out. My entire department deployed and searched for the vehicle. I'm an honorable man. I've never gotten mixed up in cartel business. My entire department is clean. Please, don't do this. You don't have to do this!"

"I have a list," Dante told him. "It's kind like Santa's list. I know who's been naughty, and who's played nice. Before I walked into this store, I checked the list twice. You deployed your officers immediately."

"I did!" Sheriff Limon said instantly.

"And you've continued to keep your ear to the street," Dante continued. "I heard the Maverick County Sheriff's Department has been asking everyone they arrest if they have any information on my daughter. You've also put out a reward for her return."

154

"Yes," Sheriff Limon said nodding. Tears formed in his eyes. "Please, I have a wife, I have a son, I have a daughter. I have a grandmother that I take care of."

"Your department, along with the Eagle Pass Police Department conducted a raid two days ago, because of a tip that a little girl may have been kept at a house used by coyotes," Dante continued.

"It was a bad tip," Sheriff Limon said. "It turned out to be nothing. We searched every inch of the place. I brought in our forensics team, and there was nothing."

"You've always refused to take bribes," Dante continued. "From my family, from the cartels, from everyone."

"I'm sorry, but I cannot" Sheriff Limon told him.

"My list said that you've been a good boy," Dante told him. "You've went way above and beyond to try to find my daughter. Stay motivated."

Sheriff Limon nodded and swallowed hard. He wiped the sweat that had formed on his brow.

Dante and his men turned and started to walk away, and then Dante stopped and turned back toward the Sheriff. He lifted his weapon.

"That one!" Dante told him. "The Scott Tissue. You get more per roll. The other ones are just a rip off."

Sheriff Limon clasped his stomach which had turned into knots when Dante turned and lifted his weapon. He nodded, and grabbed a four pack of Scotts Tissue from the shelf.

"Thanks for the tip," Limon said weakly.

Dante nodded. "And Leo..."

"Yes?"

"Stay honest," Dante told him. "Don't take bribes. From me, from them, from anyone. You're alive right now, because you're clean. And one more thing. Thanks for searching so hard for my little girl."

"I'm a father," Sheriff Limon said, finally able to stand up straight.

"And a good one," Dante told him. "Remain the type of person that your daughter can be proud of."

Sheriff Limon nodded.

Dante and his men turned and walked away.

*****

Dante stepped out of the store to see more men than the ones he brought. His men were standing in a circle, and they were surrounded by other men.

"What the fuck is going on here?" Dante asked.

Mina Reigns stepped out of a Black Escalade. "Hey cuzzin!"

"Mina!" Dante shouted. "What the fuck is going on here?"

"Boss wants to see you," Mina told him.

"What the fuck you mean?" Dante asked. "I *am* the boss!"

"Nope," Mina said, shaking her head. "The *big* boss."

"*I don't have a boss!*" Dante told her.

"Don't give me a hard time, Nigga!" Mina said smiling. "Your big head brother wants you back in San Antonio."

Dante shook his head. "You and him, are some fucking fools if you think I'm going to San Antonio tonight. Now, release my men, I have a daughter to find."

"And I *said*, Damian wants to see you," Mina told him.

Dante pulled out his pistol. "I will shoot every single man you brought with you, unless you order them to get the fuck outta my way."

Mina shook her head laughing. "Dante, go to sleep, Nigga."

Mina snapped her finger, and one of her men stepped up behind Dante, lifted a stun gun to his neck and hit him with fifty thousand volts. Two men caught Dante before he hit the ground. They carried his convulsing body to the back seat of the Escalade, where a waiting doctor tranquilized him for the ride back home.

Mina twirled her finger in the air. "Give his men back their weapons, and mount up. All of you boys who were rolling with Dante, report to San Antonio. You've all been reassigned."

Mina climbed into the Escalade and lifted her cellphone. "Yeah, I got him."

"Is he okay?" Damian asked.

"Sleeping like a baby." Mina told him.

"How?" Damian asked. "How did you arrange that?"

"A woman's touch," Mina told him. She laughed to herself. We'll be at the airport in twenty minutes, and back home in an hour. Have a car waiting at the airport to retrieve Sleeping Beauty. I'm flying out to California immediately.

"What's up?"

"Same shit," Mina said. "California problems. Got to run out there and kill a nigga. Somebody always thinks they can take Cali away from us. I'll be back by lunch tomorrow."

"Good deal," Damian told her. "And good work."

"Of course!" Mina said. She disconnected the call, and place her iPhone inside of her Birkin Bag. She crossed her legs and reclined the seat inside of the Escalade. The flight to San Antonio would be quick. It was the fact that she had to take off again immediately and head to California that seemed exhausting to her. Oh well, she said to herself, pulling off her Giuseppe heels and leaning back into the seat. A woman's work was never done.

*****

Maryland

Brandon lifted his iPhone to his ear. "Hello?"

"Hey boy, what are you up to?" Princess asked.

Brandon stiffened slightly. "Oh, nothing. Hey, what's up?"

"Just giving you a call to discuss some business with you," Princess told him.

"This isn't a secure line," Brandon warned.

"It's okay," Princess told him. "A quick question. How would you feel about a change in scenery?"

"A change in scenery?"

"Get out of those cold Maryland winters, and enjoy a warmer, much more comfortable climate."

"What are you getting at?" Brandon asked.

"Damian wants you to go to California," Princess explained.

Brandon's heart skipped several beats. He made his way to a nearby sofa and seated himself.

"B, are you there?" Princess asked.

"Yeah, I'm here," Brandon answered. "I'm just digesting what you just said. California? Like, approved by the executive board?" Brandon wanted to know if the state would be officially *his*, approved by The Commission.

"Approved by Damian," Princess told him. "It's his division. He's not looking for board approval."

"Yeah, *his* division," Brandon repeated. "Right now, I'm running my own company."

Princess didn't want to damage his ego by stating the obvious. Brandon was in Maryland, because Damian put him there and got The Commission to accept it. The soldiers he used were Reigns soldiers, and the only reason the Old Ones hadn't went after him, was because of his last name.

"Look, B," Princess started. "It's a promotion, and a big one. Forget about the name. And the salary will be much greater. Take the job. It's a big win."

Brandon exhaled. He knew that she was correct. Running California would be a big job, more responsibility, more men, more power, but also more headache, and much more dangerous. It was a promotion in all but the name.

"And you say the salary would be more than I'm pulling in now with my own company?" he asked.

"Much more," Princess told him. "Damian is willing to cut you in on a percentage for your trouble."

"Sounds enticing," Brandon said. "I'll fly down and rap with D in person."

"Good," Princess told him. "Go out to Cali, enjoy the weather, buy you a mansion on the beach, a couple of convertible exotic cars, fucks some wanna be actresses, enjoy life."

Brandon laughed. "You make it sound like it's a vacation. But you and I both know that it's not all shits and giggles."

"Of course not. That's why Damian wants someone out there that he can trust and count on to whip the business into shape."

"And my business here?" Brandon asked. "What about my company?"

"Where is Josh?" Princess asked.

"Josh?" Brandon asked. "Are you serious? Josh? You think that Josh is ready to take over my company? An entire state?"

"I think that Josh is ready." Princess answered.

"Mina," Brandon said flatly. "Mina needs to take over the business that I've built. And if not Mina, then Darius. Not Josh!"

"Mina is in California," Princess told him. "She doesn't know it yet, but she's going to stay out there and help you out for a little while. When she's done, Mina is going to Philly."

"Philly?" Brandon asked. "A city?"

"We are going to expand out of Philly, and go back into all of Pennsylvania," Princess told him. "It will be Mina's. She's earned it."

"Jesus!" Brandon whistled. "All of Penn? The competitors won't like that."

"Fuck 'em," Princess said. "We pulled out, but they haven't held up their part of the deal. So, we're going back in. We need the money, and the manpower."

"Two big moves at once," Brandon told her. "California, and Pennsylvania. Are you sure that the business has the resources to pull off such a big ass expansion all at once? Especially considering..."

"That's why it has to be done," Princess told him. "We need the money."

"You expand, you own it, which means it's up to you to keep everyone happy." Brandon warned her. He wanted to know if they considered their ability to supply all of the territory that they were trying to take and solidify.

"We know," Princess told him. "Leave that to us. It's under control."

"Okay," Brandon exhaled. "How much time do I have?"

"Not much," Princess told him. "Wrap things up in Maryland as soon as possible. D wants you in California ASAP. Where is Josh, is he there?"

Brandon froze. He had forgotten that she wanted to know where Josh was. "No, he's not here."

"He's not answering his phone," Princess told him. "I tried to locate him, but it's not working. Same with Darius."

"I'll see what I can do," Brandon told her. "You know how he is. Probably laid up with some chic."

"He knows better than to turn off his locator," Princess said. "Darius too for that matter. I can't get in touch with either of them."

"I just talked to Darius," Brandon told her. "He's fine."

"Where is he?" Princess asked.

"He was flying back to Texas," Brandon lied.

"That's strange, because I was told that he's just left Texas." Princess said. "It's too dangerous for them to be this careless right now. They both know better."

"They're young, they're trying to fuck everything that moves," Brandon told her.

"Brandon, you and Darius are the same age."

"Well, some people mature faster than others," Brandon answered. "Besides, who said that I wasn't trying to fuck everything too?"

"Eww," Princess told him. "Too much information. Look, I need you to brief Josh, and get his ass up to speed. I think he's ready. I hope that I haven't made a mistake."

"You have," Brandon told her. "Darius should take over my company."

"No."

"You've got to let him grow up some time," Brandon told her. "You can't keep him in the house under the guise of protecting him. I know he's your younger brother, cuzzo, but he is grown."

"Brandon..."

"What?"

"California. Also, since we're being all open and honest right now, I need you to remember one thing."

"What's that?"

"Your men, are also my men," Princess told him. "Same thing with Dajon's men. You can't pull guys out of Texas, Louisiana, Maryland, and Philly, and think I won't know about it. I don't know where Josh is, or what you two are up to, or what Darius has to do with it, but I'm holding *you* responsible. Wrap it up, get those men back to Texas so they can help Dante, or to Cali, so they can help Mina. And get Darius' ass out of Ohio and back to Texas."

Brandon laughed.

"He's just like his brothers," Princess told him. "He can't keep his dick in his pants, and he'll let a girl with a big ass get his nose wide open. He doesn't need to be in Ohio, it's too dangerous. If that's where Josh is, get his ass back to Baltimore and finish teaching him what he needs to know.

Chapter Fourteen

Dante awoke to find himself in familiar surroundings. He was in his old bedroom at his family's ranch on the outskirts of San Antonio. His head felt like he had an anvil sitting on top of it, and he was groggy as hell. He could focus his eyes enough to see where he was, but his eyelids were still heavy and his body was pleading for more rest.

Dante forced himself to roll out of bed, and could barely stand. The tiny bit of sunlight creeping through the blinds burned his retinas like he was staring into a nuclear explosion. His lifted his hand over his eyes trying to shield the light, and stumbled out of the bedroom.

Damian was seated on the couch with his laptop sitting next to him, staring at a piece of property in The Seychelles. He had dreamed of leaving this life behind, leaving his worries and troubles behind, and just taking up residence on an island. The Seychelles perfect location in the Indian Ocean off the coast of East African would be the perfect destination for him.

He would be able to hit Madagascar, South Africa, Kenya, Uganda, and even hit the Middle East and chill out in Dubai whenever he felt like it. He and Grace had talked about traveling Africa a few times. Just getting away, leaving everything behind. Although Grace was out of the picture, his dream was not. He still wanted out.

Dante stumbled into the living room, and upon seeing Damian, took off after him and dove into him. The force of Dante's body hurling itself into Damian, cause them to flip the couch and fall onto the floor. Dante began punching.

Damian grabbed Dante arms, and threw him off, and tried to get up. Dante grabbed Damian's legs, tripping him up, causing him to drop back down to the floor. Both rose at the same time. Again, Dante charged.

"Muthafucka!" Dante shouted, barreling into his brother.

The two of them flew back onto a console, knocking down all the expensive collectibles, vases, and pictures that had been seated on it. Both were off balance, and again, both hit the floor. This time however, glass from the broken articles caused wounds to both of their entangled bodies.

"What the fuck are you two doing?" Nicanor said, running into the room.

Damian and Dante both rose, and Dante charged again. This time, Damian lifted his brother into the air, and tossed him into an arm chair, causing the chair to tumble and his brother to hit the ground. Dante rose, and ran after Damian again. This time,

Nicanor jumped in the way. Dante reached into Nicanor's waistband and pulled out his pistol. He cocked it and pointed at Damian.

"You want to keep me from finding my daughter, muthafucka!" Dante shouted.

"Dante!" Nicanor shouted. "Put that fucking gun down!"

"Move, Nick!" Damian shouted. "Move out the fucking way!"

"Give me that fucking gun!" Nicanor shouted.

Damian rushed toward Dante.

"Fuck you, Damian!" Dante shouted. "Fuck you!" He threw the gun at his brother, barely missing him. "Fuck you!"

Assata ran up to Dante. She slapped.

Nicanor grabbed Damian.

Dante stared at Damian with fury in his eyes.

"Look at me!" Assata shouted at Dante.

Dante shifted his gaze down toward his Aunt.

"Look at me," Assata said sternly at first. She could see Dante's face changing. "Look at me, Baby."

Dante wrapped his arms around his aunt. She wrapped her arms around him and embraced him tightly.

"Dante, we're here, baby," Assata said softly. "Your family is here for you."

She could hear and feel her nephew sobbing.

"I'm running out of time," Dante said. "I can't find her. I'm running out of time..."

"You *will* find her," Assata told him. "You may not have faith in God, Baby, but I do. And Jesus said, if you have faith the size of a mustard seed, you will be able to move mountains! I have faith! Your *mother* had faith! We are going to find her, and we are going to bring her home."

Assata waved her hand for Damian to join them. Nicanor let Damian go. Damian walked to his brother and his aunt, and wrapped his arms around them both. Assata turned to Nicanor.

"You married to my niece?" Assata asked.

"Yes ma'am," Nicanor told her.

"Then get your Cuban ass over here!" Assata told him.

Nicanor walked to where the three of them were, and joined in the embrace.

Damian then hugged his brother. "We are going to find her. We never stopped looking. We won't *ever* stop looking. Whether you are there or not, we're still looking."

"I can't be here," Dante told him. "I can't *not* be out there looking."

Damian nodded. "I just needed you to come home and get some rest. I was worried about you."

"I know," Dante said softly. "I needed some sleep. How long was I asleep?"

"Three days," Damian told him.

"What?" Dante shouted.

Damian nodded. "Three days. The sedative the doctor gave you, wore off after eight hours. The rest of it, was your body needing to sleep."

Dante nodded. "I'm ready now."

Assata shook her head. "You need to eat. A lot. And you need to get rehydrated. You need a bath, a haircut, a shave. Another bath. Plenty of deodorant. Some toothpaste, and a gallon of mouthwash..."

Dante mush-faced his aunt. "You always trying to be funny. With your short ass."

"Can't whip me!" Assata told him.

"Why you smell like..." Damian asked.

"Because I was smoking, before you too fucked up my high!" Assata said, before he could finish his question. She turned to Dante. "Eat. Rest. Drink plenty of water. You'll know when it's time. Promise me?"

Dante stared at his brother, who lifted an eyebrow. He then lowered his head and nodded slowly.

Later That Day

"Thanks for dropping Lil Damian off," Damian told Grace.

"No problem," Grace told him. "I really appreciate you being so supportive of everything that's going on. You know, with my new job and the move and everything."

"Not a problem," Damian told her. "Congratulations again, on the promotion."

"Thanks," Grace said.

Damian closed the door to the bedroom where Lil Damian was sleeping, and motioned for Grace to head downstairs. He followed just behind.

"Grace, I really want to thank you for trusting me and for allowing him to spend some time with me," Damian told her. "You know, with everything going on around here. I know it can't be easy for you."

"Actually, it is," Grace said nodding. "I know he's safe. You have many faults, Damian, but being a bad dad isn't one of them."

"Thank you," Damian told her.

"How's the search?" Grace asked. She seated herself on the sofa and kicked off her shoes.

Damian took the spot on the couch next to her. "Well, we've drawn a blank. We've turned over every stone. We've searched every motel, hotel, boarding house, tunnel, rat hole, and beneath every rock from here to Mexico City. Nothing. She just disappeared."

"How's Dante?"

Damian shook his head. "Not good. He's just been getting progressively worse since the day she was taken. One minute she was playing in a waiting room and the nanny was getting her dressed, and the next minute she was gone."

"When did he realize she was missing?" Grace asked, lifting her feet onto the sofa.

"Well, the nanny was putting her into the dress she was going to wear for the ceremony," Damian explained. "She was the flower girl for Princess and Emil's wedding. Dante had checked in on her, and then come down for the ceremony. Princess sent for her sp that they could do the run through before the ceremony and she was gone."

Grace frowned. "How long between Dante leaving her, and Princess calling for her."

Damian shook his head and shrugged. "I don't know. Maybe twenty minutes."

"Twenty minutes," Grace said aloud. "And how long did you search the property for her, before calling the police?"

"Maybe, half an hour at most," Damian answered. "We had hundreds of men here, so we were able to search the grounds pretty quick."

"Fifty minutes," Grace said.

"Huh?"

"Fifty minutes," Grace repeated. "Twenty minutes between him seeing her, and Princess sending for her, plus twenty minutes of searching before the police were called. How long before they showed up?"

"Ten minutes," Damian said. "Maybe sooner."

"So, that's an hour," Grace said. "And the officer would have sent it out over the network immediately. The Wireless Emergency Alert System would have rebroadcast immediately, and TXDOT would have put it out over the road signs immediately as well."

"What are you getting at?" Damian asked.

"It takes an hour to get outside of the city," Grace told him. "When the alert hit, they would have been in the city and would have had to drive all the way through the city with every LEO in the area looking for them. Impossible."

"Unless they changed cars?" Damian asked, lifting an eyebrow. Grace now had his attention.

Grace shook her head. "They didn't change cars, they didn't have to. At least not when she was with them."

"What are you getting at?" Damian rose from the couch and began to pace.

"They found the nanny dead," Grace told him. "They found the car, abandoned and burned."

"That means, they changed cars!" Damian told her.

"That means, they had another car waiting for them," Grace told him. "That means, they were always going to kill the nanny. That means that they knew they were going to have to burn the vehicle and take another one. They had the timing down to a science. They knew about the Amber Alert, and how long it would take to get from point A to point B. They still would not have been able to make it out to where they found that fucking car. That car was *taken* there later.

172

I wouldn't be surprised if it was towed there later beneath a tarp."

"So, they changed cars in the city!" Damian said, frustrated.

"Damian, don't you understand? The time? The time it would take for them to get to the nanny! The time it took for the nanny to get to them! The time to change vehicles! All this, while every cop, and sheriff's deputy in the city is looking for you! And then all the nosey people looking for the vehicle that the signs on the highway are describing. The texted alerts with the description of the vehicle. Time, Damian! Time!"

Grace lifted her cellphone and dialed a number.

"Steward!" the voice on the other line said, answering.

"Stew, this is Grace, you at your desk?"

"Hello to you too, sexy!" Steward told her.

"Are you at work?" grace asked again.

"Of course, where else would I be?" Steward asked. "Unless you're inviting me over to your place?"

"Uh-no, and yuck!" Grace told him.

"I've never had a big booty sista before," Steward told her. "Don't believe that rumor about White men. We are holding just like everyone else. At least this White boy is."

"Steward, that's disgusting, and legally considered sexual harassment," Grace told him.

"Please, please, please, report me!" Steward told her. "I absolutely hate my job."

"Then quit," Grace told him.

"I can't, because I like to eat, and live indoors, and have clothes on my back," Steward replied.

"I need a favor, Stu," Grace told him.

"Are we going out on a date?"

"No!"

Steward exhaled. "What cha need, Sexy?"

"Amber Alert for Lucky Reigns, San Antonio Police Department," Grace told him.

"You want me to hack into the SAPD database?" Steward asked.

"You can get the info from TXDOT," Grace replied.

"Too late, already in," Steward told her. "Got it. Wait. Which one?"

"What do you mean?" Grace asked. "There's two of them?"

"Yeah," Steward told her. "Looks like they're twenty minutes apart. Issued, pulled, and then re-issued."

Grace lowered her cellphone, closed her eyes, and leaned back on the sofa.

"What?" Damian asked.

Grace lifted her cellphone again. "Stu, are you sure?"

"Uh... yeah." Steward said. "I'm looking right at it."

"Can you see who pulled it?" Grace asked.

"Nope," Steward told her. "Came from HQ. Can see who issued them though."

"Who issued them?" Grace asked.

"First one, Patrolman Lake. Second alert issued by Chief Hardberger. Oh, I found the first pull. First alert was pulled by Lieutenant Carboni."

"Give me a second, Stu," Grace told him, lowering her cellphone. She peered up at Damian. "The first Amber Alert was pulled. Another Alert was issued twenty minutes later."

"What?" Damian asked, confused. "What does that mean?"

"It means, they needed more time," Grace said, coldly. She lifted her phone. "Stu, you got the plate for the vehicle on the Amber Alert."

"Right here," Steward told her.

"That vehicle was found destroyed and abandoned," Grace told him. "Run the plate, pull the report on that vehicle."

"Give me a sec," Steward told her. "Okay, found it."

"Officer who wrote the report?" Grace asked.

"Lieutenant Carboni," Grace and Steward said at the same time.

"How'd you know?" Steward asked.

"Stu, I need you to get into the personnel database for SAPD," Grace told him.

"What's in it for me, Brown Suga?" Steward asked.

Grace exhaled. "I have a friend who may be interested in possibly going to grab a cup of coffee with you."

"Whew!" Steward shouted. "Is she mocha like the coffee. A little Caramel Macchiato while I'm having a Caramel Macchiato?"

"Yeah, Stew, she's Black," Grace told him.

"She got ass?" Steward asked.

"Yes, Stew!" Grace said. "Can you get into the data base?"

"Already there, my Chocolate Dream Drop," Steward answered.

"Any officer that has taken an extended leave of absence, since the date of the Amber Alert?" Grace asked. "Personal leave, medical leave, vacation, whatever."

She could hear Steward typing at his keyboard.

"What's going on?" Damian asked, frowning.

Grace lifted her hand, silencing Damian.

"Okay, you have a shitload of officers," Steward told her.

"Narrow it," Grace told them.

"How?"

"How many of them, are *still* on leave," Grace asked.

"Two," Steward told her. "You're not going to believe this."

"Lieutenant Carboni," Grace said.

"How'd you guess?" Steward asked. "Strange. Apparently, SAPD allows their officers to write reports while they're on leave. Carboni was officially on leave, when the car was found and he wrote the report."

"Stu, that report was written and signed, *before* that car was even found," Grace said, shaking her head.

"What the *fuck* is going on down there in Texas?" Steward asked. "What have you gotten yourself into, Sexy?"

"Nothing," Grace told him. "Stu, forget about all of this."

"Done!"

"I'll call you when I get back in town."

"Don't forget about my hookup!"

"I got you!" Grace said, disconnecting. She turned toward Damian. "Sit down."

Damian took the seat next to Grace.

"The reason the time didn't add up, is because it didn't add up," Grace explained. "They needed more time. They got more time. The Amber Alert was pulled, and then re-issued twenty minutes later."

"Who?" Damian asked. "Who would do that? Why?"

"Not who would, but who *could*?" Grace said, correcting him. "Turns out, the SAPD isn't what it used to be. Back in the day, once you bought a cop, he stayed yours. Guess this new economy isn't all it's cracked up to be."

"SAPD pulled the alert?" Damian frowned. "Intentionally? So, these monsters could get away with kidnapping my niece?"

Grace patted Damian's hand. "Calm down. They didn't pull the alert, so that the kidnappers could get away, they pulled the alert to give them more time to get to the transfer point."

"The transfer point?" Damian asked, lifting an eyebrow.

"The reason the car wasn't spotted, is because they didn't drive it for long," Grace explained. "That fucked car got towed under cover, most likely to a fucking police pound, until it was time to tow it out to the spot where it was burned."

Damian stood, and rubbed his hand over his head. "Jesus Christ! Are you fucking kidding me! *Are you fucking kidding me!*"

"Lucky wasn't taken to Mexico, Damian," Grace continued. "Lucky never made it out of the city. They wouldn't have had time."

"*That's why we fucking couldn't find her!*" Damian shouted. "That's why it's like she disappeared into thin air!"

178

"She was probably placed in the back of a patrol car, or a police van, and driven away," Grace told him. "Who would suspect a police car as the kidnapping vehicle? It was the perfect fucking cover!"

"I want them dead!" Damian shouted. *"I want them all dead!"*

"The kidnappers are already dead," Grace said calmly. "SAPD put them in the back of some patrol cars, drove them out to the country, and put bullets in the back of their heads as well. They thought they were heading for the border. In all likelihood, they were lied to, set up, and double crossed."

Damian rubbed his hand over his face, and then shouted at the top of his lungs. He was pissed. He hadn't seen it. Perhaps because he had been *too* close to the situation. They had played him. The cartels had played them perfectly. They blew their political protection, spend hundreds of millions of dollars, gotten cut off by the Yucatan Cartels, nearly lost California, *and* Florida, because all their manpower was searching the fucking border. They had been played perfectly.

"Grace, keep this to yourself," Damian told her.

"You're not going to tell Dante?" Grace asked, shocked.

"Of course, but I need to get everything together first," Damian answered. "They have her, and they'll keep her alive. She's their bargaining chip. They've been playing chess, while we've been playing checkers. It's time for us to get in the game. I want you to stick around. I have to go to a meeting, and once I return, I

179

plan on dealing with Nuni, with the SAPD, and with everyone else involved."

"Be careful, Damian," Grace told him.

Damian leaned over and kissed Grace on her forehead. "I will never be able to thank you or repay you."

"Get out," Grace told him. "You've always claimed that you want out. Handle this, and then for the sake of your son, walk away. Don't make me raise him alone, Damian. Don't make me show him pictures and tell him about you. Be alive, so that he gets to know you, by being around you."

Damian nodded, turned, and walked out of the room.

Chapter Fifteen

The Lucky Horseshoe was one of the premier casinos and gambling destinations in the country. Located in Hammond, Indiana, just twenty minutes outside of Chicago, it was 4000,000 square feet of gaming, restaurants, entertainment, bars and lounges. It was a popular destination among the Chicago and Midwest Mob families, and as such, was used to providing high level security and secrecy for meetings that wanted to be kept off the radar. It was for this reason, that The Commission was meeting there.

Arrayed around the large table was the full Commission, minus Princess, who was in Florida, Brandon, who was in Maryland, and Peaches, who was in Ohio. Damian sat at one end, while Chacho Hernandez sat at the head of the table, as it was his turn to chair the meetings of the organization. Chacho brought the meeting to order.

"Friends, associates, we are gathered here today to discuss some Commission business," Chacho told them. "We have many serious issues to discuss. But before we get started, I feel it is necessary to check in with our fellow Commission members whom we have pledged our assistance to, since we have invoked our mutual assistance agreement. Damian, how are things going in Texas?"

Damian leaned forward. "The search for my niece continues, so if anyone has any information or knows anyone who could potentially have any information as to her whereabouts, my family would be eternally grateful. As for our difficulties with our friends to the south, that issue is progressing as well."

Chacho lifted is arms. "Anything we can do?"

"Not at this time," Damian said, shaking his head. "We are all very grateful for this organization's offer of assistance. It will not be forgotten."

"That's what friends are for," Adolphus Brandt said.

The members arrayed around the table laughed. None of them were friends.

"Very well," Chacho said, leaning back in his seat. "Friends, we are gathered here today to address some very disturbing rumors floating amongst us. It has to do with the reliability of our supply. Damian, your family guaranteed the members of this organization that you could insure a reliable flow of our commodities. You ruined an opportunity for us to work with our friends in Columbia again, because you said that Mexico would be reliable. Now, we hear that Mexico has cut us off? What is going on?"

Damian smiled. Those fucking bastards in Yucatan were spreading the word in order to put pressure on his family.

"I can reassure everyone around this table, that the supply of our commodities will continue uninterrupted," Damian told them.

"You guarantee that?" Vern McMillian of South Carolina asked.

"I do," Damian said, nodding.

"And we all know how rock solid a Reigns family guarantee is," Raphael Guzman of Oklahoma sneered.

Laughter went around the table.

"I've never gone back on my word," Damian told them. "My word has always been bond."

"Except when you take people's territory," Cesario Chavez of New Mexico said.

"Or when it suits you to kill someone, despite this organization's rules," Barry Groomes added.

Chacho lifted his hand to silence the others and to try and restore order before the meeting got out of hand.

"You will have your supply, gentlemen," Damian told them.

An unsure silence engulfed the room. They had all heard that the Reigns family had been cut off by the Yucatan Cartels. They suspected that the Reigns family had a significant supply of cocaine stored, but knew that it couldn't possibly be enough to supply all the organizations that were arrayed around the table. They suspected that either Damian was lying, or that the Reigns family was up to something. Both options made them uneasy.

"And then there is the matter of Las Vegas," Chacho said, continuing the meeting. "We need to bring in someone to head Nevada, and represent that state around the table."

"The Old Ones aren't going to go for that," Damian told them. "They will fight us tooth and nail, if we try to help someone consolidate Nevada. They want to keep not only the casinos, but the drug business to themselves. And I for one, don't want to go to war over Nevada. It's not worth it."

"Is that because you are already supplying Nevada through California?" Cesario asked. "It's no secret that most of the supply in Vegas comes out of Cali. You're trying to have it both ways. We ain't stupid, mother fucker."

"I'm not trying to secretly supply Nevada, Cesar," Damian told him. "And you *are* fucking stupid, don't sell yourself short. I'm not interested in Nevada, because it wouldn't just be the Vegas families, but the Chicago families, the New York families, the New Jersey families, all of them. It's the Russians, the Serbs, the Albanians, hell, even the fucking Croatians now have a piece of the action in Vegas. It ain't worth it. We'd be sticking our hand inside of a hornet's nest."

"But the people we bring onto the Commission, are people who basically already control their states," MiAsia told them. "They would need just a little help, right?"

Damian leaned back in his seat and exhaled.

"I believe that we should find someone," Chacho told them. "Who is in agreement?"

184

The majority of hands around the table went up.

"Then it is decided," Chacho announced. "We will begin the search for someone who is strong enough and powerful enough to maintain a hold on Nevada, and offer them a seat and the backing of this organization."

Damian shook his head. "You people are making a huge mistake. You are heading down an expensive, unnecessary road to war with the old families."

"Speaking of expensive, unnecessary wars, your family's activities in Mexico and Texas are causing us all to lose our political and police protection," Barry Groomes of Arkansas told Damian.

"My family's war was not started by us," Damian told them. "But have no doubt, we will finish it. We *will* see it through."

"Yes, but when?" Adolphus Brandt asked. "When the federal government has hauled us all off to prison? My Congressman warned me that unless the drug violence in Texas subsided, and soon, he would have no choice but to vote for the Hanson Bill."

"What's the Hanson Bill?" Bo Henry of Kentucky asked.

"The Hanson Bill is a bill making its way through Congress right now, that would completely devastate us all!" Jamie Forrest of Tennessee explained. "It gives a ton of money to the DEA, the FBI, and Homeland Security. It classifies drug organizations as narco terrorists, and changes the federal minimum mandatory sentencing guidelines for

185

everyone convicted as being a member of a drug organization, to an automatic sentence of life in prison. It allows for the creation of Federal Narcotics Task Force districts all over the country, Task forces that will be able cross state and federal judicial lines, it goes after our money, our properties, our businesses, our spouses, everything. The Bill will set up secret drugs courts, like FISA Courts, that issue secret indictments, secret surveillance, and warrantless wiretaps! It's a fucking nightmare!"

"Your family has to end its war with the Northern Mexico cartels!" Rick Shorts of North Carolina told Damian. "You don't and we're all fucked!"

"You want us to stop a war we didn't start!" Damian shouted. "They kidnapped my niece!"

"Damian, make peace!" Raphael Guzman shouted.

"Damian, you are going to have to bring this war to a conclusion," Chacho told him.

"And my niece?" Damian asked. "Do you people honestly believe that I would end a war without getting my niece back? Do you honestly believe that could happen?"

"It's business, *Puto*," Cesario told Damian. "That's what you always like to say, right? It's just business?"

"No, it's *not* just business," Damian told them. "Kidnapping my niece is personal. Let me make something clear to all of you. I am not going to abandon the search for my niece. Not now, not *ever*. I will lose every single dollar I have, I will fight the cartels to the last man, and if I have to, I will fight every single member of this commission to the last man. Ask yourselves, if I call off the search for my niece, and I end the war with the cartels, and do it because this commission forced my hand, what do you think that I would do with the thousands upon thousands of men that I would have just sitting around? Don't get me fucked up. Don't mistake me for being some other muthafucka! I will bury all of you!"

Silence engulfed the room. They had never heard Damian talk like that. They were used to threats from Princess, and *very* used to threats from Dante, but when they came from Damian, they somehow sounded even more deadly.

"We want you to find your niece," Steve Hawk of Kansas told Damian.

"Nobody is talking war, Damian," MiAsia told him.

"You need to make peace, and soon," Raphael Guzman told him. "You are going to destroy us all. So, if we have to go to war with the Reigns family, then so be it. Fuck it. I will fight you to the last man, before I go to prison for life, or let the fucking Feds take away everything that I've built for my family. Your family ain't more important than mines!"

"Gentlemen!" Chacho said, lifting his hands again. "We are *not* going to war. Damian, how long? You have to be reasonable. You can't continue this war and this search forever. Dante is killing too many people, too many police officers, too many federal agents, and causing too much attention. It's hurting us all. It's hurting your family as well. You have to turn it off, and you know it. How much longer?"

Damian knew that the search for his niece was about to be over, but he wasn't going to give them a date. He couldn't give an inch, or appear to show any weakness. The next time, they would press for more, or demand more, or demand something that he really couldn't give. He had to show them who he was.

Damian shrugged. "As long as it takes."

"Turn it off," Cesario told him. "If that bill continues through Congress, we're all fucked."

"You keep talking, you'll be fucked anyway," Damian said coldly.

"Bring it," Cesario told him.

"Gentlemen," Adolphus Brandt, said, interjecting. "We don't need this right now. I'm sure the Reigns family is doing everything that they can to find their child. And I'm sure Damian understands the urgency of the situation."

Damian decided to give a little. He nodded.

"Damian will expedite the search, and then bring the war to a conclusion," Adolphus continued. "And we will focus on Nevada."

"We also have the matter of the new states," Chacho said, taking control of the meeting again. MiAsia?"

MiAsia shook her head. "My state is under control. I have complete control of Missouri."

"DeAndre?" Chacho said, turning toward him.

DeAndre shrugged and brushed his waves. "I'm progressing. Taking over shit. A little resistance, but nothing I can't handle."

"Not what I'm hearing," Malcom 'Baby Doc' Mueller of Alabama said.

"You can hear shit about Michigan all the way down there in Alabama?" DeAndre asked.

"I can hear Hassan's name everywhere," Baby Doc said smiling.

"Who is Hassan?" Chacho asked.

"Hassan ain't shit!" DeAndre shouted. "Just another dead nigga! I got my state, Dog! Don't worry about my shit!"

"Hassan is the young brother who should be sitting in his seat," Baby Doc said, nodding toward DeAndre. "He's the one who *really* controls Michigan. This Commission chose all the wrong muthafuckas in the Mid-West. We got this Asian bitch in St. Louis, we got a hood rat in Ohio, who almost got herself killed, and who has about as much control over Ohio as I do. If we don't remedy this shit, we are all about to be exposed?"

"Exposed?" Adolphus Brandt asked, leaning forward. "What are you talking about?"

"I got your Asian bitch!" MiAsia said, staring at Baby Doc.

Chacho held up his hand, silencing everyone. "What are you talking about, Malcom?"

"These muthafuckin losers!" Baby Doc told them. "They are going to end up in federal custody, singing like birds. They don't have control over their shit. This nigga is about to get run out of Michigan. That little hood rat bitch is running for her life and almost got herself killed. Why do you think she's not here? She couldn't afford the airfare to fly in! She never controlled her state in the first place! We need to install the real muthafuckas in those seats!"

"I got my state!" MiAsia said. "Nobody is challenging me in my shit! The last person who challenged my control, has been worm food for the last two years!"

"I got my shit too!" DeAndre protested. He brushed his waves nervously.

"So, you say this Hassan person, really controls most of Michigan?" Barry Groomes asked.

"And this young brother named Kharee controls Ohio," Baby Doc said, nodding.

Glances were exchanged around the table.

Damian knew what the others were thinking. DeAndre was about to be a dead man.

"We all agreed that new members have some time to bring their states *fully* under their control," Damian told the others. "He needs more time."

"We don't need any more dust being kicked up!" Baby Doc said. "Your family is stirring up enough bullshit for all of us. The bullshit needs to stop!"

"The agreement is, they have time to bring their states under full control," Damian told the others. "They get the same courtesy everyone else got."

"And Ohio?" Chacho asked.

"He says that she controls nothing?" Cesario asked.

"Same thing," Damian told the others. "She gets time."

"Yes, but how much time?" Steve Hawk asked. "If she doesn't even control her own city..."

"We don't know that," Damian told the others. He shot Baby Doc a glance. "No one does. And she's not here to speak for herself. But I do wonder, how it is that Malcom knows so much?"

The members arrayed around the table turned toward Baby Doc.

Baby Doc smiled. "I have my sources. Like everyone else around this table, my reach is nationwide."

"You need to get your state under control," Chacho told DeAndre. "All of you new members do. Bring your states under control immediately. We're not going to give you that much time. You were brought into this organization because it was understood that you pretty much ran your states. You were supposed to be the biggest dealers in your respective states, and if we made a mistake in believing in you, that mistake will be corrected."

DeAndre stared at Baby Doc with fury. He wanted him dead. He thought of Baby Doc as being a sellout.

"If there is nothing else, then we are all in agreement," Chacho said, peering around the table. "The Reigns family will expedite its search, and conclude its war with the Northern Cartels, the new members will bring their states under their control expeditiously, and we will look to fill the Vegas seat."

"Which is empty because of the Reigns family," Cesario said.

"You just couldn't help but get in one last dig, huh?" Damian asked with a smile.

"This meeting is adjourned," Chacho announced.

Damian rose, walked into the casino and pulled out his cell phone.

"Hello?" Princess said, immediately answering her brother's call.

"How are things in Florida?" Damian asked.

"Progressing," Princess said.

"Wrap things up ASAP. I need you back in Texas."

"What's the matter?"

"Just leaving the meeting," Damian told her.

"Everything okay?" Princess asked.

"Of course not," Damian told her. "I need you home. We need to wrap things up with Lucky. I think I have something."

"Are you fucking kidding me?" Princess nearly shouted. "You found her? Is she okay? Please tell me she's alive and okay!"

"I think I know where she is," Damian said. "Actually, Baby Momma found her. It's time to bring her home, and finish up our business with our friends down south. I also have a feeling that Ohio wasn't just a local issue. Our Haitian friend has been playing in other people's playgrounds."

"That son of a bitch!" Princess said.

"Get here!" Damian told her. "It's time for us to remind everyone who the Reigns family is."

Chapter Sixteen

There was luxury, and then there was *luxury*. Barton G's in South Beach was a redefinition of the word and the concept. The famous restaurant combined elegant dining, with showcase presentation, to present an experience unparalleled anywhere else in Florida. It also boasted a price and exclusivity to match. It was here that Princess had paid nine thousand dollars to shut the restaurant down for her meeting with Analiza Arriago Sataenilia. Her men were everywhere.

Analiza showed up with only two men. Princess had guaranteed her safety, and she had also been guaranteed her safety by Cedras, the head of the Medellin Cartels. She strutted into the restaurant in her Versace heels and matching Versace gown with the confidence of a woman who thought herself untouchable.

Analiza was escorted to Princess' table, where she removed her Versace sunglasses and smiled. Princess took her in. Analiza was Cuban, and the Afro Caribbean blood running through her veins was evident in her figure. She had an ass like only a descendant of Nubia could be graced with, and her brown skin, full lips, and long dark hair were also a testament to Cuba's racial integration. Her eyes spoke to the Spanish side of her lineage, they were greyish-green, with flecks of emerald. Princess thought her gorgeous, and was immediately turned on by her.

"Have a seat," Princess said, nodding at the seat across from her.

Analiza seated herself at the table, placing her Birkin in the chair next to hers. "Nice restaurant."

Princess lifted a Glock with an enormous silencer attached to it, and put a bullet in the head of Analiza's two bodyguards. They dropped instantly.

"Fuck!" Analiza shouted. "Do you know what the fuck you've done? Do you know who you've just fucked with? My safety was guaranteed by the Medellin Cartels!"

"If you would have done your homework, you dumb bitch, you would have known that the Reigns family doesn't give a fuck about the Medellin Cartels, or any cartels in Columbia. Our supply comes from Mexico. We killed El Jeffe. How do you think Cedras came to power?"

"So, you're going to kill me now?" Analiza asked. "You're going to go back on your word?"

"No," Princess said, shaking her head. "I just wanted you to understand, that Cedras can't protect you. No one, can protect you. You are alive, because I gave you *my* word, not because of Cedras. And my family's word is always good."

"And if you let me walk out of here, you don't think that they'll be war?" Analiza asked.

"Maybe," Princess said, shrugging. "But you will lose. You cannot win a war against the Reigns family. My family will soon wrap up its war against the cartels in Mexico, and we will eventually end the search for my niece. After that, I will have enough men to crush you. There will be so many Black men in Little Havana, that you will think you were in Lagos, Nigeria."

"You didn't bring me here to threaten me," Analiza told her. "You could have done that over the phone. And since you're not going to kill me, that means I'm here for some other reason."

Princess smiled and nodded.

A server brought Analiza a plate and a cup. Another server poured her a bottle of her favorite wine. Analiza looked at the plate and the wine and smiled.

"Your favorite," Princess said nodding. "I know. I know everything about you. I know what you like, where you live, where you grew up, how you came to America, your favorite color, your birthday, your favorite song. I know what you wore in your school play in fourth grade back in Havana. That's power, Analiza. That's who we are. I can even tell you who you favorite Little Pony was, and which Spice Girl you wore your hair like while growing up."

Analiza Sataenilia smiled. "Okay. But we're not here to film an episode of This Is Your Life."

"Correct," Princess said nodding. She waved her hand toward Analiza's plate. "Enjoy your meal."

Analiza lifted her fork, and began to eat.

Princess leaned back in her chair and got comfortable. "I'm here to tell you about my life, actually."

Analiza lifted an eyebrow. "This should be interesting."

"Oh, it's a very interesting story," Princess said with a smile. "My story, began when my brothers went off to college, and just after I graduated. My parents had a construction company, that my father grew into a pretty large and successful business. But my father suffered a small coronary, and he had to step back from the business, so that left things up to me and my mother. Now, Momma, she wasn't into the company, and the company that she once helped run, had grown in size and scope beyond her ability or comfort level to run. And she hadn't been involved in day to day operations in years. So that left me."

Princess lifted her glass of wine and sipped. "Anyway, the economy changed. Things went south, and it was up to me to save my parent's company. There was no way that I was going to let their life's work, their legacy, go bankrupt. That, and we had hundreds of families depending on us for their income. So, I had a boyfriend who was into the street life. I took some money from the company, and I bought my first one hundred kilos of pure Columbian cocaine."

Analiza smiled. "Always the boyfriends, isn't it? Always family obligations that make our lives difficult. If only we could walk away like men."

Princess returned her smile. "Ain't that always the truth."

Analiza lifted her wine glass. "To strong women."

"To strong women," Princess lifted her glass, and sipped. "Anyway, I was pretty good at it. The business. The cocaine business that is. I bought up plenty of other businesses to wash the money, and made a fortune. And then, Damian graduated from Harvard and came home and took over my family's businesses. And he had the magic touch. Damian took all our companies to a whole other level. In fact, he was making more money legitimately, than I was making in the drug game. I knew that I should have stopped, I should have given it up, but I couldn't. I just couldn't."

"Addicted to the money?" Analiza asked.

"Not just the money," Princess told her. "It was something else. It was something that *I* had built. And the fact that I had to do things to build it, to maintain it. I couldn't just shut it down, because by then, I needed to keep going in order to protect my family from the things that I had done to build up my little empire."

Analiza nodded.

"Dante graduated from college the following year and came back home, and slowly but surely, he got into the business. He helped Damian on the legit side, and me on the other side, and we were all doing well. And then one bright sunny day, Damian decides that we need to shut down my side. We had enough money, we had invested well, all the other businesses were booming, and there was no need to stay involved in the other business. They couldn't see my side, they couldn't see that we needed the muscle, the protection, the money and fear and respect that came along with my side of things. Eventually, things got bad, and they made a move to shut me down, and shut me out. I was not going out without a fight. It was war. If I had to take Damian out, in order to keep the rest of my family safe, to keep my Momma and Daddy safe, then that's what I would do. I took my men, ran to Florida, and took this state."

"That was the war between you and your brothers?" Analiza said, now understanding.

"We fought," Princess smiled. "Dante sided with Damian, and the two of them fought me to a standstill. I was surprised as hell. Dante is ruthless, and Damian is smart and conniving, and the two of them made the perfect pair. Eventually, the war between us ended. Thankfully, it ended with all of us alive. I went back home to Texas, to run the family's dark business once again, and things went back to the way they were before. But, I still controlled Florida. I still had underbosses, men who were loyal to me, men who fought with me against my brothers, my own family. I owe them my loyalty, like they gave me theirs."

"And so, that brings us here," Analiza told her.

"I don't need Florida," Princess told her. "I don't want to run it, at least not the day to day operations. But as you know, Florida is full of ports. You see, what my family learned, is that you don't have to control all of the drugs coming into the country, you just have to control the ports. We make money not just as a direct supplier, but as the middleman. We get the shipment coming across the border through Mexico, or from other places into our ports, and we distribute it with a slight markup. We get to control the market, keep down the violence, and decide who gets how much, and who gets none."

"Brilliant," Analiza said nodding. "Why are you telling me all this?"

"I need to be in Texas to run my family's empire," Princess told her. "I can't be in Florida, because everything is based and run out of Texas. I need someone with balls to run Florida for me."

"Excuse me?" Analiza said, almost choking on her wine.

"I want you to run Florida for me," Princess said with a smile.

"Why would I do that?" Analiza frowned. "Why work for you when I have my own organization? I control my own destiny, and I get as big as I want."

"You can get as dead as you want," Princess told her. "I'm not giving up Florida. My family is never going to give up those ports. It's why we are fighting so hard to keep California. Like I said, our war in Texas will be done soon. And we will have thousands of soldiers, battle hardened soldiers, sitting around doing nothing. Florida is going to get real crowded with Black people. I will wipe your little Dominican allies in Orlando off the map. And I will personally, put a bullet, in that pretty little face of yours. Either that, or you can run Florida, and make money beyond your wildest dreams."

"I would be under you?" Analiza asked.

"You would answer only to me, and to my brothers of course," Princess told her. "But you would basically run Florida."

"What about your loyal underbosses?" Analiza asked. "They won't listen to me."

"They only thing they want is their supply," Princess said, sipping from her wine. You will get the shipment, arrange the distribution, and keep shit in check and running smooth. Anyone else tries to move in, you smash them."

"What's in it for me?"

"You get to live," Princess told her.

"I'm alive right now."

"Right now, is the operative word," Princess said coldly.

Analiza peered down at the bodies of her men, which Princess had her men leave on the floor of the restaurant while they ate.

"I'm just kidding," Princess told her. "I'll also give you one percent. One percent of everything coming into Florida. You will have money beyond your wildest dreams. You get our police protection, our political protection, a peaceful Florida, and a nice long life."

"How do you know you can trust me?" Analiza asked.

"I can trust you, because you're smart," Princess told her. "You're a survivor. I'm offering you the keys to the kingdom. *Plata o Plomo.* Silver, or lead. Your choice, Sweetheart."

"I've always been partial to silver," Analiza said with a smile. "I will work for you."

"Good decision." Princess told her. She nodded at her men. They immediately produced two body bags and began gathering up Analiza's men. Analiza didn't notice the third body bag that they had brought with them.

Princess lifted her glass in toast. "To business."

"To our new relationship." Analiza told her.

"You'll have to tell me how you got the name, Black Widow," Princess said with a smile.

"Of course," Analiza said, smiling back.

"You're also going to have to give me something," Princess told her.

"What's that?"

"You knew where I was going to be, and how to hit me," Princess told her. "You're also getting dope into Miami. Someone has been naughty. I want to know, who sold me out."

Analiza lowered her head and smiled. She hesitated for a few moments. "You're the boss."

*****

Texas

Dante hadn't been home in ages. He walked into his penthouse and tossed his keys on a nearby table. He felt refreshed, more energetic and alive than he had felt in a long time. He truly needed the rest that Damian had ordered. He felt healthy again, and he was ready to get back into the hunt.

Yessenia walked from the bedroom into the living room upon hearing the door to the penthouse open. She saw Dante and a smile appeared across her face.

Dante was slightly surprised. It was as if he had forgotten about his guest. "Yessenia..."

"Dante," she said, walking to him and wrapping her arms around him. "You look exhausted. And thin."

"Really?" Dante said with a smile. "You should have seen me before I got some sleep and some food in me."

Yessenia pulled Dante to the sofa and practically shoved him onto it. "Sit down. I'm going to cook for you."

"Naw, I'm good," Dante said, pulling her onto the sofa next to him. "I can't eat another bite. My aunt has been stuffing me with food."

Yessenia caressed the side of his face. "How have you been? How is the search going? Have you heard anything?"

Dante lowered his head. It was her brother that he was at war with, and her brother who was responsible for his daughter's kidnapping. The conversation was uncomfortable at best, awkward at worse.

"I haven't found her," Dante said, shaking his head. He lifted his head toward her. "Why are you still here?"

"I want you to find her," Yessenia told him. "If keeping me here is going to help you get your daughter back, then this is where I'll be."

"Yessenia, there's no sense in keeping you here," Dante told her. He nodded toward the door. "You can go."

Yessenia placed her hand beneath his chin and turned his face toward hers. "I'm not leaving, until you find her. If you need me to talk to my brother, to convince him to let her go, I will do it. If he truly believes that you are going to kill me, he may trade me for your daughter."

Dante shook his head. "If Nuni was going to do that, he would have already. He knows that I have you. He may not be able to. He may not have her, or it may even be too late..."

"Don't say that!" Yessenia told him. "Don't even think like that. I know my brother. To many people, he may be a monster. But Nuni is not a child killer. Trust me, if he has her, she is alive. You will find her. You believe that? Say that you believe that!"

Dante hesitated, before finally relenting. He smiled and nodded to placate her. "I believe that."

"Good." Yessenia told him. "In the meantime, you need to eat, to rest, and then go out there and find her."

Yessenia pulled Dante's head to her shoulder and caressed his face. She turned and shifted her body so that her legs were now in his lap, and his head was lying on her stomach. Dante could smell the lotion on her body, and feel the softness of her silky skin. He eyes made their way up and down her tight stomach, and then came to rest of the mound resting between her legs. The only thing fat on her body, was what he was now staring at. He could feel himself beginning to throb.

Dante kissed Yessenia on her stomach. It had been a long time for both of them, so it didn't take much to get either of their motors going. Yessenia lifted her leg over his head and rested it on the top of the sofa. His head was now perfectly placed between her thighs. He rubbed the front of her thong, caressing the camel toe print that was clearly visible. He pulled down her underwear and kissed her smooth, shaved, privates, causing her to adjust her body and moan.

Dante's tongue came out, and he licked the surface around her canal, before parting it and finding her labia. The warm wetness of his tongue again caused her to stir and moan. Dante's hands made their way to Yessenia's vagina, where he parted her opening so that he could get to her good. His tongue glided over her, in and out of her, and every once and a while he pulled her pearl into his mouth and sucked gently on it.

"Aye, Papi!" Yessenia screamed, clutching the back and Dante's head. "Right there! Right there! Right there, Papicito! Aye!"

Dante licked and sucked until Yessenia couldn't take it anymore. She screamed, clinched her thighs around his head, orgasmed like there was no tomorrow. Dante made his way up her stiffened body, stopping briefly at her breast, where he engulfed each of her hardened nipples in turn. Kissing her, he made his way up to her neck, and then sucked gently on her ear lobe. Yessenia took his rock-hard manhood, and placed it inside of her.

"Oh! Oye! Oye! Aye, Papi! Fuck me! Fuck me!" Yessenia screamed.

Dante got his stroke going. He placed his hands beneath her large, round, firm ass and pulled her close so that she couldn't get away. The soft cushions of the couch were saving her from his down stroke, and he wanted her to feel all of him deep up inside. It worked. Yessenia stopped screaming for him to fuck her and started biting on his shoulder and digging nails into his back.

Dante went up inside of her with the fury of a man on a mission. He could feel her trying to slide back to soften the blow, but his hands behind her ass wouldn't let her escape. He was stroking so hard and she was screaming so loud, that neither of them heard the door to his penthouse open.

"You sorry mother fucker!"

Dante turned to find his girlfriend, Desire staring at them in shock. He leapt off the couch.

"You bastard!" Desire shouted. She lifted a vase from a nearby table and threw it at him. "You sorry, cheating, no good mutherfucker!"

Dante stood in the middle of his living room with his manhood rock hard, dodging items that Desire was throwing. "Des, stop!"

"Fuck you!" Desire shouted. "Fuck you, and you're little Latina whore! You want that bitch! That's what you want? You can have that bitch, you sorry mutherfucker!"

"Desi, wait!" Dante shouted.

Desire turned over more tables, raked a lamp off a nearby coffee table, and then headed out the door. Dante, manhood swinging, ran into the hallway after her. Yessenia, still laying on the couch, covered her face in laughter.

"Desi!" Dante shouted, chasing Desire down the private hall.

The elevator came instantly, and Desire climbed on board. Dante made it to the elevator as the door was closing.

"Desi!"

"Fuck you!" Desire shouted, as the doors shut.

Dante covered his privates, and made his way back to his penthouse. How much Desire knew about his family and their business, he didn't know. But he knew that she wasn't stupid. He really had feelings for Desire. In fact, he knew that she would probably be the one he would settle down with. Desire had the entire package. She was drop dead gorgeous, extremely well educated, and real. Lucky loved her, and she was good to his daughter. And now, he faced the possibility that he had truly fucked up a good thing.

Dante walked into the penthouse and closed the door. Yessenia uncovered her face and sat up.

"You okay?" Yessenia asked.

Dante nodded. "Yeah, I'm good."

"I'm sorry." Yessenia told him.

"Not your fault," Dante said, shaking his head.

"I didn't know you had a woman," Yessenia told him.

Dante seated himself on the couch next to Yessenia.

"How long you two been together?" Yessenia asked.

"Not long," Dante told her.

"You love her?" Yessenia asked, lifting an eyebrow.

Dante nodded.

"She obviously loves you," Yessenia told him. "What are you going to do?"

Dante shook his head. "I don't know." He pounded his fist into his other palm. "Fuck!"

"She knows what you do for a living?" Yessenia asked.

Dante shrugged.

Yessenia exhaled forcibly and caressed the side of Dante's face. "I can't believe you fell in love. Especially with a woman who isn't a part of this world. I thought that was rule number ten or something."

Dante smiled and turned to her. "I think it's rule number eighteen."

"She gonna blow you up?" Yessenia asked.

Dante shook his head. "Don't think she can."

"Good," Yessenia said. She climbed off the couch and stood. "Let her live. Give her some time. Call her, blame everything on me. She loves you. She'll take you back. Just give her a story that is remotely plausible. Her heart will make her head believe it. She'll *want* to believe it. Love is a fucked-up thing."

Yessenia walked back into the bathroom. Dante could hear his shower come alive.

He wondered if he should take Yessenia's advice, or if he would have to kill Desire.

Chapter Seventeen

Darius grabbed his Glock when he heard the knock at his hotel room door. The knock wasn't the coded knock that his men used, so that told him that it wasn't one of them, nor was it Peaches or DeMarion. He peered through the peep hole.

"Holy fuck!" Darius said, opening the door.

DeFranz Reigns stood smiling at his cousin. "Get your Black, ugly, water bucket head ass back to Texas, muthafucka!"

Darius laughed, and he and DeFranz embraced.

"Get your ass in here, nigga!" Darius told him.

DeFranz walked into his cousin's room.

"What the fuck are you doing here?" Darius asked. "How the fuck you know where I was?"

"Muthafucka, I know, Brandon knows, and Princess knows, which means pretty soon, Damian's ugly ass is gonna know," DeFranz told him. "Nigga, what the fuck is you doing in Ohio? What? You trying to get killed?"

"Fuck!" Darius shouted.

"You chasing that pretty yellow bitch ain't you?" DeFranz asked.

"Man, why she gotta be a bitch?" Darius asked. "You always been a disrespectful muthafucka!"

"Disrespect this muthafucking Purple People Eater!" DeFranz told him, pulling out a large blunt and lighting it. He took a deep pull on the cigar, blew a ring of smoke in the air, and passed it to Darius. "Pussy always have you niggaz going crazy. She look like she got some good pussy too. Is it good, kinfolk?"

"Goddamn, nigga!" Darius said, taking a puff from the blunt. "Even if it was, you ain't gonna hit."

"Oh, it's like that?" DeFranz asked. "You don't wanna share with your kinfolk. Nigga, give me my blunt, ole, in luv ass muthafucka!"

Darius laughed. DeFranz was from the other side of the Reigns family. The side that grew up in the hood. He was a street cat through and through. No filter whatsoever.

DeFranz hit the blunt again. "Brandon sent me here to get you niggaz outta here. Real talk, Princess is on to you niggaz. Where is Josh ass at?"

"Helping Peaches put her shit together again."

"He out helping yo bitch?" DeFranz said loudly. He broke into laughter. "Now wonder you sitting here all sore as a muthafucka! Nigga sitting in the dark in ya drawers and shit. What, you about to commit

211

suicide or something, ole depressed ass nigga! Up in the room watching pornos and shit. You know Josh a take a nigga bitch. You better watch that nigga!"

Darius shook his head and snatchws the blunt away from his cousin. "Do you ever shut the fuck up?"

"Nigga, where pretty ass DeMarion?" DeFranz asked. "I know that nigga up here too!"

Darius shook his head. "Just shut up and listen."

DeFranz went quiet and silence engulfed the room. They could hear Vendetta screaming in the next room.

"Gotdamn, he killing that bitch!" DeFranz said, laughing. "I'm finta go fuck that nigga stroke up!"

DeFranz rushed out of Darius' room and banged on the door of DeMarion's suite.

"Who the fuck is it?" DeMarion shouted.

"It's the pussy police!" DeFranz shouted. "We got a called about a 211 on some pussy!"

They could hear laughter coming from the room. DeMarion threw open the door and hugged DeFranz.

"What the fuck you doing here?" DeMarion asked.

"Nigga, get your sweaty ass off me!" DeFranz told him. "You got pussy juice, dick juice, ass juice, all kinds a juice on yo muthafuckin hands and you wanna hug a nigga and shit!"

Vendetta flushed the toilet and opened the door to the bathroom. Seeing Darius, DeFranz, and DeMarion all standing next to one another made her laugh. They looked like triplets.

"V, this is my crazy ass cousin DeFranz," DeMarion said, waving toward DeFranz. "Franz, this is V."

"I would shake your hand but you got dick juice on it," DeFranz told her.

Darius and DeMarion laughed.

DeMarion adjusted his boxers to try and hide his still bulging semi-hard penis. "What the fuck you doing here?"

"Princess knows we're here," Darius answered.

"Damn!" DeMarion said.

"We got to wrap shit up and get the fuck outta here," Darius told them.

"But we ain't ready," Vendetta said. "We still need you guys. We still need your men!"

"That's why I'm here," DeFranz said, winking at her.

"You?" Vendetta asked. "You brought more men?"

"I did," DeFranz told her. "But more importantly, I brought me."

"You?" Vendetta asked again. "And what are you going to do?"

"I'm the cleanup man, baby!" DeFranz said, lifting his arms. "I'm here to kill everybody that's keeping my people from being able to get back to Texas. I'm here to take care of whatever boogeyman is keeping you from sleeping sound at night."

"Sounds like a big job," Vendetta said.

"Not really," DeFranz said shaking his head. "And that's a good thing for you."

"Why is that?" Vendetta asked. Suddenly, she wasn't feeling DeFranz.

"Well, right now, I'm here because Brandon sent me," DeFranz told her. "That's completely different than when Damian sends me. Once Damian wants me here, things will take a completely different turn. You see, when Brandon sends me, I'm here to fix shit. When Damian sends me, I'm here to wipe all the pieces off the board."

A slight uncontrollable shiver shot through Vendetta. DeFranz scared her.

*****

Texas

Dante strolled into the dining room at the family's ranch to find Damian and Nicanor staring at a large map. One look at the map told Dante that something big was up. The map was not only marked 'classified', but it also had the markings of the National Security Agency on it.

"What the fuck is this?" Dante asked Damian.

"A gift from the United States Southern Command," Damian answered with a smile. "It was given to them, by the NSA."

"How did we get it, and why do we have it?" Dante asked, examining the map.

"Well, apparently your boy Nuni, made a huge mistake," Damian said, still smiling like the cat that caught the canary. "He used some key words in a phone call, and got caught up in the NSA's system. It triggered an automatic monitoring of his communications, and a location trace. The NSA turned the information, the location, the map over to Southern Command, instead of the DEA because they were afraid that the DEA would fuck it up and possibly even share it. The Pentagon can't go after him because he's not a fucking terrorist, and they don't want to share it with the Mexican military because they're all on the take. Our contacts inside of Southern Command got a copy of it to us. See this?"

Dante's eyes shifted to where Damian was pointing on the map. "What is that?"

"The Sierra Madre Oriental Mountain Range," Damian told him. "This is Cerro San Rafael in Coahuila. Half way up the mountain, there is a massive log cabin estate hidden in the trees. That estate, is where the calls came from."

Dante peered up at his brother and smiled. "Nuni?"

"Confirmed by NSA's voice recognition software, and other intelligence." Damian told him.

215

"We got his ass!" Dante said, clapping his hands.

Nicanor hung up his cellphone. "The pilot has received the money."

"Pilot?" Dante asked, staring at Nicanor.

Nicanor turned looked at Damian.

"The compound is heavily defended," Damian told him. No way we can make it up the mountain to get him, not with the number of men he has, and the system he has. They have cameras, and sensors all over the mountain. They can shift men around, and put up a helluva fight. I have another way to end this thing."

"Jesus, Damian!" Dante shouted. "A plane? And you mother fuckers have the nerve to call me cold hearted, cold blooded, crazy, and a bunch of other shit! Seriously?"

"It's not a passenger jet," Damian told him. "It's a cargo plane."

"And the pilot?" Dante asked.

"Dying of cancer," Damian told him. "Terminal. His company doesn't know yet, so he is still flying."

Dante shook his head. "And so, he's just going to Kamakazi his way out."

"College is expensive," Damian told him. "Seven kids. A wife, a mortgage, car payments. Wants to make sure she never has to work again, his kids' colleges are paid for, kids are set up after college. His insurance won't take care of all that."

"Where'd you find..." Dante started to ask.

"Bio One," Damian answered. "He's a patient at Bio One's Yancy Hospital."

"Co-pilot?" Dante asked. "He dying too?"

"Not from cancer," Damian said. "Co-pilot is a fucking Klansman. Fuck him!"

"You forgetting something?" Dante asked.

"What's that?"

"My daughter could be inside that fucking place!" Dante shouted.

Damian nodded at one of his men. The man disappeared, and returned with Grace following him.

"How are you doing, Dante?" Grace asked. She and Dante exchanged hugs.

Dante nodded toward the map. "You?"

Grace shook her head.

"Grace didn't do this for us, but she did do something else for us," Damian told his brother. He pulled out a taser and sat it down on the table on top of the map.

"What is this?" Dante asked. "You ain't fucking tasering me, bro! Fuck that! That shit ain't happening twice."

"I'm going to fucking taser you if you don't fucking listen to me," Damian told him. "I need you to listen to everything Grace is about to say, and don't go off with your fucking hot ass head. We have these people. Listen to me, we have a chance to end all this bullshit, immediately! But you can't go off with a hot head! You can't ruin it!"

"Is my daughter okay?" Dante asked Grace.

A smile appeared across Grace's face. Tears began to flow. "She's alive." Grace wiped her tears and sniffled. "She's alive, Dante!"

Dante fell into Grace's arms and the two of them embraced.

"She's not in Mexico," Damian told his brother.

"Where is she?" Dante asked.

"Are you willing to listen?" Damian asked. "Am I going to have to fucking use this, to keep her safe from you doing dumb shit?"

Dante peered at the taser and back at his brother. "She's safe?"

Damian nodded.

"Do I need to sit down?" Dante asked.

Again, Damian shook his head. "You need to stand up, so that you can hug Grace. She's the one who found her."

"You found my daughter?" Dante asked.

Still crying, Grace nodded.

"Where is she?" Dante asked.

"She's safe," Damian told him. "But we know where she is."

"Where the fuck is she?" Dante shouted.

Damian placed his hand on the taser.

Dante lifted his hands. "Okay, okay. Where is she?"

"Are you going to listen?" Damian asked.

Dante nodded.

Damian nodded at Grace.

"The timing was off," Grace told him. "They wouldn't have had enough time to get her out of the city. I checked into it. The amber alert was pulled, giving the nanny time to hand her over to the kidnappers, and give the kidnapper time to hand her over to people who now have her."

Dante bit down on his knuckles.

"The people who have her, killed the kidnappers, and have been hiding her in the city. She never left the city," Grace told him.

"Fuck!" Dante shouted, raking everything off the table. He was furious, and breathing heavily.

"We got played," Damian said, patting his brother on his back. "They played us big time."

"Where is she?" Dante asked.

"Dante, she is with the only people who could pull an alert, and then re-issue it later. The only people who could drive her passed all the patrol cars looking for her, and all the other cars on the highway after the alert went out. She is with the only people who could murder a bunch of people from Mexico, bury their bodies, hide the car, and then transport it to the spot where it was burned and found, and then doctor the report."

"Are you fucking kidding me!" Dante shouted at the top of his lungs. "I'm going to kill them! I'm going to bury all of them mutha fuckas!"

"The chief, at least one of his lieutenants, a sergeant, and one patrolman are involved, as far as we can tell." Damian told him. "Grace had her people check, and only one of them has been off since the kidnapping. She also had agents from her office roll by the lieutenant's house with a thermal imaging system. The lieutenant has one daughter, but two children are sleeping upstairs in a bunk bed. She's safe. She's playing, she's happy. She probably thinks she's been having a giant sleepover."

"I checked the wife's credit cards, and pulled the grocery receipts," Grace told him. "She's eating well, they're buying her favorite snacks, she's fine. I even checked their cable company, Netflix, and Amazon accounts. She's watching cartoons, and just being a child. She's okay, Dante. Children are resilient. She's going to be okay once she comes home."

Damian knew the look on Dante's face. He was not just going to kill all those involved, he was going to do it slowly. He was going to torture them and make them regret that they had ever been born.

"Are you okay?" Damian asked.

Dante was bent over the table in silence.

"Are you with me, brother?" Damian asked again.

Dante turned toward Damian and nodded. "You're asking me to leave her there?"

"I'm asking which one of them do you want to kill?" Damian asked. "The lieutenant, who has her, or the Chief who set things up?"

"The chief set things up?" Dante asked.

Damian nodded. "But lucky is staying at the lieutenant's house."

"I want you to get my daughter," Dante told him. "You bring Lucky home. I want to talk to the chief."

Grace shivered at the way Damian's last sentence came out.

"Princess has to wrap something up in Florida, and then she's on her way," Damian told him.

Dante shook his head. "I don't want to wait for Princess. You can't ask me to wait, Damian. Knowing where she is, you can't ask me to wait. I need to bring my baby home."

Damian waved his hand, and one of his men came forward and pulled out a gun. Damian took the gun from the man, and handed it to Dante.

"Who the fuck do you think I am" Damian asked. He clasped the back of Dante's neck and pulled his face close to his. "I'm your fucking brother. I love you more than life itself! I would never ask you to wait. What I was asking, is that you don't run outta here before you know the whole story. Everything is set up. I just wanted to know which one you wanted to kill, and which one you wanted *me* to kill. Let's go and get our baby back. Lucky comes home, tonight!"

Chapter Eighteen

A Quinceanera is a major turning point in a young lady's life. It is the time when she passes from childhood to a young lady, and this momentous occasion is heavily celebrated in the Latin and Spanish communities. Religious ceremonies are performed, a ball filled with rituals and dance, and an elaborate dinner usually caps off the day's festivities. Parents spend tens of thousands of dollars to commemorate their daughter's fifteenth birthday. In this instance, Vasco Cardenas spent well over a hundred thousand dollars to celebrate his daughter's coming of age. The elaborate ballroom was just one of the event's expenses. It was this ballroom inside of the Ritz Carlton Miami where the day's events would come to a close.

Vasco leaned over and kissed his wife Guadalupe on her cheek. "I've got to drain the main vein, Sweetie."

"Don't take too long," Guadalupe told her husband. "It's going to be time for you to change her flat shoes to heels."

Vasco rolled his eyes and shook his head. "I'm still not ready for this."

"She's a young lady now," Guadalupe said with a smile.

Vasco made his way through the crowded ballroom out the door and down the hall to the nearby restroom. He stepped to the urinal and proceeded to relieve himself.

"Don't forget to shake," Princess told him. "But only twice. You shake it more than twice, you're playing with yourself."

Vasco turned, and hurriedly zipped his fly. "Princess! What are you doing here? You should have told me you were coming, I could have prepared a special place for you at my table."

"I think, you've prepared enough surprises for me, Vasco," Princess told him. "The little ambush in Palm Beach was surprise enough."

"What are you talking about?" Vasco asked.

"I talked to The Black Widow," Princess told him. "We had a nice dinner together. In fact, she agreed to work for me. In exchange, she told me who the Judas was in my organization."

"That bitch is lying!" Vasco shouted. "You can't believe that *Pinche Bruja!* She's trying to turn us against each other!"

Princess shook her head. "Naaa. She knew where I was going to be, and she knew who to hit up in order to get her shit through the port. Someone turned her on to the right people. Someone on the inside. That meant it had to be one of my underbosses. When she named you, it made sense. You were always smart, so you probably figured you were throw your hat in the ring with her. She's in Florida, she was taking over territory, I was always in Texas, so..."

"Princess, I've been loyal to you from the beginning!" Vasco told her. "From day one, I've been by your side."

Princess held out her hand, and one of her men placed a silenced pistol in her hand.

"This is my daughter's Quinceanera!" Vasco shouted, holding up his hands. "Please! Not here! Not now! I don't want her to find me! Please, not today. This can't be how she remembers her fifteenth birthday for the rest of her life!"

"What did you think the consequences would be, once I found out about your betrayal?" Princess asked. "Did you think I was going to slap you on the wrist? You set me up to be killed, and that bitch almost succeeded."

"I understand the consequences of my decisions," Vasco told her. "This is the business we're in, but my daughter shouldn't have to be in this building when I'm found. For all my years of loyalty and service to you, please take me away and kill me. Don't let them find me until long after this night has passed."

"Analiza works for me," Princess told him. "*All* of Florida belongs to me. Your men, are now under her control. Spend the next thirty days with your daughter. In thirty days, I want you to drive your car off a bridge. I want you to drink a gallon of Tequila, take a bottle of pills, climb in the tub with a radio plugged into an outlet, I don't care how you do it. You have thirty days. And there is no place in this world for you to run."

Vasco nodded.

Princess nodded toward the bathroom exit. "Go and change your daughter's shoes."

Vasco rushed past her to the bathroom door, and stopped just short. He turned back to her. "Thank you."

"I was a Daddy's little girl once," Princess told him. "She shouldn't remember this night as the night her father was killed. You have thirty days."

Vasco nodded, and walked out of the bathroom.

*****

Ohio

The caravan of black Escalades made its way through the tree lined streets of New Albany, Ohio, passing mansion after mansion, until coming to a massive secured compound with its own gatehouse and impressively massive mansion sitting in the distance. The grounds of the compound were immaculate, with symmetrical floral gardens, neatly trimmed hedges, and manicured lawns covering the entire property.

One of the Reign's men inside of the guardhouse pressed a button, opening the massive black intricate wrought iron gates, allowing the motorcade access to the gorgeous property. The caravan pulled up to the enormous French Country style estate and halted, allowing its passenger to disembark. Peaches was the first one out.

"What is this place?" she asked.

DeFranz lifted his arms and spun around slowly. "Your new, highly-secured residence."

"*My* residence?" Peaches asked.

"Jesus!" Vendetta said, taking in the size of the mansion.

"Ten acres of manicured, secured, private grounds, covered by the most elaborate security system money can buy," DeFranz told her.

Peaches shook her head. "I can't afford this. Not right now!"

"It's already paid for," DeFranz said with a smile. "Considerate a gift, from the Reigns family."

"Why?" Peaches asked. "Why would you do this?"

DeFranz leaned in. "Because you need security, I need to get my men out of this shit hole, and because I know my cousin would be safe out here."

Peaches peered at the Escalade Darius was riding in. He hadn't bothered to get out of the SUV. The two of them hadn't spoken since the run-in with Chesarae.

"I can't pay you back for this," Peaches told DeFranz.

DeMarion wrapped his arm around Peaches. "Just accept it. Don't look a gift horse in the mouth."

"For real, girl!" Vendetta added. "This beats Dublin, and you know how much I love those big ass cribs in Dublin. Girl this is old, long, paper out here!"

"Your men should be able to secure this place," DeFranz told Peaches. "One road in, and it's covered by cameras and motion sensors. You'll know if anyone is coming, long before they even get to the main gate. River in the back, along with other properties. New Albany Country Club is just over there, we have cameras, beam breaks, pressure sensors, and motion detectors covering the entire property, and all access points coming in. Even the golf course of the country club is covered. The house itself is built out of insulated concrete forms with steel rebar and steel Fibermesh in the concrete. You have bullet resistant windows, and it would take a tank to get through the wrought iron fence surrounding the property. There's an armory, a safe room, back up whole house generator, and plenty of other tricks."

"All of this, because you want to keep *Darius* safe?" Peaches asked, lifting a suspicious eyebrow.

DeFranz smiled.

"I'm afraid of what this is really gonna cost me," Peaches told him. "And I'm not talking about money. I suspect the price is going to end up being way too high."

She didn't like the way DeFranz smiled at her. She knew that he knew that she had made a deal with the devil. Or more accurately, a deal with the devil's family.

"Girl, let's check out the inside!" Vendetta said excitedly.

Peaches turned back toward Darius, who was peering down into his cellphone. She wanted to know what he thought, and what he knew that she didn't. She followed V into the house. The house was gorgeous, she thought, there was no doubt about that. It wasn't her taste though. Her crib in Dublin was French Country style, but the interior was a lot more modern. The house she was standing in now was distinctly old world and old money. The furnishings looked like a Versace furniture store threw up inside of the place. There was Louis XV, Louis XVI, Louis, XIV, and every other Louis' chairs and sofas. There was gold leaf, frescos, French and Italian vases, shiny marble floors, wrought iron stair cases, silk wall coverings, and crystal chandeliers everywhere. It wasn't that it was gaudy, it just wasn't *her*. But still, it was better than staying in a hotel room.

"Girl!" Vendetta shouted from the other room. "You should see the pool! And there's a damn bowling alley in the basement!"

Peaches turned to DeMarion, who seemed like he was avoiding eye contact. She shifted her gaze toward DeFranz, who maintained that slick Cheshire Cat smile of his. It was the kind of smile that made you want to slap the fuck outta him. She held out her hand.

DeFranz handed her the keys.

"Thank you," Peaches told him.

"Oh, Sweetie, you're more than welcome," DeFranz told her.

"Why do I get the feeling that this is less of a home, and more of a gilded cage?" Peaches asked. "Am I a prisoner?"

"In your own home?" DeFranz asked. "Seriously?"

"Why are you doing this?" Peaches asked. "And don't give me some bullshit about keeping your cousin safe! He hasn't said two fucking words to me, and he's going back with you when you leave, so that's all bullshit!"

"We want to keep you safe," DeFranz told her.

Peaches turned to DeMarion. "What's the deal? Am I a fucking prisoner?"

DeMarion shrugged. "If my cousin says that it's to keep you safe, then it's to keep you safe."

"I thought we was better than that!" Peaches told him.

"We good," DeMarion told her. "But even if it was something else, don't ever make the mistake of thinking that I would go against my family."

Peaches stormed out of the mansion and up to the Escalade Darius was sitting in. She tapped on the window. Darius lowered the window.

"Am I in danger?" Peaches asked. "Am I a dead woman? Just fucking tell me. Be a man, and tell me! Don't have me waiting around if you're just going to fucking kill me! Do it now, Darius! Do it!"

Darius opened the door and climbed out the SUV. "What the fuck are you talking about?"

"This!" Peaches said, flailing her arms toward the massive mansion. "What the fuck is this really about?"

"It about keeping you alive," Darius told her.

"Why the fuck is your family so interested in keeping me alive all of a sudden?" Peaches asked. "What the fuck do I mean to them?"

"You're a friend on the Commission," Darius told her.

"Bullshit!" Peaches shot back. "You ain't spending this kinda bread for a vote!"

"We also think that we know who is pulling the strings," Darius told her.

"D!" DeFranz shouted.

Darius waved him off. "It's cool, Franz! I got this!"

DeFranz shook his head.

"Pulling the strings?" Peaches asked, folding her arms.

"Those soldiers weren't from Ohio," Darius told her.

"No shit!"

"We are going to keep you safe," Darius told her. "We ain't gonna let nothing happen to you. I wouldn't let nothing happen to you."

"What is this?" Peaches asked. "Are they coming at me again, is that what you're saying? What? I'm some fucking *bait*? Is that what this is about? Making sure that I'm alive, so that you can play politics with my *life*?"

"Peaches!" Darius shouted, placing his hands on her shoulders. "Listen to your fucking self, Man! I ain't gonna let nothing fucking happen to you! Do you fucking understand that?"

"I don't know, Darius," Peaches told him. "I don't know anymore."

"Is that what you really think about me?" Darius asked. "That's the type of nigga you think I am?"

"I know you're pissed off about Chesarae!" Peaches told him. "You ain't even give me a chance to explain."

"Ain't nothing to explain," Darius told her. "You got a man."

"I don't have a man!" Peaches shouted. "He was in *prison*! He was supposed to be gone for *life!* Yes, I visited him, yes, I sent him money, yes, I wrote him letters! I stayed down! But I never counted on him showing up at my fucking door!"

"If you stayed down, then you are *his* woman," Darius said with a smile. "Did you fuck with anybody after he left?"

Peaches folded her arms and shook her head. "No."

"Why not?" Darius asked. "He was gone for good."

Peaches shrugged.

"Because you fucking love the nigga!" Darius told her. "A blind man can see that!"

"I'm not in love with him!" Peaches shouted. "What we had was special! Yes! But I'm not that little girl anymore! I've moved on with my life. I... I..."

"You what?"

"I fell in love with somebody else..."

"Really?"

"I fell in love with you," Peaches said softly.

"How do you figure that?" Darius asked.

"If I could explain it, then it ain't real," Peaches said, stepping closer.

Darius wrapped his arms around her and pulled her close.

DeFranz and DeMarion exchanged glances. They knew that they were in trouble. Getting Darius to leave Ohio wasn't going to be easy.

Chapter Nineteen

Damian unlatched the back gate to the police chief's home and strolled into the back yard. Despite that fact that it was two o'clock in the morning, Chief Hardberger was up, sitting at his outdoor table next to his swimming pool. A glass of Hennessey was sitting on the table next to a half empty bottle of the same spirit.

Damian and his men, made their way up to the chief, who was wearing a bathrobe, some boxers, and some slippers. The chief peered up at Damian and smiled.

"I knew you'd be coming by," Hardberger told him.

Damian, holding a handgun with a long silencer attached to it, motioned to the wrought iron chair across from where the chief was seated. "May I?"

"Of course," Hardberger said, motioning for Damian to join him.

"How'd you know I'd be dropping by?" Damian asked.

"We had a data breach at the station," Hardberger told him. "The computer geeks I have working for me are pretty damn good. Smart kids. They traced the breach back to a computer at Homeland."

"So how did that tell you that I'd be coming by?" Damian asked.

Chief Hardberger lifted his bottle of Hennessey offering Damian a drink. Damian waved him off.

"That's right!" Hardberger said, laughing. "You don't drink. A drug dealer without vices. Except one, that is."

"And which one would that be?" Damian asked.

"You don't smoke or drink, but you'll kill people," Hardberger told him. He allowed himself a drunk, alcohol induced laugh. They could all tell that he was drunk. "Or better yet, you *have* people killed. You don't get your hands dirty."

Damian held up the large pistol, showing it to the chief.

"Surprising," Hardberger told him. "I thought it would be your brother coming by. I pulled out an extra glass." Again, the chief let out an alcohol tinged laugh.

"You know why I'm here?" Damian asked.

"Of course, I do!" Hardberger said, pounding his fist on the table. "You're here for your pound of flesh!

You're here, to settle the score, to take your revenge, to end my pain."

Chief Hardberger broke down into tears. He was clearly drunk. Damian suspected that the half bottle of Hennessey wasn't all that he had to drink.

"I sent them away," Hardberger told him. "I sent them all away."

"You sent who away?" Damian asked.

"My family," the Chief said with a smile. He stuck out his chest with pride. "I said my goodbyes to my family, to my wife, and I sent her away. She shouldn't have to see this. I even made all the arrangements so she wouldn't have to."

"You made your funeral arrangements?" Damian asked, shaking his head. "If you knew it was going to come to this, then why did you do it? Why did you betray my family? We've always paid you well."

Chief Hardberger backed away from the table and held up his leg. He showed Damian a long scar. "Same thing in both legs. Double knee replacement surgery. When you get old, this is what waits for you. Pain, knee replacement, hip replacement, hands full of pills."

"I pay you more than enough money to pay for that," Damian told him.

"It's not about the got damned money!" Hardberger shouted, banging his fist on the table. "It's about the pain." Again. his alcohol induced tears flowed. "The pain."

Damian peered at the chief confused. Hardberger sniffled, and straightened up.

"You're a goody two shoes," Hardberger told him. "Don't use. So, you don't know what it's like. You don't know what it's like to want to kill yourself to ease the pain. So, you turn to pain relievers. Bottles of Advil, bottles of Aleve, bottles of Motrin. They give you Demerol, Percocet, Oxycodone, Vicodin, OxyContin, and finally, the daddy of them all, Fentanyl. I started with the patches at first, and they worked a little at first. And then they stopped working. And then you're back on the hunt for something stronger and stronger, just to help with the pain. And then you wake up one day, and you realize that the pain has gone away, and that the pain you have, is from needing your fix."

"You sold me out, for some dope, Man?" Damian asked. "All of this, because you're a fucking junky!"

Chief Hardberger started crying again. "I wasn't going to hurt her. I wasn't going to let them hurt her. They wanted her, but the deal was, they weren't going to take her to Mexico. I wasn't going to let those monsters take her to Mexico."

"Monster?" Damian asked, lifting an eyebrow. "That's a relative term."

"If that ain't the pot calling the kettle black," Hardberger told him. "At least I saved her."

"She didn't need saving!" Damian shouted. "She was taken from her family!"

"At least she's alive!" Hardberger shouted. "That's better than all the people you've come across.

You kill everything, Damian! You... you're a murderer."

"Don't you doze off, you son-of-a-bitch!" Damian said, tapping the chief's forehead with the silencer on his pistol. "Wake your ass up."

"I'm up," Hardberger said, slurring his words. "I'm tired. Just get it over with, I need to sleep."

"You could have gone to rehab," Damian said, standing up. "Instead, we're here. You could have even come to me, and I could have helped you."

"Help me from what?" Hardberger shouted. "They had me! They fucking had me! They had pictures, they had videos of me scrapping fentanyl gel from a patch and smoking it! They had me doing stuff on film, stuff that no one should have to do, no children should have to see their father doing. No wife should..."

Damian stared at the chief and shook his head. He was staring at a man's whose life had been over, long before he got there. He was a man who needed to be put out of his misery. He had gone to the chief's house to wake a man up and execute him. Now, he found himself having to do a mercy killing. The anger and bloodthirst had left his body. He was staring at broken man who had succumbed to addiction.

Damian lifted his pistol and pointed it at the chief.

"Please..." Chief Hardberger said, breaking into tears again.

Damian lowered his weapon.

"If you don't, I will," Hardberger told him.

"No, you won't," Damian told him. "If you were going to do it, you would have done it already. My brother was going to come here, and he was going to put a bullet in your head, but only after he had tortured you. I convinced him to go and get his daughter. After tonight, you'll be no good to the cartels, and more likely than not, they're going to expose you. If you're on film sucking cock for Fentanyl, then that's on you. The world is about to find out. What I'm going to do, is have my men send you a box of pure Fentanyl, and a key of pure uncut Bolivian cocaine, and let you finish off what you've started. You'll overdose, I have no doubt about that. I hope your children find your body."

Hardberger lowered his head to his wrought iron table and began crying heavily.

Damian and his men walked out of the chief's backyard, leaving him crying heavily.

*****

Dante tapped Lt. Frank Carboni on his head with the tip of the long silencer attached to his pistol. Carboni woke from his sleep, to find his bedroom full of Black men in suits.

"What the fuck?" Carboni said, sitting up and wiping to sleep out of his eyes.

Jennifer Carboni was awakened by her husband's loud voice. Upon seeing all the strangers inside of her bedroom, she bolted upright and clasped her husband's arm. "Honey, what's going on?"

"Awww, Honey, you know what's going on?" Dante told her.

"Leave her out of this!" Frank told him. "She has nothing to do with this!"

"Did you fix my little girl sandwiches when she was hungry, Frank?" Dante asked. "Did you make her dinner? Did you wash her cloths? What about when she had to go to the potty, Frank? Did you wipe my little girl after she went to the potty?"

Jennifer Carboni covered the lower half of her face.

"I didn't think so," Dante told him. "She's as guilty as you are."

"She has nothing to do with this!" Frank reiterated. "Let her go! Just let her take my daughter and leave. I don't care what you do to me, but she ain't got nothing to do with this!"

"Oh, what are you saying, Frank?" Dante asked. "Are you saying families are off limits? Is that what you're trying to tell me? Because that's what I thought too, and then you helped the fucking cartel kidnap my little girl."

"Dante, you don't understand!" Frank told him.

"Help me, Frank!" Dante told him. "Help me to understand. Please explain to me what kind of sick fuck you got to be, to kidnap a child!"

"They just wanted the war to end," Frank told him. "They just wanted leverage. They wanted to get you to listen."

Dante nodded. "The war is about to be over, that's for sure. Perhaps not the way they suspected it would end, nor the way they would like it to end, but it's about to be over. All over. You, the chief, Nuni, his whole fucking organization. Everybody who had anything to do with this, and everyone who fucked with my family, and tried to take advantage of the situation. All of you, are going to hear from me. You chose the wrong side, Frank."

"We didn't choose!" Jennifer told him. "What makes you think we had a choice!"

"You had a choice!" Dante shouted. "You could have turned this piece of shit in! You could have told him that you didn't want anything to do with it! You could have made him bring my daughter home!"

"He works for the chief!" Jennifer shouted.

Dante stared at Lt. Carboni. "Do you, Frank? Do you really work for the chief? Something tells me, that it was the other way around. Sure, he's the chief, and during the day, you officially work for him, but something tells me that it was really you who was calling the shots."

Jennifer quickly turned toward her husband. Frank lowered his head.

"You see, Frank, the chief has worked for us for a long time," Dante continued. "And if the cartel would have approached him, he would have immediately let us know. It wasn't the cartel that approached him, it was you. You probably found out that he was dirty. You found something on him, and you wanted in on the payroll. And it had to be something that would prevent him from killing you, or having us kill you. What was it Frank? Go ahead, tell your wife the reason why we are all here tonight. What brought us to this little tete-a-tete?"

"Frank?" Jennifer Carboni asked softly.

Frank exhaled. "He was dirty."

"Everyone's dirty," Dante told him.

"He's a junkie," Frank admitted. "The cartel found out that he was a junky. They approached me, and I went to the chief. They had pictures, video, receipts, pawn tickets, all kinds of shit."

"Frank!" Jennifer shouted. "How could you? He was your friend!"

"What was I supposed to do, Jennifer?" Frank shouted. "Vacations cost money! This big ass house, cost money! Emma's private school, cost money! That fucking Mercedes truck you're so in love with, cost money! The cabin on the lake, the fishing boat, all that shit cost money! Besides, they said that I had to choose. I could take the money, or they could take Emma. What choice did I have?"

"You could have come to me," Dante told him.

"Come to you?" Frank sneered. "Why would I go to a got damned drug dealer to protect me from other drug dealers!"

"Because that's what we do," Dante told him. "You pick a side, and you stay the fuck out the way. You just picked the wrong fucking side!"

Jennifer Carboni began to climb out of bed. "I'm going to go and check on Emma!"

"No, you're not!" Dante told her. "Emma is going to be just fine."

"What's that supposed to mean?" Frank asked. "I didn't hurt your little girl. I took really good care of your little girl!"

"I'm going to take really good care of yours," Dante said with a smiled.

Jennifer Carboni's hands flew to her face and she began crying.

"Leave my little girl outta this!" Frank shouted.

"Kinda like you left my little girl out of it?" Dante asked.

"She's innocent!" Jennifer screamed.

"So is my daughter!" Dane shouted back.

"Dante, please..." Frank said, placing his hands together and pleading.

"When I was on my way over here, I thought about all the things that I was going to do to you," Dante told him. "I thought about barbecuing your ass, and pulling you apart with salad tongs, bit by bit. I thought about pulling out my old trusty electric saw, and cutting you up piece by tiny piece while you were alive. I thought about using rose bud clippers, and snipping you apart piece by piece. I was going to take

243

my time and have fun with both of you. And after it was all done, I was going to take my daughter and go home. And then I thought about your daughter, coming downstairs, finding your bodies, trying to get you to wake up. I thought about her being hungry, and going in the kitchen and trying to fix herself something to eat. Maybe she would fall down trying to climb onto the counter and reach the cereal, maybe she would turn on the stove and burn her little body trying to cook food like mommy, I thought about so many things. A little girl living in a house starving slowly, while her parents rotting bodies lay in the bedroom. Thinking about that on the way here, bled all of the vengeance out of me. I'm not going to do that to your daughter."

Jennifer Carboni was in full blown tears, listening to Dante.

"Please, call my mom, or her mom, call someone to come and pick her up," Frank told him, shaking his head. "Don't let her find us, don't leave her here alone. Please, let her grandmother take her. Please."

Dante shook his head. "I'm not going to do that either. You took my daughter, so now I'm going to take yours."

"Nooo!" Jennifer wailed.

"Dante! Please, no!" Frank shouted.

"Emma is going to go home with me," Dante told them. "She's going to grow up a Reigns. She's going to go to the best schools, get the best education, and have everything she can ever dream of, while growing up. But she's also going to get an additional education. Emma, is going to grow up, to become the

244

Reigns family's number one assassin. She's going to use that White privilege to get close to people we can't get close to, and she's going to take them out."

"Dante, please, no!" Frank said, crying heavily.

"She's going to go to Harvard, like all Reigns family members do," Dante continued. "She's going to be groomed to be a trained killer and to always seek opportunity and advantage. She will be extremely loyal to her new family. She may marry a future Senator, a future Governor, and perhaps even a future President, or become those things herself. Emma, is going to be my family's greatest weapon in the future. And it's all your doing."

"Keep your filthy Black hands off my daughter!" Jennifer Carboni screamed.

"Shut up, bitch!" Dante said, lifting his weapon and putting a bullet through Jennifer Carboni's skull. She died instantly.

Frank Carboni shouted, and clasped his wife's hand. "No! Oh God! Jenny! Jenny! Don't! Come back to me! Jenny!"

"Frank, all I can say is, do better next time!" Dante told him.

"Fuck you!" Frank shouted.

"Is that really what you want your last words to be?" Dante asked, lifting an eyebrow.

Breathing heavily, Frank thought about his life for a few moments. "No! No, it isn't. Tell Emma, that I love her. That *we* love her! Tell that I'm sorry! No matter what, I'll always love her, and I'll always watch over her! Tell her to please forgive me! And that if I could do it over again, I would. She meant more to me than life itself, and for the time I got to share with her, I will be forever grateful. She was my light, my sunshine, my joy. Tell her... Tell her to keep her eyes open when she's riding her bike so she can see where she's going. And tell her that she's right, light bugs are magic. And one day, she *will* find a unicorn. Wash her princess costume, Dante. She'll wear that thing seven days a week, twenty-four hours a day. Take care of my little girl!"

"Bye, Frank!" Dante lifted his weapon and squeezed the trigger repeatedly. The first round went through Frank's hand and into his neck. The second into Frank's abdomen, and the third into Frank's heart. He turned to his men. "Where is she?"

"Upstairs."

Dante made his way up the stairs and down the hall which was lined by his men. One of them opened the bedroom door and he stepped inside. Lucky was sound asleep on the bottom bunk. Tears flowed from Dante's eyes. Lucky was alive.

Dante bit down upon his fist to keep himself from weeping out loud, as he stood and took in the sight of his daughter alive and sleeping peacefully. He had never been big on church, or been much for prayer or faith. It wasn't that he didn't believe in God, he did. He just figured that his fate had been sealed a long time ago. Still, he turned his face up toward heaven.

"Thank you!" Dante whispered through his tears. "Thank you!"

Dante leaned down, and scooped a still sleeping Lucky into his arms, and begin to carry her out the room. Emma woke up.

"Are you her Daddy?" Emma asked.

Dante nodded. "Yes, I'm her Daddy."

"Lucky is my best friend," Emma told him. "We pretend like we're sisters. Can I come and sleep over your house, we've already had a long sleep over at my house?"

"You want to come and sleep over?" Dante asked.

Emma shook her head.

Dante nodded for her to come with them. Emma used the bunk beds' ladder to climb down.

"Can I bring my favorite stuffed animal?" Emma asked.

"You can bring all your toys," Dante told her. He looked up at his men. "Get all her toys, clothes, everything. Go and pick up an exact copy of her carriage bunk bed, and have it assembled at the ranch."

"The ranch, or the penthouse?" he man asked.

"The ranch," Dante told him. "We're moving to the ranch. Children should be raised on a ranch, not in a damn penthouse. They need horses to ride, they need room to run and play, they need fresh air. Have my clothes moved to the ranch as well. Let everyone know that I have the package, and that we're on our way to basecamp."

Dante kissed Lucky's face uncontrollably, and then looked down when he felt Emma clasp his hand. "You're going to love the ranch, Emma. You like ponies? You can have your own pony, and everything you want. You and Lucky can be sisters and best friends forever. Neat, huh?"

Emma nodded excitedly. She was happy to be going on a long sleepover, with her new family.

Chapter Twenty

Princess threw open the doors to the Reigns family homestead and raced into the living room, where she shoved everyone aside and scooped Lucky up into her arms.

"Auntie!" Lucky shouted, kissing Princess on her cheek.

"My baby!" Princess shouted, showering Lucky with kisses all over her face. Tears flowed from eyes continuously. "I love you! I love you! I love you so much!"

"I love you too!" Lucky said, rubbing her nosed against Princess' nose, giving her an Eskimo kiss. "Auntie, this is my best friend and new sister, Emma!"

Princess looked down and was taken aback. "Why, hello, Emma! Please to meet you."

"So, are you my auntie too?" Emma asked.

Princess looked at Damian, and then at Dante, and then back at Emma. "Why yes, I guess I am. Do you know how to do Eskimo kisses?"

"Nope, the Eskimo kiss is all mine!" Lucky said, holding her hand up.

Everyone in the room burst into laughter.

Damian took his niece from Princess, and put her back down on the floor. "Lucky, show Emma the rest of the house, and then you can take her and show her all the animals on the ranch."

"Okay, Uncle Damian," Lucky said.

"Sounds like fun!" Emma shouted.

The two of them raced off.

Princess turned to Dante. "What the fuck did I miss?"

"I wasn't going to put a bullet in her," Dante told her.

"Of course not!" Princess told him. "But to bring her here? That little White child? Every FBI agent in the country is going to be out looking for her. And her fucking name is Emma, and she got blue eyes and blood hair? Fuck a milk carton, they putting her ass on cereal boxers, cans of Spaghetti O's, Fruit Roll ups, every damn thing!"

"Not if they think she's dead," Dante told her.

"Dead?" Princess asked, lifting an eyebrow.

"Three burned bodies were delivered to the morgue, all three of them unrecognizable," Dante told her.

"And dental records?" Princess asked.

"She still has her fucking baby teeth!" Dante told her. "Besides, the parents kept all the teeth she's lost, I gave them over to the coroner. Plus, he works for us. So do the fucking local FBI pukes. Everything has been taken care of."

"Dante, what the fuck are you going to do with a little White child?" Princess asked. "And what are you going to do when she decides that she wants to go home? What happens when she starts crying for her mommy?"

"I'll make it so fun, that she doesn't want to go home," Dante said. "What child ever wants to end a sleepover? And when it comes to that, I explain to her that her house burned down, and her mommy and daddy are in Heaven, so she can stay with Lucky and they can be sisters forever."

"That is so fucked up, on so many levels!" Princess protested.

"Her parents are dead!" Dante told her. "She's not going to have them ever again. So, what, give her to some other family member?"

"Yes!" Princess said. "We don't need the headache!"

"It's not a headache," Dante said.

"Damian, you went for this bullshit?" Princess asked.

Damian shrugged. "Not my call."

"I understand you were pissed," Princess told him. "I understand you wanted revenge. But this shit... C'mon?"

"Here, she's good," Dante told her. "I don't know what the grandparents are like, what the uncles or aunts are like, what the cousins are like. Here, she's safe."

"So, you feel responsible for her?" Princess asked. "Her father fucked up."

"That's right, she didn't!" Dante told her. "Why should she suffer, or be put in an unknown situation. Princess, here, she'll have Lucky. They'll be sisters. Here, she'll have horses, and goats, and pigs, and cows, and chickens, and every other animal to play with. She'll have tutors, maids, nannies, cooks, Christmases filled with toys, birthday parties out of this world, Disney vacations, everything her heart could ever desire. She'll get the best education, and end up going to fucking Harvard! She'll have an unbelievable life!"

Princess shook her head. "I don't like it. But it's your call. Now let me ask you this, have you forgot that this bitch is an FBI agent?"

"Hey, fuck you, Princess!" Grace shouted.

Dante laughed. "It's all good."

"Oh, so you two muthafuckas is all Kumbaya now, huh?" Princess asked. "What the fuck has the world come to?"

"Grace, give us a minute please?" Damian asked.

Grace nodded, rolled her eyes at Princess, and then left the room.

"Grace is the reason we found Lucky in the first place," Damian told his sister.

"Well, I *still* don't trust the bitch!" Princess said. "Hell, she may be just trying to get close to your dumb asses again. Ever thought about that?"

Damian glared at his sister.

"Leave me out of whatever plans you have, if it involves *that* bitch!" Princess told them. "I'm too pretty to go to prison."

Dante wrapped his arm around his sister. "But just think about all that coochie in there!"

Damian laughed.

"Fuck you, and you!" Princess said, pointing at both of her brothers.

Damian nodded for them to walk to the large dining room table. They followed him, and gathered around the map that was laid around the table.

"We have our baby back," Damian told them. "Now, it's time to bring this war to an end. Dante, you know where Nuni is hiding out. I already have men in Mexico waiting for you. Everything else is already set up."

"Do I even want to know?" Princess asked.

"You might not," Dante told her with a smile. "Might not fit your *moral conscience.*"

"*My* moral conscience?" Princess asked, pressing her chest. "I would have put two bullets in the little bitch's forehead and called it a day. You want to Save the Children and shit."

Dante laughed and shook his head.

"Princess, I want Baby Doc to get the message to stay out of Ohio," Damian told her. "We put Peaches on the Commission, and his going after her, is a disrespect to our family. Let him know that."

"If we kill him, The Commission is going to be up in arms," Princess warned. "Remember, we agreed, no more killing Commission members."

"He broke the deal," Damian reminded her. "He tried to kill Peaches. What you saw in her, I'll never understand. If it were me, I would have backed the other young cat. Anyway, make sure he gets the message. See if there's a way for him to understand not to fuck with us, without pissing the Commission off."

Princess shrugged. "Another soft muthafucka. I go to Florida, and you two niggaz get extra friendly. Fuck the Commission."

"Alive, Princess." Damian told her. "Besides, I don't want to fight a war with them, *and* the Old Ones at the same time."

"Pennsylvania?" Dante asked.

"Not just Pennsylvania," Damian said, shaking his head. "That's going to piss them off, but I have a suspicion that they've been pulling some strings behind our back."

"Really?" Princess asked. "How so?"

"Because Baby Doc would have never pulled that move on Peaches alone," Damian explained. "Not knowing how the Commission would come down on him if he was caught. Also, Baby Doc has been getting shipments in from Columbia."

254

"No shit!" Dante said smiling.

"Our people at the port in Mobile are pretty sure," Damian said nodding. "And, the markings on his keys are the same markings that have been turning up in Jersey."

"Are you fucking serious?" Princess asked. "You telling me that Old Malcom has been sleeping around with Columbian dogs behind our back."

Damian nodded. "He's fucking with Cedras and the Medellin cartel on the low."

"And allowing the Old Ones to bring in Columbian dope through his port," Princess said, shaking her head.

"When did you find out about this?" Dante asked.

"Just got the confirmation from our people in Jersey this morning," Damian told them. "After our people in Mobile laced me up, I went to that last meeting and saw how Baby Doc was acting. He was cockier than a motherfucker. That told me that he was in bed with the fucking Sicilians and the Columbians."

"Yeah," Princess said, nodding. "Time for Baby Doc to get scratched. Get some of them Columbian fleas off his ass."

"And its also time for Don Biaggio to retire," Damian told them.

"Seriously?" Princess asked.

Damian nodded. "Nicanor will help. Dante, take care of Nuni, Princess you deal with Baby Doc, and then I want the three of you to handle the Old Ones."

"And what are you going to be doing?" Princess asked.

Damian smiled. "I have a Commission member I have to catch up with in Chicago. And then, I'm going to pay a visit to Senator Hanson, the author of the infamous Hanson Bill. He's trying to have drug organizations declared as narco-terrorist, and treated with the same penalties as political terrorists. His daughter died from a Meth overdose, so now he's trying to wage a one-man war. I can't let this bill pass."

"Fuck no, you can't!" Princess told him.

"We have the men, the search is over, now let's deal with all of our enemies once and for all," Damian told them.

Nods went around the table.

Damian looked at his watch. "I have to fly out right now. Dante, you have to catch a plane too."

"Dante," Princess said, calling out to her brother.

"What?" Dante asked, stopping in his tracks.

"Don't bring no little kids back from Mexico, you friendly muthafucka!" Princess told him.

Dante threw his head back in laughter, and lifted his middle finger up at his sister.

Chapter
Twenty-One

The Magnificent Mile was Chicago's answer to Beverly Hills' Rodeo Drive. It was home to such high-end retailers as Versace, Hermes, Gucci, Fendi, Prada, Escada, Louis Vuitton, Chanel, Armani, Burberry, Zegna, Rolex, Cartier, Patek Phillipe, and many many more. Within the fabulous Mag Mile, was also some of Chicago's finest dining, as well as other upscale novelty shops. One such novelty shop, Sprinkles, was home to the cupcake ATM. It was in this shop, where MiAsia found herself this afternoon. Her hands were full of shopping bags from most of the aforementioned luxury retailers. So much so, that she was now regretting that she only brought two men with her on her secret shopping excursion.

"Let me have a red velvet cupcake, and a peanut butter chocolate one," MiAsia told the girl working the counter. She handed the girl her American Express Centurion Card.

Collecting her neatly packaged cupcakes, MiAsia lifted her shopping bags, and headed out the door. It had been a long day of shopping, and she was ready to head back to her club level suite atop the nearby Ritz Carlton. Stepping out the door, she found herself, and her men, being quickly surrounded. Her bags were taken out of her hands, and a black Rolls Royce Phantom pulled up. The rear door to the Phantom was opened for her to climb inside.

"What is this?" MiAsia demanded.

The man said nothing. He opened his jacket so that she could see his pistol, and then motioned for her to climb inside of the waiting Rolls. MiAsia turned back to her men, who were vastly outnumbered, and then climbed into the back of the waiting car.

"What is going on?" MiAsia asked the driver. Again, she received no response.

The man who showed her his weapon, climbed into the Rolls Royce with her, and the car pulled off. The first thing she noticed, was that they were not alone, they were part of a caravan composed of four more vehicles. The ride she took was a short one, as the motorcade took her directly to a pier on Lake Michigan. There, she found a massive yacht waiting alongside the pier.

MiAsia's first thought was on finding an escape. The fact that there were men lining the pier, men watching her from the yacht, men behind her getting out of the other vehicles in the caravan, all put an end to her thoughts of *immediate* escape. Her second thought, was who in the hell would put a two-hundred-foot yacht on the Great Lakes? A yacht of that size, price, and magnitude was made to cross oceans, not roam around the Great Lakes. Someone was either an idiot, or had money to burn.

The man who showed MiAsia his weapon stepped in front of her, and patted her down. He found the gun she had hiding in a tiny holster in the small of her back, and relieved her of it. Once he searched her a second time, and was confident that she was unarmed, he waved his hand for her to board the massive yacht.

MiAsia came to the end of the gangway and stepped onboard, where another gentleman motioned for her to head below deck. She eyed the distance to the water, wondering if she could make it overboard before being shot in the back. A man stepping in between her and the edge of the boat killed that option. He waved for her to head down the stairs to the deck below. She was certain that she was about to see her last bit of sunlight forever. MiAsia took in a deep breath, and walked down the steps. In the living room below, she found her abductor.

"Damian, what the fuck is the meaning of this?" MiAsia shouted.

One of Damian's men walked in, sat her cupcake box down on the table, and then disappeared.

"You went against me at the last Commission meeting," Damian told her.

"I didn't go *against* you!" MiAsia shouted. "I asked a fucking question! I *am* allowed to ask questions, aren't I?"

"Not when they are against me," Damian told her.

"What?" MiAsia shouted. "Are you fucking serious? What the fuck is all this? Where are my men? Why the fuck did you kidnap me? Is your little ego that fragile that you can't be questioned?"

"I'm wrapping up all family business," Damian said coldly. "We recovered my niece."

"That's good!" MiAsia rejoiced.

Damian held up his hand silencing her.

"I'm taking out the heads of the Northern Mexico cartels," Damian continued. "I'm dealing with Baby Doc, because I know he sent soldiers into Ohio. I also know that he had the backing of the Old Ones, and so I'm having them dealt with as well. Today, is the reckoning. Today, everyone who has stood against my family, will feel me."

MiAsia swallowed hard, to get rid of the lump in her throat. "Damian, I'm not your enemy. I never went against you or your family."

Damian pushed the box of cupcakes toward her. "Have a bite."

MiAsia spied the cupcake box. "I'm not hungry."

"Eat the got damn cupcake," Damian told her. "You bought them. Eat up."

"I'm not hungry!" MiAsia told him. "What? What the fuck is this about?"

"Like I said, I'm bringing all unfinished business to a close." Damian pulled out a pistol, and then a long silencer. Slowly, he screwed the silencer onto the barrel of the pistol. "Eat up."

MiAsia swallowed hard. "I'm not..."

"Eat the got damned cupcake!" Damian shouted.

MiAsia pulled the box closer and opened it. She lifted the red velvet cupcake and bit down on it. "Happy?"

Damian kissed the barrel of his pistol. "You'll know when I'm happy. Eat."

MiAsia took another bite, this time she found an object inside of her mouth. She didn't know what it was.

"Eat!" Damian said forcefully.

MiAsia used her tongue to clear the cupcake debris from around the object, before finally realizing what it was. She spat it out into her hand. It was a five-carat diamond engagement ring, on a platinum base. "What the fuck is this?"

Damian pointed his pistol toward her and squeezed the trigger. Water shot out, squirting MiAsia's face and blouse.

"Eat the cake, Anna Mae!" Damian said laughing.

"You bastard!" MiAsia shouted, throwing the rest of the cupcake at Damian. "You sorry motherfucker!"

MiAsia's two bodyguards walked into the room laughing.

"You two were in on this?" She shouted.

They shook their heads.

"They didn't know shit!" Damian said, walking up behind her and wrapping his arms around her. He turned her hand over, and she opened it, exposing the ring. Damian took the ring from her palm, turned her around, and dropped down to one knee.

"I told you, I'm tying up all loose ends, and wrapping up all family business," Damian said. He placed the ring on her finger. "MiAsia, will you marry me?"

MiAsia lifted the ring into the light, taking it in. "Of course! Of course, I'll marry your retarded ass!"

Damian rose, lifting MiAsia into the air, and began kissing her passionately. He motioned for everyone to leave the room.

"After this bullshit, how could I say no?" MiAsia asked. "I found someone as crazy as I am!"

Damian and MiAsia laughed. She kissed him again.

"You know how beautiful you are?" Damian asked.

"Of course!" she said with a smile. "Do you know how sexy you are?"

Damian sat her down on the table, and unbuttoned her blouse.

"Careful!" MiAsia told him. "This is Chanel, baby!"

Damian stopped, pursed his lips, and then ripped her blouse open.

"You bastard!" MiAsia shouted.

"I'll buy you a fucking Chanel boutique!" Damian said kissing her neck. "Hell, I'll buy you the company!"

MiAsia tore Damian's shirt off. She kissed his shoulder, his neck, and his chest. He unclasped her bra, and tossed it onto the floor, and then took one of her nipples into his mouth. MiAsia leaned her head back and moaned. Damian, pulled up MiAsia's skirt, and pulled her panties off and tossed them onto the floor, while she unbuckled his trousers, and yanked down his pants and boxers simultaneously. He pushed his erection into her.

MiAsia spread her legs wide, and leaned back on the table slightly, while Damian stood in front of her going to work. He scooted his hands beneath her ass, and lifted her off the table and into the air, sliding her up and down on him. MiAsia wrapped her arms around his neck and held on for the ride.

Damian worked MiAsia furiously, bouncing her up and down on his pole, while she cried out in his ear. She wanted him bad, and she was letting him know it.

"Fuck me!" MiAsia told him. "Fuck me harder!"

Damian lowered MiAsia to the floor, turned her around, and pushed her onto the table. He grabbed his meat, and pushed into back inside of her, hitting it from the back. MiAsia quickly found herself banging her ass against him, trying to give him all of her. Damian slapped her ass.

"That's it!" he told her. "Work that ass! Give it to me! Give it *all* to me!"

MiAsia bit down upon her lip, as Damian was now fully inside of her, and hitting her in her deepest pleasure spots. She had to stop throwing it back because he was going in hard on his own, and she was now feeling all of him.

Damian grabbed her long, silky hair, wound it around his hand, and pulled. "You ain't getting away from this dick! You ain't escaping this!"

MiAsia griped the edges of the table while Damian pounded her from the back. He clasped the back of her neck and gripped her tight. The forcefulness of his grip and the rough way he was fucking her, turned her on more than she had ever been turned on. She had never been fucked like this. Most of the men she had been with, wanted to be gentle, to stare into her eyes, to make love while staring at her beauty. Damian was doing the complete opposite, he was fucking her rough and raw, and doing it well. He slapped her on her ass and she orgasmed instantly.

"Ooooooh, Damian!" MiAsia cried out. "Right there! Right there!"

Damian could feel her body tighten, and saw the way her eyes were rolling back as she peered at him over her shoulder. He knew that she was coming. He started hitting it even harder.

MiAsia's screams drove him to climax. He got in a few more strokes before he too found release. His body went stiff, and he shot his seed deep up into her. MiAsia turned, and took him into her mouth and drained him completely. He almost collapsed.

Breathing heavily, Damian walked to where MiAsia's panties were, and tossed them to her. "Get out."

"What?" she asked, breathing heavily.

"Get the fuck off my boat," Damian told her.

"Come again?" MiAsia said, frowning.

"You fucked me, and threw me off your jet," Damian said with a smile. "Now, I'm throwing you off my yacht. Recognize it when you see it again."

"You're kidding me right?" MiAsia asked, pulling down her skirt.

"Payback is a bitch," Damian said smiling.

"Sorry ass muthafucka!" MiAsia told him.

Damian popped her on her ass. "See you back in Texas?"

"I ain't going to Texas!" MiAsia told him.

"Have your ass at my house waiting for me, completely buck naked, Mrs. Reigns," Damian told her. "You got that?"

"I'm starting to not like you," MiAsia said with a smile. "You want me to be barefoot and in the kitchen too?"

"I want you barefoot and in the bedroom," Damian told her. "You probably suck at cooking."

"Fuck you!" MiAsia said. "I can burn in more than just the bedroom."

"We'll see," Damian said, kissing her. "You have a lifetime to show me."

"Are we really doing this?" MiAsia asked.

"Fuck yeah!"

"You sure?" she asked, lifting an eyebrow.

"I know you're crazy as fuck," Damian said, kissing her forehead. "I wouldn't have it any other way. Besides, my sister is batshit crazy. I've been training for this my entire life."

MiAsia laughed. "I forgot about your family. How are they going to take this?"

"They'll be happy for me," Damian told her. "They'll be suspicious of you at first. Well, truthfully, they'll *always* be suspicious of you. And, they'll probably kill you if we ever get divorced."'

"Well, then maybe we shouldn't ever get divorced."

"My thoughts exactly."

"The Commission isn't going to like this," MiAsia told him.

"Fuck 'em." Damian told her. He nodded toward the door. "See you back in Texas."

"You're really going to do this?" MiAsia asked. "You're really kicking me out?"

"Payback," Damian told her. "Get off my boat."

"Isn't this *our* boat now?"

"Not until we're married."

MiAsia closed her torn blouse, grabbed her heels, and headed up the stairs. "Payback is a mutha, Damian."

"Remember that!"

"Promise me something," MiAsia said, hesitating at the stairs.

"What's that?"

"That being married to you will *always* be this fun."

"I'll tell you what," Damian told her. "I promise that it won't ever be boring. And I promise you that I'll always try to make it an adventure. I also promise that I'll love you and protect you."

"Don't need your protection, Damian," MiAsia said, heading up the stairs. "Just your love."

"You had that from the first moment I laid eyes on you," Damian told her. He lifted his ringing cell phone. "Hello?"

"It's done," the voice on the other line said. "The chief overdosed this morning."

"Good," Damian said, disconnecting the call. It was one down, and a few more to go. He would take care of his enemies, and then get to planning a wedding.

Chapter Twenty-Two

Malcom Baby Doc Mueller leaned back in the dental chair and placed the dark shades over his eyes to block out the dentist's light. The dentist leaned Baby Doc back in the chair, and turned on her light, causing him to close his eyes. She inserted her dental dam into his mouth, and began to drill.

Malcom was completely surprised when the handcuffs went around his wrist, securing him to the chair, and a belt went around his chest, securing him to the back of the dental chair. He opened his eyes to find Princess peering down at him.

"That is one big ass cavity," Princess told him.

Baby Doc tried to break free of his restraints, but found that he couldn't. The dental dam in his mouth prevented him from screaming. And even if he could shout for help it would be of no use, Princess standing next to him meant that all his bodyguards were dead.

Princess lifted the drill, leaned in, and placed it on Baby Doc's tooth. "I've always wanted to do this. When I was a little girl and I would visit the dentist, this always seemed like it was so much fun."

Princess pressed her foot on the peddle spooling up the drill, and then placed it against Baby Doc's tooth. She quickly ground through his tooth and hit nerve, causing him to cry out in pain.

"Awww, did that hurt?" Princess asked. "So, sorry about that Malcom. I must have struck a nerve. Kinda like you did. You know, you really struck a nerve when you invaded Ohio and went after someone who we backed to be on the Commission. Kinda like spitting in my family's face."

Princess lifted the rinse tool and sprayed water down Baby' Doc's throat, choking him. "You need to spit again? You want to spit in my face again?"

Princess again lifted the drill, and went to work on another of Baby Doc's teeth. Again, she drilled straight through the tooth and hit nerve. Baby Doc went crazy screaming and bucking in the dentist chair. The pain was unbearable.

"What's that, Malcom?" Princess asked, leaning forward. "You're sorry? You know you made a mistake? You know that you shouldn't have sent men into another member's territory? You know that you shouldn't have crossed the Reigns family? What's that, boy?"

Again, Princess went after another tooth. She leaned into the drill, grinding straight through the tooth and into his gum, where she hit nerve. Blood, water, and tooth particles flew out of Baby Doc's mouth when he screamed.

Baby Doc was finally able to maneuver his tongue behind the dental dam and push it out of his mouth. "You fucking bitch! Do you know what will happen to you if you kill me? Do you know what the Commission will do?"

Princess shrugged. "We made a deal. We wouldn't kill another member of the Commission, without the permission of the *entire* Commission. But you broke the treaty we had to not go into another member's territory."

"You still need permission to kill me!" Baby Doc told her.

"What makes you think I *don't* have it?" Princess asked. "What makes you think I give a fuck whether I have their permission or not?"

"You can't take on the entire Commission, bitch!" Baby Doc sneered.

"Is that why you invaded Ohio?" Princess asked with a smile. "Is that why you thought you could fuck over my family? Is that why you cut a deal with the Old Ones? Huh? Speak up, Malcom. Is that why you cut a deal with Cedras, and why you're bringing Columbian cocaine into the country, and supplying La Costa Nostra?"

"Even if what you say is true, you still can't kill me!" Baby Doc, said, shaking his head and laughing.

"See, Malcom, that's where you're wrong," Princess told him. "I can afford to take on the *entire* fucking Commission. I can fight them, until they decide they want to make peace. I have soldiers on top of soldiers, and they have nothing better to do than to kill muthafuckas, now that the search for my niece is over with."

Baby Doc's eyes went wide.

"That's right, Fat Boy!" Princess said, patting Baby Doc's growing stomach. "My niece is safe and sound back at home. The war with the cartels is about to be over as well. No search, no war, nothing but thousands and thousands of men, sitting around bored, waiting for some action. I don't give a fuck about fighting The Commission!"

"Princess..."

Princess waved her finger at him. "Uh, uh, un, don't you started going soft now, Malcom. You were talking cash shit a minute ago. I can't kill you, I can't afford a war, blah, blah, blah. I'll tell you what, Malcom. You stay out of Ohio, and I won't kill you. Deal?"

"Deal."

"Not that easy!" Princess lifted the drill and shoved it into Baby Doc's mouth and started drilling. She cut through a tooth, and right into gum, causing blood to fly everywhere. She then punched him in the mouth repeatedly with the drill, knocking out some teeth and chipping others. She then pulled out her pistol and screwed on the silencer.

"Princess no!" Baby Doc shouted. "Please!"

"I need you to stay out of Ohio," Princess told him.

"I will!" Baby Doc said, spitting out blood with each of his words. "I swear!"

"I'mma need you to stop supplying the Old Ones," Princess added. "And I'mma need you to quit fucking with Cedras."

"Okay!" Baby Doc shouted.

"The coke coming into this country, comes from us, you got that?" Princess asked.

"Yes!" Baby Doc told her.

"Glad we had this little talk," Princess told him. "I hope that I don't ever have to come back to this backwater shit hole and have this conversation again. You got that?"

Baby Doc nodded.

"I don't believe you really understand," Princess told him. She lifted her weapon and fired a round into Baby Doc's thigh. He screamed like a wounded animal. Princess tilted her head to the side and examined the bullet hole. "Oh, Malcom, quit screaming like a little girl. It's just a flesh wound. I just wanted to make sure I had your full attention, and that you really understood what I was saying. No more bullshit from you, right?"

Baby Doc nodded. Beads of sweat poured down his face, and mixed with the blood pouring out of his mouth.

"No more adventures in Ohio, no more fucking with Columbian dogs, or racist Italians, got it?"

Baby Doc nodded profusely.

"They're racists," Princess continued. "They don't like us anyway."

She lifted her weapon and placed a round into Baby Doc's other thigh. Baby Doc screamed for dear life.

"Okay, that one looks pretty bad," Princess told him. "I don't even know why I did that one. You know, sometimes I just do shit. It's like I just can't help myself. I get off on torturing people. Makes my pussy wet. Like with a *capital* W. A fucking *capital* W, Malcom. Nothing like a little torture, to give a bitch an orgasm."

Princess waved for her men to leave. "See you later, Malcom. You're gonna want to get those legs looked at. And you're probably gonna need to reschedule with your dentist. Your teeth look pretty fucked up."

Princess and her men strolled out of the dentist office, stepping over the bodies of Baby Doc's dead men.

*****

Mobile Alabama Docks

Nicanor lifted his walkie talkie. "Everyone in place?"

"Roger."

"Zeus, in place."

"Apollo in place."

"Go!" Nicanor said, into his walkie talkie.

The guards patrolling the inner perimeter of the dock side warehouse, paced leisurely alongside the metal fence. The shipping containers had already been loaded onto the waiting trucks, and were sitting safely inside of the warehouse, waiting for nightfall to ship out. At night, the weigh stations of the Alabama Highway Patrol were closed, and that meant less of a chance of getting caught. The weights of the trucks were vastly understated, as each container was filled to the brim with pure uncut Columbian cocaine.

Zeus, the first Reigns' family sniper, was perched high inside of a loading crane on the dock. He had a view over the entire warehouse, all of the pier, and most of the port. Apollo, the second sniper, was hidden in the antennae mast of a ship just off shore, and had an excellent view of the port as well. Both were using expensive, silenced, high-powered competition rifles with match grade ammunition.

Zeus fired first.

The Chey-Tac M200 Intervention Sniper Rifle sent a .408 caliber round down range at more than 3000 feet per second. The first guard didn't know he was dead. He took two more steps before finally collapsing.

Zeus quickly adjusted his aim, and took out another guard, before Apollo joined in. Together, the two snipers managed to drop ten guards in less than a minute.

"Clear," Zeus said, into his walkie talkie.

Nicanor patted his driver on his shoulder, and the black G Wagon they were in, raced across the dock up to the guard house of the warehouse. Nicanor jumped out of the SUV, and approached the guardhouse. The guard stepped out holding a clipboard in his hand.

"I'm sorry, sir, you can't..."

Before he could finish his sentence, his head exploded and he collapsed. Nicanor reached inside of the guardhouse and pressed the button, opening the gate. He waved for his men to enter into the secured area, before climbing onto the running boards of the last SUV for the quick trip up to the warehouse door. He heard a barely audible subsonic screeching sound, and then saw a guard fall off the roof and onto the ground next to him. Two more screeches, told him that two others had just bit the dust as well.

Nicanor lifted his silenced pistol, aimed it at the door lock, and pulled the trigger. The door lock flew off. Nicanor threw open the warehouse doors, and stormed inside. He lifted his pistol and dropped one and then another. He shifted his aim to drop a third man, but was beaten to the punch by his men. The Reigns soldiers went through the warehouse with their silenced pistols and made quick work of the rest of Baby Doc's men. Once they were done, Nicanor made his way to one of the trucks, shot off the lock, and opened the rear door.

"Holy fuck!"

Nicanor himself was in shock. There was not one truck, but eight, and each of them was filled to the brim with kilos of cocaine. He lifted his cellphone. "Damian, we have a problem."

"What's up?" Damian asked.

"There are *eight* semi-trailers, and they're all full," Nicanor told him.

"Get the fuck outta here!" Damian told him. "Eight, eighteen wheelers?"

"Not bullshitting," Nicanor said, lifting one of the kilos and examining it. "Silver foil, red scorpion. Cedras for sure."

"Eight?" Damian asked again.

"All full," Nicanor told him.

"That's too much!" Damian said.

"Too much for Alabama, and even too much for New York, and New Jersey," Nicanor told him.

"That means the Old Ones are probably pushing into Boston, Connecticut, Delaware," Damian told him.

"Philly, and probably making a push for all of Pennsylvania," Nicanor told him.

"That means, Pennsylvania is going to be a fight," Damian said.

"So will Jersey," Nicanor told him. "And Delaware. We warned them to stay out of Delaware."

"Get the shipment, and get out of there," Damian told him. "Brandon's men are already in New York waiting on you. Everything is set up. Get the stuff on the ship, and you get to the airport."

"We planned on shipping out one, not eight," Nicanor told him.

"They'll fit," Damian told him. "Just hurry up. One truck, they'll be pissed. Eight, they aren't going to let you get outta there without a helluva fight."

"Gotcha!" Nicanor said, disconnecting. He turned to his men. Get these trucks outta here. Back to the dock, and back onto the ship."

"All of them?" one of his men asked.

"Of course, all of them!" Nicanor shouted.

He watched, as the trucks drove out of the warehouse, back to a waiting container ship that belonged to a Reigns' family holding company. They were going to steal Baby' Doc's drugs, by shipping them out of the Port of Mobile. No highway patrol to worry about, no local police, none of Baby Doc's men chasing them through the state. They were going to get onto the ship, and take a nice quiet trip down the coast to Galveston, Texas. While Baby Doc, would be wondering where the hell they were. He was going to owe the Old Ones tens of millions of dollars, and the Columbian's tens of millions as well. They didn't need to kill Baby Doc, the Old Ones or the Columbians would do it for them, while they got away with truckloads of free cocaine.

Chapter
Twenty-Three

The Estafeta delivery truck sat pulled to the side of the road midway up the mountain. Estafeta was Mexico's version of Fed Ex, they were a national delivery service that dropped off everything from heavy freight, to parcel and package delivery. They were well known, and everywhere. It was the perfect cover.

Inside, Dante sat in the cargo hold of the van at a communications console, with a headset over his ears. The headset had a mic that extended down to his mouth so that he could communicate with everyone involved in the operation. At this moment, he was watching a blip on the console screen, and that blip, represented the large 777 UPS cargo plane that was approaching the mountain.

"UPS, check your altitude," Dante said into his mic.

"Roger," the pilot replied. "Flight 8770, holding steady."

Dante smiled, the pilot's reply told him that it was a go, and that everything was right on time.

"Roger that, Flight 8770," Dante replied. "Looking good."

The pilot smiled. Dante had just given him the code word that informed him that the rest of the money had been transferred, and that his family was going to be well taken care of. He turned to his left and looked at the body of his now dead co-pilot. He could see the Swastika tattoo peeking out from beneath the cuff of the dead man's sleeve. He shifted his gaze back to the rapidly approaching mountain. He could clearly see his target. Nuni's mansion was in his crosshairs. The pilot pushed forward on the airplane's throttle, and then started his terminal dive. His speed didn't really matter, as the jet fuel inside of the nearly full fuel tanks were going to incinerate the mansion, and pretty much everything surrounding it. He placed his fingers on his lips kissing them, and then planted the kiss on the photo of his wife and children that he had taped to the airplane's control panel in front of him.

Dante took off his headset, and placed a pair of earplugs inside of his ears. He knew that the explosion was going to be loud.

Nuni's men saw the 777 barreling toward them and their initial shock paralyzed them from reacting. A few of them started firing weapons at the massive airplane. With the size and speed of the airplane barreling toward them, they may well have tossed their shoes at it. Nothing was going to stop this massive explosive projectile from incinerating the mountainside.

The 777 hit the compound with the force of an asteroid. The collision and subsequent explosion shook most of the mountain. Even Dante felt the effects inside of the van. The blast waves sent a thunderous rumble down the mountain through the van, and into his chest. It was as if God Himself had struck the mansion with a bolt.

"Let's go!" Dante shouted to the driver, while pulling out his ear plugs.

The two Estafeta vans raced up the mountain road toward the mansion, being joined on the way by two vans from the Comision Federal de Electricidad, which was the Mexican power company, as well as two vans from Telmex, the largest telephone company in Mexico. The six vans joined in formation as they made their way through the gates of Nuni's now obliterated compound. Dante was the first one out of the vans.

The weapons of choice for today's incursion into the compound were silenced FN SCAR assault rifles. Dante lifted his, and took out a burnt and blackened survivor who was crawling on the ground. The man's pants legs were still on fire. Dante placed two rounds in the back of the man's skull.

"Fan out!" Dante told his men. "Whoever is still alive, make sure they're not alive when we leave this shithole."

Dante's men fanned out over the compound, searching for survivors. The buildings were all gone, and the scattered pieces of logs which made up the buildings, were burning energetically. The entire area wreaked of jet fuel, burning wood, and cooking flesh. A dark black smoke from the fuel billowed throughout the area, obscuring the air. Dante and his men had prepared. They pulled out gas mask and placed them over their faces, as they made their way further into the destroyed compound.

Methodically, Dante shot each man that he came across, whether the man was moving or not. He was there for vengeance, but he was also making sure that the rest of the Northern Cartels got the message. He wanted no survivors, he wanted to sap the manpower of the cartels, and he wanted to suck their fighting spirit out of them. Soon, he came across the body of the person he was looking for. Miraculously, Nuni Nunez was still alive, even if it was just barely. Dante lifted his foot, and kicked Nuni in his ass.

"Roll over," Dante told him.

Nuni stopped crawling along the ground, and with all the strength he could muster, turned himself over. His face was bloodied and charred, and his hair had melted onto his skull. His eyebrows were gone, so was his mustache and beard. Blood poured from his right eye.

"Look at you," Dante sneered. "It didn't have to come to this. It didn't have to be this way. You could have negotiated. *Esta, Jodido!* You crossed the line when you brought my daughter into this."

"It was always going to be this way," Nuni said, barely mustering a half smile. "You can't stop destiny."

"I have my daughter back," Dante told him. "The chief, he's dead. The other officers, they're dead too. Once you're dead, the other cartels will make peace. This was all for nothing."

"Not for nothing, *Cabron!*" Nuni smiled. "I'm Nuni fucking Nunez, mutherfucker! I'm the baddest motherfucker Mexico ever seen! So, pull that *pinche* trigger, you ain't gonna change nothing! *Me vale madre! Vete al carajo, Puto!*"

Dante smiled and shook his head. "No, Nuni, you go fuck yourself!"

Dante tossed his weapon, and pulled out a giant Bowie knife with a sixteen-inch blade. He was going to do this the old-fashioned way. Nuni was about to get a Juarez smile. In other words, he was going to slice his neck so deep, all the way across, that it would behead him.

"*Chinga tu madre!*" Nuni screamed, as Dante ran the blade around his neck, cutting through flesh and bone. Blood shot everywhere. Nuni was dead halfway through the cut.

Dante lifted his bloody hand and wiped sweat away from his forehead, leaving Nuni's blood all over his face. He turned to his men. "Let's wrap this up and get the fuck outta here!"

Nuni's body would stay there. And when the recovery team lifted it, his head would fall off. That was the beauty of the Juarez smile. The other cartels would definitely get the message. It was old school, and it meant that there would be no quarter given. The Reigns family was prepared to fight this war to the death of the last man.

*****

282

New York

Nicanor and his men followed loosely behind Don DeLuca's limousine. Nicanor's driver was careful to remain at least five cars back at all times, and to make sure that he didn't draw any suspicion. DeLuca's Cadillac limousine made a right and came to a stop light. Traffic in the borough was heavy, as usual, and so today's commute would be the usual crawl. The fact that the Reigns family had men dressed like construction workers, and were intentionally routing traffic in order to insure the jam, helped matters of course. Nicanor lifted his walkie talkie.

"Deploy the toy," Nicanor told his men.

"Roger."

One of the men dressed as a city worker reached inside of a van disguised as a city work truck, and pulled out an Radio-Controlled vehicle. This particular model was less of a kid's toy, and more of a workhorse. It was a heavily modified Traxxas Stampeded VXL, with a special heavy-duty lithium ion battery and an aluminum chassis. Although it had the ability to hit over one hundred miles per hour, this one was designed less for speed, and more for payload and stability. The small remote-controlled monster truck was carrying forty-five pounds of high explosives designed to explode upwards. He placed the RC vehicle on the ground, flipped the switch turning it on, and then activated the explosives. He then lifted his walkie talkie.

"Big Foot deployed."

Nicanor flipped open his computer screen, and he could now receive the image from the stabilized camera mounted on the remoted controlled vehicle. He then lifted the remote, and began to guide the vehicle.

It was no secret that the Don's limousine was armored. The only people in their business who rolled around in unarmored vehicles were idiots, and soon to be dead people. Especially at this level. The shaped charged explosive would attack the least armored part of the vehicle, which was the undercarriage. He didn't know what level the Don's armor package was, so he didn't know if the warhead would gain full penetration. What he was counting on, was that the explosion beneath the vehicle, and the one he was going to deliver to the top of the vehicle, would combine to weaken the armor enough for his men to finish the work. If was New York City, and they wouldn't have a lot of time to fuck around. They needed to get through the armor, get to the old man, and then get the fuck off the scene. He guided the small remote-controlled vehicle beneath Don DeLuca's limousine.

"Here we go," Nicanor said to his men, before pressing the button on the remote to detonate the explosive charge.

The forty-five-pound Astrolite bomb created an explosive equivalent of more than a hundred pounds of TNT. Don DeLuca's limousine was lifted slightly off the ground by the pressure waved created by the blast. Another one of Nicanor's men stepped out onto a balcony with a shoulder fired AT-4 rocket and fired at the roof of the limousine, engulfing the vehicle in fire. The two back to back explosions aimed the armor's weakest points, caused the armor to suffer a catastrophic fail. Nicanor could see that the ballistic windows were blown out, and the limousine had split into two sections, opening up the cabin.

"Go! Go! Go!" Nicanor shouted into his walkie talkie.

The Reigns family's men, wrapped black mask around the lower half of their faces, pulled out the FN .308 assault rifles, and ran up to the Don's limo, where they poured massive armor piercing rounds into the vehicle. The massive .308 rounds took chunks out of the vehicle, blasting away at the weakened armor, tearing into the cabin and into the Don's flesh. He didn't stand a chance. Don DeLuca, the youngest and toughest of the old New York dons took more than a hundred rounds through his body. They pumped so many rounds into him, that some of his body parts actually fell off. The don's arms, and legs had both become detached. The Reigns family men fled into the city, ditching their construction uniforms, revealing business suits beneath. They ditched their assault rifles, lifted briefcases, and caught cabs, and hit the subways. The disappeared into the New York City landscape, leaving a dead Don, and a still burning limousine as the only evidence that they had been there.

Chapter Twenty-Four

Don Biaggio felt the motor controlling the table of the MRI machine come alive. Today's scan seemed to have been much quicker than the previous scans, he thought. Either that, or he had been asleep for far longer than he realized. The table slid out of the giant machine providing the old don with all the answers he was searching for. The sight of Princess standing next to him, made him smile.

"You're prettier than the nurse that sent me in there," Don Biaggio told her.

"It was a male nurse," Princess told him.

"You're still prettier," Biaggio told her with another smile.

Princess laughed. "You old snake charmer you. A sense of humor is the quickest way to a girl's heart."

"If only I were fifty years younger," Biaggio told her.

"Fifty years younger?" Princess asked. "You don't look a day over sixty-five."

"You're playing with an old man's ego." Biaggio told her. He sat up on the table, with Princess helping him. "Well, you're not here to flirt with an old man's ego, so... To what do I owe the pleasure of this visit?"

"Malcom, New Jersey, Ohio, Columbian cocaine," Princess said.

Don Biaggio smiled and shook his head. "I told that dang Malcom, to stay the hell out of Ohio. It had nothing to do with business."

"And Jersey?" Princess asked.

Biaggio shrugged. "It's ours. Always been ours. Our families were running Jersey before your great parents were born. Jersey's nothing to you. Means more to us that it does to you. Don't know why you didn't just give it to us."

"You're right," Princess shrugged. "Don't get me wrong, the money out of Jersey is good. But we keep Jersey just to piss you guys off. Plus, it gives us plenty of soldiers for Maryland, and for New York just in case you guys act up."

Biaggio laughed. "Your honesty scars me. That's the kind of honesty that people give on their deathbed."

"I'm not going anywhere," Princess said with a smile.

"So, Malcom turned on us?" Don Biaggio asked.

"No," Princess said, shaking her head. "He's careless, an idiot. He went after a young lady we put on The Commission. He was a little too bold in his moves, so we were able to figure out that he must have had some major muscle behind him."

"Is he alive?" Biaggio asked.

"Barely," Princess told him. "Gonna need a lot of dental work. Maybe some surgery, some time in therapy to walk again. But, he'll live."

Biaggio gave a slight laugh. "Dumb kid. I told him to leave Ohio alone. It was a sideshow, a useless distraction. He thought that it would help. That it would get you to commit more men. The plan was to stretch you so thin..."

"Then you could just walk into Jersey uncontested," Princess said, finishing his sentence. "The search for my niece is over. The war with the cartels in Mexico is over. The disturbance in Florida is over. And soon, my brother will take care of Senator Hanson, while Dante has already taken care of Nuni. It's over. All of our enemies are gone."

Don Biaggio smiled. "What a feeling! I can remember when we had that kind of power. Back in the good old days, no one dared challenge the old families. And now..."

"Now, things have changed," Princess told him. "You still wield that kind of power. The only difference these days, is that now others have it as well."

"I'm dying," Biaggio said softly.

"I know."

"Why finish a job that cancer is perfectly capable of finishing?" Don Biaggio asked. "It's a brain tumor. I have eight months, a year at most."

Princess shook her head. "Can't do that, Don."

"Time is a person's most precious commodity," Biaggio told her. "Time to say good-bye, time to get one's affairs in order. Time to kiss one's wife and kids. To have one last stroll in Central Park, one last trip to Sicily, one last taste of Maggiano's Pizza. It's got to be worth something."

"We can't cheat the reaper, Don Biaggio."

"No, but maybe the reaper could be persuaded to give an old man a little more time?"

"And why is that?"

"I have a billion reasons why," Biaggio told her. "One billion reasons for you to walk out that door."

"A billion dollars?" Princess asked, lifting an eyebrow.

"Plus, all my interest in Vegas, and Atlantic City," Don Biaggio told her. "Your brother has always been about business. That's what I've always liked about Damian, he was a businessman first and foremost. Surely, he could put a billion dollars to use?"

Princess whistled and smiled. "I'm sure he could. The problem with that offer, is that my family backed a young lady in Ohio. We put her in a seat at a table of vicious wolves, and they went after her. If that goes unchecked, then what happens the next time the Reigns family offers its backing and support to someone? If we all turned our back because of money, then what kind of world would we live in? My family's word has to be worth more than money."

Don Biaggio nodded. "And that's why I've always respected your family. You must have Sicilian in your blood. The war to come, will not be pretty, you know that?"

"The old New York families will make peace," Princess told him. "It's not a secret why you haven't retired after all these years. Your oldest son, is not built for this business. He will try to make noise, and he will try to fight us. Trust me, two weeks after you've been in the ground, he'll make peace. And the others will follow."

"You don't know Don DeLuca," Biaggio said with a wry smile. "DeLuca is old school. A bulldog. Don DeLuca will fight you to the last man, and he'll get the others to stand up and fight alongside him. You won't be able to stop DeLuca, nor negotiate with him."

"Let us worry about DeLuca," Princess told him.

"I don't want my wife to see a bullet in my head!" Don Biaggio said forcefully.

"Of course not," Princess told him. "I'll make sure you're a handsome corpse. Much like you are now."

Biaggio laughed, and Princess joined in the laughter.

"Old person jokes?" Biaggio asked. "Is that how you're going to send an old man on his way? Telling him how old he looks?"

"You know you're quite handsome," Princess said, caressing his face. "If I were fifty years older, you'd be a heck of a catch."

Don Biaggio lifted his arms. "So, how are we going to do this?"

Princess opened her hand, and one of her men placed two pills in her palm. She placed the pills into Don Biaggio's hand. "You'll take a nice, long, relaxing sleep, my old friend."

Don Biaggio pointed toward a medical cup next to the sink. "I hate taking pills dry."

"Water?" Princess asked, lifting an eyebrow. "Do you think we're barbarians?"

One of Princess's men handed the Don a wine glass, and then handed one to Princess. Another of her men handed her a bottle of wine, which she held up so that the Don could see it.

"Masseto Toscana!" Don Biaggio exclaimed. "Bravo!"

Princess poured some of the Merlot into the Don's wine glass, and then some into her own, before handing her man the bottle. The don sniffed the wine and then took a large gulp from his glass. He closed his eyes and savored the taste.

"Bravo, Princessa!" Biaggio told her. "Tell, me, you wouldn't have to have one of those fruit phone things."

"A fruit phone?" Princess asked, lifting an eyebrow.

"You know, the little phone, it plays the music, takes the pictures, does everything," Biaggio explained.

"You mean an Apple iPhone?" Princess said, laughing. She nodded. "We have phones."

My granddaughter, she plays music on hers," Biaggio explained. "Can you play music?"

"Sure," Princess said, nodding. She snapped her fingers and one of her men pulled out an iPhone.

"I would like to hear, *Mi votu e mi rivotu*, by Rosa Balistreri," Don Biaggio said with a smile.

Princess' man did a quick search for the song, found it, and pressed play. Music poured from the phone into the room. Don Biaggio slid off the table and stood. He extended his arms toward Princess.

"May I?" Biaggio asked.

Princess placed her hands into his, and Don Biaggio twirled her around and then pulled her close as the two of them danced slowly to the old Sicilian ballad.

"I love this song," Don Biaggio said, singing along to it.

"Sounds sad," Princess told him. "So much emotion, so much pain..."

"That's life, my dear," Don Biaggio told her. "The trick to it, is the make sure the good days, outnumber the bad ones."

The short ballad came to an end, and Don Biaggio sat back down on the table, with Princess helping him up onto it.

"I'm tired," Biaggio told her.

"It's time to take your rest, Don Biaggio." Princess told him. Her men began to filter out of the room. Princess walked to the door and flipped the light switch, dimming the room. "Lay down, close your eyes, and rest."

"How long?" Biaggio asked.

"You'll be asleep before we leave the parking lot." Princess told him.

"That fast?" Biaggio smiled. "Cure cancer, not in my lifetime. Invent a poison that can kill someone in less than ten minutes, sure. We got everything wrong. Humans..."

Princess smiled at the old don. "You can spit the pills out."

"Huh?" Don Biaggio asked, peering up at her.

"The pills you're holding in your mouth, they're placebos." Princess said with a smile. "They're aren't going to do anything to you. I laced the wine glass."

Don Biaggio spat the pills into his hand and then threw them onto the floor. He smiled at her.

"*Che il Signore sia con te,*" Princess told him.

"No, Princessesa!" Don Biaggio shouted, as she exited the room. "*May God be with you! You are going to need Him!*"

*****

293

San Antonio

Dante walked into his penthouse, pulled off his tie, and tossed it onto the couch. He was shocked when Desire walked out of his bedroom and into his living room. She folded her arms and stood just in front of him.

"I'm listening." Desire told him.

"I'm tired," Dante said, shaking his head. "I just want to shower, grab some clothes, and go to the ranch and see my daughter."

"I don't give a fuck how tired you are!" Desire shouted. "You owe me an explanation!"

"Desire, I don't know what you want to hear," Dante told her. "Anything I say is going to sound like bullshit. I can't give you an excuse, because I don't have one. I'm not going to play games with you, I can't make you believe me, or forgive me, or trust me again. I fucked up."

"Because you're weak, you're not going to even attempt to try to explain? This isn't worth saving to you, Dante? Did it mean anything to you?"

"You know it did."

"Then how could you do that to me?" Desire shouted. "How could you do that to *us*? I thought you were different! I thought you were better! You're just like the rest of these sorry ass niggas!"

"Desi..."

Desire started for the door. Dante clasped her arm, and she jerked away.

"Don't you *fucking* touch me!" Desire shouted.

"Desi!" Dante shouted.

Desire stopped and turned back to him. "Who was she, Dante? Tell me that? Who was she? And why was she worth throwing everything away?"

"She's not important."

"Bullshit!" Desire shouted. "She has to be! She meant more to you than *I* did!"

"She doesn't!"

"Then why was she here?" Desire shouted, pointing toward the sofa. "And why were you fucking her?"

"She was here, because her brother was responsible for kidnapping Lucky."

Desire hesitated, allowing what Dante had just told her to sink in. "Her brother kidnapped your daughter, so that made you want to *fuck* her? Are you fucking serious, Dante? You can't do better than that? At least rehearsed a better fucking excuse!"

"It's true," Dante said, trying to pull her close. She pulled away from him and folded her arms. "I know it sounds fucked up. Hell, it sounds crazy as fuck, I know. But it's true. Her brother, kidnapped Lucky. She was here, to help me get her back. I needed to use her so that her brother would keep Lucky alive."

"Even if by some miracle, that what you're saying is true, why would you fuck her?" Desire shouted. "What does her brother have to do with you lying on the couch making love to that bitch!"

Dante threw up his hands. "Nothing! It has nothing to do with it! That's what I'm trying to tell you. There was no reason for me to do what I did. I was wrong. I hurt you, I violated your trust. I'm sorry."

"That's not good enough, Dante," she said, shaking her head.

"I know," Dante said, lowering his head. "If there was any way that I could make it up to you, I would. And if I were you, I would feel the same way."

"I can't trust you."

"I know, and I'm sorry."

"So, what comes next?" Desire asked. "Where does this leave us?"

"I hope that one day you can forgive me," Dante told her. "I hope that one day, you'll be able to trust me again. I love you, Desi. What you walked in on, you should have never been put through that. I don't know how that happen, or why that happened."

"You're stronger than that," Desire said, shaking her head. "You did, what you wanted to do. What has me fucked up more than anything, is that you didn't think about me. You didn't think about us. Cheating is a selfish act. It shows a person that you are all about you, and all about your pleasure, your happiness, and not about theirs. You have a lot of growing up to do, Dante. A boy will fuck anything and everything that comes his way. A man, a real man, knows how to be faithful. Call me when you become a man."

Desire turned, and stormed out of the penthouse, leaving Dante alone.

Chapter Twenty-Five

H. Huntsman & Sons was without a doubt the jewel of London's bespoke suit makers. Huntsman's has been making suits and clothing for the monarchy since 1849. It has been *the* go to marquee shop on Savile Row for Oil Sheiks, Robber Baron's, European nobility, the famous, the extremely wealthy, and the fabulous since its inception. In fact, the premiere clothier of men's bespoke suits has been such a tour de force within the industry for so long, they decided to branch out and spread their wings. They opened a shop in Manhattan in 2016, and the company's wealthy American clientele couldn't wait to line up and spend nearly seven thousand dollars for one of the company's exquisite suits. It was within Huntsman & Son's 57th street Manhattan shop where the powerful Senator Hanson found himself today. Senator William Winthorpe Hanson VI was New York old money. A descendent of the Rockafellas, the Vanderbilts, and the Carnegies, he had a pedigree that made him as close as one could be, to being considered American royalty.

Senator Hanson lifted two ties into the air comparing them, and then holding each up against the luxurious Tengri fabric that would constitute his new fourteen-thousand-dollar suit.

"The one on the left," the voice from behind told him.

Senator Hanson spun, to find Damian in his fitting room.

"I'm sorry, this fitting room is occupied," Senator Hanson told him.

"Of course, it is," Damian said with a smile. He stepped further inside, and waved toward a Queen Anne chair.

"And you are?" Senator Hanson asked.

Damian seated himself in the chair, leaned back, and crossed his legs. "Damian Reigns."

Senator Hanson nodded slowly. He knew who Damian was. He knew of Energia Oil, Bio One, and about the Reigns family's more nefarious business enterprises.

"To what do I owe the pleasure, Mr. Reigns?"

"The Hanson Bill," Damian told him.

Again, Senator Hanson nodded. This time, it was his turn to smile.

"There are more appropriate venues to express your concerns," Senator Hanson told him. "You could contact my office. Maybe even hire yourself a lobbyist. A private fitting room..."

"I'm not going to allow the bill to pass," Damian said, interrupting him. "I cannot."

"I wasn't aware that you had been elected to the United States Senate," Hanson said with a Cheshire grin.

"That bill, is a direct danger to me, to my family, and to many people that I know and love," Damian told him.

"I don't see why a crime bill would be a danger to a legitimate businessman," Senator Hanson told him. "You are a legitimate businessman, aren't you? At least you've always claimed to be."

"I'm a family man, and a businessman," Damian told him. "If that bill passes, you've unleashed law enforcement tactics and judicial penalties equivalent to The Patriot Act. FISA Courts issuing warrants against American citizens who are *suspected* of dealing drugs, you'll have sneak and peak warrantless searches, federal agents reading correspondence, documents, and mail without a warrant or court order. And death penalties for leader/organizers convicted under RICO or CCE charges. You are going after my family's money, and our lives."

"Get out of the drug business, Mr. Reigns," Senator Hanson told him. "If you're clean, you have nothing to worry about."

"If you're dead, then I won't have nothing to worry about," Damian countered.

"Oh, you think killing me is going to solve your problem?" Hanson asked. "You think putting a bullet inside the head of a United States Senator isn't going to have repercussions? The FBI will hunt you to the ends of the Earth. This crime will get solved. And my colleagues, they will pass that bill in my honor. So, you'll have gotten nowhere, Mr. Reigns. All your little efforts, all of your violence, it'll all be for naught."

Damian smiled. "We don't put bullets into the heads of United States Senators. Precisely for all of the reasons you named. Senators, Congressmen, judges, Governors, State Attorneys Generals, United States Attorneys, no, you get to die tragically. Senators die in skiing accidents in Switzerland, Aspen, Vail. They die in boating accidents in the Mediterranean, off the coasts of Martha's Vineyard, or Key West. They die tragically in plane crashes, or by running their cars off the road and into creeks. They die well. They're still dead nonetheless, but they get better deaths."

Senator Hanson walked to the chair across from where Damian was seated, and sat down. He leaned in. "Surely, a man of your intelligence, foresight, and business acumen can see the benefit of having a friend in the Senate."

"I believe the time for that type of friendship, has passed," Damian told him. "You're too dangerous for me to allow you to live. The bill has too much momentum, and it would be politically impossible for you to walk away from a bill that you've spent so much time, energy, and political capitol pushing. And even if you could drop it, your co-sponsors in the House and Senate would keep pushing it. No, the bill has to die along with you."

"And just how do you plan on doing that, Mr. Reigns?" Senator Hanson asked. "My death, will only push that bill forward, and it'll push it forward with so much speed that you won't know what hit you. My death, will only bring it to fruition that much faster. Let me help you. I *can* kill the bill. And you will have a powerful friend in the Senate."

"You're right about that," Damian said nodding. "Your death would only make the others want to pass the bill in your honor, so just killing you is not enough. I have to kill your reputation. I have to make the others think of you as a fraud, I have to make them want to run away from you, to distance themselves from you, I have to make you an embarrassment to the Senate."

"Don't do that," Senator Hanson said, shaking his head. "Don't do that to my wife and kids. At least let them have their dignity."

"Dignity?" Damian asked, lifting an eyebrow. "Don't worry about your wife's dignity. She's banging the yoga instructor, the chef at Nobu, and the captain of your yacht. And she knows your banging your assistant, just like you know about all of her little tryst. Your marriage is a sham. But that's not how I'm going to destroy you. No, in order for me to make sure that bill doesn't pass, you have to have a shit load of Oxycontin in your system. The housekeepers are going to find Oxycontin in your room, and some staffers are going to find it in your office. The man who is proposing draconian laws to punish drug dealers, is an addict. That's what the headlines will read."

Senator Hanson allowed himself a slight laugh before lowering his head and applauding softly. "Bravo, Mr. Reigns. Bravo. Make me a junkie.

Turning me into a hypocrite will make others wonder about the other sponsors of the bill, which in turn will cause them to quickly run away from it. Well done."

"I'm not here by accident," Damian told him. Damian rose from his seat. "Under different circumstances, I would have loved to have worked with you, Senator. Two Harvard men working together, we could have made great allies."

"I don't want to die, Mr. Reigns," Senator Hanson told him. "Surely, there is something I can offer, something I could do?"

"Nobody wants to die, but we all have to take a ride in the back of that big Caddy one day," Damian told him. "Unfortunately, you hurried your trip up by opposing Caesar."

"Caesar?" Senator Hanson asked, lifting an eyebrow.

"I am Black Caesar," Damian told him. "And you tried to take away my empire, to destroy my family. And all enemies of Caesar, must die. My men will take you to your home in the Hamptons. Enjoy the trip, take in the views, feel the sun on your face. You're going to die tragically in a yachting accident in a couple of hours. Take comfort in knowing, that you'll have a lot of company where you're going. Many men have tried over the years to destroy me and my family, and like you, they failed also. Tell all of them that Damian said, what's up."

Damian turned, and walked out of the fitting room. His men walked in to collect the Senator for his trip to his mansion in the Hamptons. Damian stepped outside of H. Huntsman & Sons onto the streets of

Manhattan. He peered up and the crystal blue sky, pulled out his Gucci shades, and put them on. His white Rolls Royce Phantom pulled around, and one of his men opened the rear door for him. Damian climbed inside.

*****

Veracruz, Mexico

The meeting was in San Lorenzo, Tenochtitlan, an area in southeastern Veracruz. San Lorenzo was most famous for being the capitol of the once mighty Olmec civilization, and today boasted several massive carved sculptures known as The Olmec Heads. The Olmec heads were massive ancient carvings of the heads of the Olmec kings. The carvings, which date back to 1700 BC, clearly delineate the origins of this great Mesoamerican civilization; the noses were broad and flat, while the lips are wide and thick, clearly showing the rulers to be of African descent. Mexican and Spanish architects deny vehemently the African origins of the civilization, and it remained sore point and bone of contention. To except the obvious, would also call into question the true builders of the Mexican Pyramids and other pre-colonial structures. The Reigns family chose this meeting site for precisely those reasons. Meeting the Mexican Cartels at the site of a great Black empire in Mexico, would not be lost on anyone. A modern day Black empire hosting a meeting at the site of an Ancient Black empire was the family sending a 'fuck you' to the cartels. There were hundreds of Black Reigns family soldiers spread throughout the site providing security. It would also send a message to the Yucatan Cartels, as Veracruz was part of the Yucatan peninsula. It was clearly a show of Reigns family power to all.

Galindo Ortega climbed out of his Mercedes Maybach and peered around. While Veracruz had always had Black Mexicans, the number of Blacks at the meeting place today, made it look like they were in Chicago. He marveled at the number of Reigns family soldiers in his country, and the amount of money, resources, and power that that they had in order to take on all of the Northern Mexico border cartels simultaneously, while conducting a search all over Texas, while holding onto Florida, California, Texas, Louisiana, and all of their other territories like Philly, New Jersey, Maryland, and Virginia. He peered across the landscape, until he spotted Dajon Reigns, standing near one of the Ancient statues having his picture taken. He headed over in his direction.

Dajon spied Galindo heading in his direction. Galindo looked like he had aged years. Even from a distance, he could see the grey in his hair, the new wrinkles on his face, and the fatigue in his demeanor. Galindo had lost a lot of men in the war. He lost two sons, and his best friend and right-hand man, Nuni Nunez. He looked like a man who was tired of war, tired of loss, tired of bleeding money, of moving from location to location to not get caught. Galindo was the most powerful don of all the Border Cartels, and yet he looked as though he had one foot in the grave and one foot out.

Galindo walked up to Dajon and stopped. "I thought Dante would be here."

Dajon shook his head. "Couldn't chance it. Dante would just as soon pull out his pistol and put a bullet in your head than make peace with you. Taking his daughter, was over the line."

"I agree," Galindo told him. "Nuni thought that it would get Damian to wait. We never wanted a war, we just wanted you to wait, until our war with the other cartels was over with. But you went to those bastards in Yucatan. And your commission voted to go back to the Columbians. Nuni thought it would bring you back to the negotiating table. No one, was ever going to hurt that little girl."

"Kidnapping children, is over the line," Dajon told him. "Our children, our women, our parents, they are off limits. What happened to the old days? Something like that, the person would have been executed, and their head sent as tribute with an apology."

"You went to war!" Galindo said forcefully. "There was no negotiation, just instant war."

"What did you think was going to happen?" Dajon asked. "You kidnap a child, and you expect a polite phone call?"

"I've lost people," Galindo told him. "I lost my sons. No father should ever have to bury their sons."

"No father, should ever have to go through the nightmare of having their daughter taken by strange men."

"She was safe, my friend," Galindo said, placing his hand over his heart. "You have my word, that no harm was ever going to come to her. It was business."

"It was *bad* business."

"It was a horrible mistake," Galindo told him. "Nuni, he paid for his miscalculation. I paid for it, my wife paid for it, two of my sons paid for it with their lives. Hundreds of my men paid for it with their lives, their families have paid for it, their orphaned children who will grow up without them, have paid for it. I am tired of war."

"Wars are easy to start, but not so easy to turn off," Dajon told him.

"Let us stop this bleeding," Galindo told him.

Dajon peered around the archeological site. He rubbed his hand on top of the massive carved Olmec head that he was standing next to. "Empires. They rise, they fall. They make war, they make peace. Sometimes history remembers them, sometimes they are lost to the centuries. My family, we are an empire. Dante is not here, because Dante arrived in Juarez this morning, with two thousand men."

Galindo stumbled back before catching his balance. Dajon clasped his arm, helping to steady him.

"Princess is in Texas," Dajon told him. "She has another two thousand men and is about to hit Nuevo Laredo. Nicanor is about to hit Matamoros. And I am here, to send a clear message to our friends in Yucatan."

Galindo's hand made his way to his face, where he wiped his tired eyes. "No more."

"Damian is heading to a meeting with the Commission," Dajon continued. "By the end of the week, all of our enemies will be dead."

"Why are we here?" Galindo asked. "If you are going to shoot me in the head and kill all my men, then just get it over with. I'm tired."

"You were never our enemy," Dajon told him. "You let Nuni cross the line. Other than that, you did good business with us for years. Time to lay all the cards on the table. How are things with the other cartels."

"We are at peace," Galindo told him. "We defeated them, and then every time we took someone out, we brought the rest of their organizations into ours. There is no more war between the border cartels."

"And your supply?" Dajon asked.

"Same as before," Galindo told him.

"Reliable?" Dajon asked, lifting an eyebrow.

"Of course," Galindo said nodding.

"If Dante blows through Juarez and all of Chihuahua, it'll be the rest of your men, he's killing?" Dajon asked.

Galindo nodded. "Same thing with Princess."

Dajon nodded. "The only war going on right now, is the war between our organizations, and the remnants of the other border cartels?"

Galindo nodded.

"And you speak for them?"

"I'm here to make peace on behalf of *all* the border cartels," Galindo told him.

Dajon nodded. "Cut your price in half."

"Half?" Galindo shouted.

"Half of what we were paying before," Dajon told him. "Right now, what we are getting from Bolivia is half of what you were charging, and even better. At least give us the same pricing."

"Fuck!" Galindo shouted. "You're eating my lunch."

"You're paying for Nuni's mistake," Dajon told him.

"What fucking choice do I have?" Galindo asked. "I can't fucking refuse. "You have two thousand fucking men in my territory, along with another two thousand sitting across the border waiting to come in."

Dajon shook his head. "No, I said Dante brought in two thousand men this morning. We already *had* two thousand muthafuckas in Mexico. And I have four thousand waiting to come in. Nicanor is also waiting, not just Princess."

"What are you going to do with Mexico?" Galindo asked. "You can't just move down here! You can't just take it and hold it."

Dajon smiled. "We don't *want* Mexico, and we know we wouldn't be able to hold it. But by the time we finished, it would take a generation to rebuild the cocaine industry. And by then, the Fedrales might have the drug trade on lock. It would also serve as an example to the next muthafuckas. We're real big on sending messages."

Galindo exhaled. "Half the price."

Dajon opened his arms wide, and Galindo wrapped his arms around him and the two men embraced.

"Peace," Dajon told him.

"Peace," Galindo replied. "Now, can you tell your people to get the fuck outta my country!"

Dajon laughed. "Of course. We'd much rather send them to California. Also, we're taking all of Pennsylvania again. We need them in Jersey, and the Commission is going back into Las Vegas. And Princess needs men in Florida. Trust me, they'll be out of Mexico before you can blink. We need them in other places. Like I said, the Reigns family is on a mission, to wrap up all family business."

Galindo shook his head. "Must be nice."

Dajon nodded. "It is. Now, if you'll excuse me, I have to go and meet with those Yucatan muthafuckas and let them know how much we didn't appreciate being cut off."

"Please kill some of them for me!" Galindo said with a smile.

"First shipment?" Dajon asked.

"Truck or ship?" Galindo asked.

"Both," Dajon told him. "Both pipes are open for business."

"That was quick," Galindo said, shaking his head.

"They've been open," Dajon said. "Just waiting on you to get your shit together."

Galindo nodded. "You tell Dante that I'm sorry. That I never meant for this to happen, and that it shouldn't have ever been like this. You tell him that I swear on my Father's grave, that no harm was going to come to his daughter. I swear it."

"Galindo, my advice to you, is to stay away from Dante, for the rest of your life," Dajon told him. "Never let him see you again. You will never meet with him again. More importantly, don't ever cross the line like that again."

Chapter Twenty-Six

Cruise ships come into port, drop off their passengers, and then get ready to board passengers for the next cruise. During the time in between unloading the old passengers, and taking on the new ones, the ship is taking on fuel, the crews are taking on food, supplies, and water, while the technicians and crew are getting the ship cleaned, performing maintenance, and getting the rooms ready. It is also during the dead time, where people are able to move on and off the busy ship unnoticed. Thus, it was the perfect place to hold today's secret meeting.

The Commission was meeting in Galveston, Texas aboard the massive cruise ship, the Carnival Breeze. The Breeze was an enormous Dream Class Cruise Ship, which meant that it was basically a one-thousand-foot floating luxury hotel. And like all hotels, this one had a private dining area with a bar, which is where the meeting was being held.

The full Commission was present at today's meeting. The message was that urgent matters needed to be discussed in regards to cleaning up the Commission, and righting its membership. They were also going to discuss inter-Commission violence, as well as their supply issues. It was not going to be a good meeting.

Damian knew ahead of time what the meeting was going to be about. They were pissed about Malcom, they were nervous about supply, and they were probably going to go after Peaches' seat. He knew that it was definitely going to be an interesting meeting. And just as they had a surprise for him, he had one for them as well.

Damian strolled into the room, and the members inside stood and clapped and cheered.

"Congratulations!" Chacho shouted. "I knew that you were going to get her back safe!"

"Cheers to Damian!" Barry Groomes shouted.

Adolphus Brandt patted Damian on his back. Damian did something he hadn't done in a long time, he walked to the head of the table, and stood there, waiting for the person sitting there to move. New to the Commission, a nervous Bobby Blake moved and took a side seat at the table. The applause in the room slowly died down, and all the members took note of what Damian had just did.

"Thank you, gentlemen," Damian told them. "I can't even begin to tell you how much of a relief it is to have my niece back unharmed. It was truly a blessing."

Cesario Chavez made the sign of the cross and kissed the tip of his fingers. "A blessing."

Princess walked into the room, and the others were shocked. She walked to Jamie Forrest who was seated on the side of Damian. "Jamie, could you be a darling, and just scoot on around there. I want to sit next to my brother."

Jamie exhaled, rose, and took another seat.

"Princess, what a pleasant surprise." Raphael Guzman told her. "Not use to seeing both of you hear together. I was starting to think you were really one person. Like, Damian just wearing a wig or something."

Laughter went around the table.

"Aww, did you miss me, Boo?" Princess asked.

"Like a hole in my fucking heart!" Raphael said, clutching his chest.

"And you know how bad I would just love to put a great big ole hole in that tiny little heart of yours," Princess said with a smile.

Again, laughter went around the table.

"Glad you're back," Cesario told her. "And I'm glad you found your niece. So, does this mean the war is over?"

"Maybe," Damian told them.

"Maybe?" Steve Hawk asked. "What the fuck does that mean?"

"It means that the war between my family, and the border cartels is over," Damian explained. "The question is, is there going to be another war to take its place? If there is, then it needs to happen now, while I have a shit ton of soldiers with itchy trigger fingers and plenty or experience."

A chill went through the room.

"Hi, who are you?" Princess asked, turning toward Hassan.

"He's representing Michigan," Baby Doc snarled. "And my man right here, is representing Ohio."

"God, Baby Doc, you look terrible," Princess told him. "What, did you fall down or something?"

"Fuck you!" Baby Doc shouted. He rose. "I'll kill you right now, and not give a fuck what anybody else in here says."

Damian turned toward Baby Doc. "What you gonna do, is sit your ass down before I drown you in a fucking toilet. Don't you ever disrespect my sister again." He turned to the rest of the Commission members. "This is not what we discussed."

"Some disturbing information has come to our attention," Chacho told him. "The people you backed, don't even control one percent of their states. This is unacceptable."

"And these two, they control Ohio and Michigan?" Damian asked.

"It appears so," Cesario answered.

"And you know this how?" Damian asked.

"It appears that your little tart in Ohio, damn near got herself killed," Jamie Forrest told him. "She practically got run out of Ohio, she's on the run, she's done with."

"Really?" Damian asked, lifting an eyebrow.

"Yeah," Baby Doc said nodding.

"Well, I think she did pretty good for a new comer, seeing as how she had to fight off dudes in her territory, plus soldiers flown in from Alabama, plus soldiers sent by Don Biaggio," Damian told them.

Murmurs went around the room.

"Bullshit!" Baby Doc shouted. "That's a bullshit ass lie! Ain't nobody went after that bitch territory!"

"Don Biaggio confirmed it, right before I killed him," Princess told them.

"Fuck that shit!" Baby Doc shouted. "Ain't nobody worried about some delusional old man, and some deathbed confession shit!"

Cesario shook his head. "This is bullshit! You were warned, Baby Doc!"

"Going into another member's territory is an act of war!" Chacho told Baby Doc.

"Where the hell is she at, anyway?" Vern McMillan asked. "She's never here."

"She hasn't been to the last two meetings," Rick Shorts said.

"She was recovering from wounds she received when Malcom's men kicked in her door," Princess told them.

"And you've spoken to her?" Chacho asked. "Is she ready for this? I mean, *really* ready? Doesn't sound like she's in control of anything."

"She never had time to consolidate her state," Damian told them.

"Why do you care so much about her?" Steve Hawk asked. "And where's that other fella, the one from Michigan? Why isn't he here? Did you kill him too, Malcom?"

"You seem to have a lot of questions, why don't you ask her directly?" Princess told them.

"She's here?" MiAsia asked, lifting an eyebrow.

Princess nodded at one of her men standing in the door way, and he disappeared. Seconds later, Peaches walked in to the room.

"Hello everyone," Peaches told them. No one responded. "Baby Doc tried to kill me. I didn't know it at the time, but he conspired with my friend Kharee over there, to wipe out my entire organization. And they pretty much did. I lost a lot of good men that night. And good women. Friends, and they were people with families. I thought I had lost my brother, and two women who were like sisters to me. They took so much away from me that night, they took so much away from so many people."

"This ain't the girl scouts, Sweetie," Bobby Blake told her.

"I know what the fuck this is," Peaches told him. "But what I didn't know, was what I had. I thought I had built an organization, and I thought my system was perfect, and I was moving cocaine all over Ohio. It was after I was lying in bed recovering, that I realized what I had done wrong. I was saved by Darius Reigns, and he took me to Maryland, and then to Texas where

I recovered. It was in Texas where I learned where I went wrong. I saw the Reigns family first hand. The brothers and sisters, the cousins, everybody. They were a *family*. I took over my boyfriend's *organization,* and I kept it an *organization,* and that was my mistake. I should have been building *a family*."

"Thanks for the history lesson, but nobody gives a fuck!" Baby Doc shouted.

"Malcom, if you ever send men into my state again, I will kill you," Peaches told him.

Baby Doc laughed at her. "With what, your looks?"

"Ohio belongs to me!" Peaches told them. "It's where I'm from, it's where I grew up, it's where my *family* lives. I was in it for the money at first, and that was my mistake. I'm awake now. You fucking animals have woke me up. I'm no longer in it for the bread, now I'm in it, because I have to protect my family. I have to take care of the people that I love. I will do anything, to make sure that they're safe. If I have to pile bodies up from here, to Alabama, and all the way up to Dayton, I will. Nobody is going to take Ohio from me, because I need it, to protect my family.

Peaches walked to where Kharee was sitting. DeAndre Michaels walked into the room, peering around like a timid cat, observing from the door.

"Get the fuck outta my chair, Kharee," Peaches told him.

Baby Doc rolled his eyes and Kharee and shook his head.

"If you're not outta my seat by the time I count to three, you're a dead man," Peaches told him. "Omar and my soldiers are sitting outside of a house in Ohio. Trap, along with more of my men, is sitting outside of another. And inside of all these houses, is someone you love. Get the fuck up!"

Kharee pushed back from the table and rose. He eyeballed Peaches with a hatred the made his face glow red with fury. Peaches seated herself at the table. Deandre walked up behind Hassan.

"If you don't get your five-dollar ass away from me, I swear I'm going to embarrass you!" Hassan told DeAndre.

DeAndre lowered his head and nervously brushed his waves. "You need to get up."

"You heard the man!" Peaches told Hassan. "Get the fuck outta his seat!"

"I ain't going nowhere!" Hassan declared. "I own Detroit! I owned Michigan! That's my shit, and I've *earned* this spot."

"You need to be on a plane right now, and you need to be worrying about where Chi-Chi and Vendetta is," Peaches told him.

"What the fuck is that supposed to mean?" Hassan asked.

"We don't just sit outside of houses in Ohio, muthafucka!" Peaches told him. "Catch that flight, and make sure your family is straight."

"You sure you want to go there?" Hassan asked. "You know what it is?"

319

"You don't have much time," Peaches whispered. "You can save them, if you leave now."

Hassan pushed his chair back and stood up. He stormed out of the room.

"There you go, Baby Girl!" Princess told her. "You have to fight for your seat at the table! No one is going to give you anything. As a matter of fact, they think that since you're a woman, they can bulldoze. You have to show them, that nothing is more fierce than a woman protecting her family."

Peaches nodded.

"The war with the border cartels is over," Damian told them. "I ordered the hit on Malcom, in response to the hit he did on Peaches. The shipments from Mexico are starting immediately. All of you who doubted me, fuck you! A bunch of you snake muthafuckers made secret deals with the Columbians. Cut the deals. Ain't no Columbian cocaine coming into any ports that I control. Get that shit out of your mind. And another thing, nobody better not go after Peaches or DeAndre. If they lose their wars with motherfuckers in their states, so be it. But none of you better intervene. Malcom, I'm tired of you trying me. Do it again, and Alabama is going to be full of niggaz with Texas accents."

"Are you going to put your thumb on the scale in Ohio?" Cesario asked.

"No, why?" Damian asked.

"Cause I want to set up a dead pool!" Cesario said, laughing. "Without your support, she won't last two months. No offense, *chica!*"

"None taken," Peaches said shrugging. "Just make sure you let me in on that action, because this bitch right here, ain't going nowhere."

Cesario nodded. "That's the attitude."

"Oh, one last thing," Damian told them. "You're all invited to the wedding."

"Wedding?" Princess asked. "What wedding. Emil and I haven't set another date yet?"

"Not your wedding," Damian said, holding out his hand. "Our wedding."

MiAsia clasped Damian's hand.

"What the fuck?" Princess asked.

"Fuck no!" Chacho shouted. "This Commission ain't a fucking family affair! Is she going to give up Missouri?"

"Try to take it," MiAsia told him.

"If she wants to," Damian told them. "If she doesn't want to, then she doesn't have to. That means, Missouri is protected by the Reigns family. Anybody fuck with my wife, I will chop you up, feed you to the fish in my fish tank. The war is over, it's time for peace and good, quiet business again. Let's celebrate a wedding, and be happy."

James Speech rose, and lifted his glass. "To Damian and MiAsia, may God bless your union."

The others around the table rose and lifted their glasses. "To Damian and MiAsia!"

After the meeting had broken up, Princess walked to where Peaches was siting, and leaned against the table.

"Bold move," Princess told her.

"Thank you," Peaches said.

"When you pull a move like that, you have to be prepared to back it up," Princess explained. "What would you have done, if either one of them had called your bluff?"

Peaches shrugged.

"That's what I thought," Princess said, exhaling. She folded her arms. "This is a dog eat dog business. These men in here, they'll eat you alive. You can never show emotion or anger. When you show anger, they know you've lost control. Anger shows weakness, it shows desperation, it tells them that you're not in control. Understand?"

"Yes, ma'am," Peaches said, swallowing hard.

"I see a lot of me in you," Princess said with a smile. "You know it wasn't Damian that picked you for this, it was me."

Peaches peered up at Princess. "Why?"

"Because I believed in you," Princess told her. "Because I knew your story. Your boyfriend went to prison and left you with nothing but legal bills. You took over his organization, you took over his connection, and you didn't miss a got damned beat. You got yourself out of debt, and despite all the threats and deals that the Feds threw at you, you kept your mouth closed, stayed strong, and didn't snitch. I admired that."

"Thank you," Peaches told her. She was almost giddy at what Princess was telling her.

"I wanted you to take over all of Ohio," Princes continued. "I figured, if you could bring those niggas in Columbus, Cincinnati, Dayton, and Youngstown under control, then you could damn sure run Florida for me."

"Run Florida?" Princess asked. Her eyes went wide with confusion.

"I wanted to see if you could put together an organization and run it, and if you could, I was going to have you give up Ohio, go to Florida, and run that state for me. It would have been a promotion, trust me. More money, more power, beautiful weather, you would have loved it. But, I don't need you to do that anymore. So now, Ohio is all yours. You control it, you run it. Let me give you a tiny piece of advice," Princess said, leaning in. "Dressing the part, is a big part of being the boss. This is the big league, you're not running a crew or a posse, you're trying to control all of the cocaine coming into an entire state. You have to look like you're the boss. No more Michael Kors, we carry Hermes. Go to Gucci, Louis, Christian Lacroix, and get you a wardrobe. Giuseppe, Louboutins, Manolo's, those are all good shoes to start with. Get you a couple of armored G Wagons, an armored Rolls Royce Phantom, some armored Navigators for your bodyguards, and a small private jet. It's time to step it up. When they see you *looking* like a boss, dressing like a boss, and carrying yourself like a boss, then the people in Ohio will start *treating* you like a boss. You make them bow down. And no more shouting and displays of anger. Never let 'em see you sweat."

Peaches smiled. "Thank you."

Princess rose from the table. "No problem. If you need anything, any advice, or just want to talk, call me."

Peaches nodded. "I will. Thank you."

"Consider me a big sister," Princess told her. "Not a big sister in law, but a big sister."

"Huh?"

"I was born *at* night, but not *last* night," Princess told her. "Right now, you are in a very precarious situation, Sweetie, make no doubt about it. Everyone will be gunning for you, as you try to establish your control over Ohio. You are about to go through some bloody times, as you move across Ohio into different turfs and different cities. People aren't just going to roll over for you. Like I said earlier, you're going to have to *take* what you want. That makes Ohio a very dangerous place for my brother. I like you, Peaches, but I *love* my brother, and I don't want to see him hurt. If he were to get caught up in some bullshit in Ohio, or get shot or killed because someone is gunning for you, I would not be happy. I would have to come to Ohio, and I would have to do things, horrible things, terrible things. This business we've chosen, is a fucked up one, and can be an extremely lonely one. Sometimes we have to push away the people we love, in order to keep them safe. We sacrifice our happiness for their safety. That's the price we pay, for the life we've chosen. When you get back to Ohio, break up with my brother. Send him home where he'll be safe. And maybe, just maybe, one day when Ohio is safe, you two can be together. But that day, is not today, nor is it anytime soon. Send my baby brother home. Understand?"

Peaches nodded.

Princess walked out of the room, leaving her sitting alone at the conference table.

Chapter
Twenty-Seven

Darius dropped the top on his rented Camaro and then fired up his blunt. He was running late to catch his flight back to Texas. He needed to drop off his rental car, get his clothes through baggage check, and then board his flight. John Glenn International Airport wasn't exactly known to be a model of efficiency.

Darius puffed on the blunt hanging off his lips and blew thick rings of smoke into the air. He had planned to stay in Ohio and wait for Peaches to get back from the meeting with The Commission, but then got the text informing him that his family was having a huge get together at the ranch to celebrate Lucky's safe return. It was his chance to see all his aunts and uncles and cousins and other family members that he hadn't seen in years. There would be barbecue, Dominoes, Spades, potato salad, pecan pie, and plenty of aunts and uncles talking trash. He wasn't going to miss this family gathering for nothing in the world.

Darius thumped the ashes from his blunt over the door sill and took another long puff. He wished that he would have left with DeFranz, who used the family's Net Jets account and chartered the last available private jet out of Columbus. Brandon had taken one of the family's own private jets and headed to California two days prior, leaving him having to catch a last minute commercial flight to Texas. And he hated flying commercial. You couldn't blow Cush on a commercial flight.

Darius wheeled the Camaro around the corner and picked up his pace. He hoped that the airline was running behind and that boarding would be late. His mind was so focused on ways to clear security that he was slow to notice the White Chrysler 300C that had pulled up alongside of him. When he finally did peer in its direction, he was taken back by the fact that all the occupants were wearing clown masks. Once it hit him, it was too late. The two passengers on his side came out of the window with a pair of old school Tech - 9 pistols and opened fire.

The first bullets ripped through Darius' side, his arm, and right upper chest. He took another to the neck as he swerved, while trying to maintain control of the Camaro. It was his swerving that turned the potential head shot to a neck shot, thus saving his life. The bullets kept coming, penetrating the doors, the windshield, and the hood of the Camaro, turning the car into a bullet riddled homage to Grand Theft Auto. The final bullet struck Darius on the other side of his chest, finally causing him to lose complete control of the car and veer off the road. Darius barreled over the side walk, through a parking lot, and into a Skyline

Chili Restaurant. He slumped forward, laying on the horn, while black smoke poured from the car's engine.

Chesarae pulled off his mask, and peered out of the window back at the crash. A broad smile went across his face, as he knew he had just done some good shooting. He sat back in the seat of the 300 and pulled out his cellphone and dialed up a number.

"Hello?"

"Hey, girl, where fuck have y'all been?" Chesarae asked.

"Who the fuck is this?"

"It's Chesarae."

"What do you want?" Analiza asked. "Why are you calling me?"

"You're the only muthafucka I can get in touch with," Chesarae told her.

"What do you mean?"

"I can't reach Baby Doc, I can't reach Don B, I can't get in touch with nobody," Chesarae told her. "Y'all better not be trying to fuck over me!"

"What the fuck are you talking about?" Analiza asked, growing impatient.

"I did the job, now it's time to pay up."

"Job?" Analiza asked. "What job?"

"Don't fucking play with me, bitch!" Chesarae shouted. "You know what fucking job I'm talking about! The Reigns muthafucka, he's done! Now, I want my fucking dope! You and Baby Doc promised me enough yea-yo to supply Columbus, and take my shit back. I want what we agreed upon!"

"You didn't!" Analiza shouted. "No! No! No! Are you kidding me! You, dumb stupid fuck! You killed a Reigns? Do you know what you've done? Do you know what you've fucking done!"

"What the fuck you mean?" Chesarae shouted. "You wanted it done!"

"You, stupid fuck!" Analiza shouted. "You can't get in touch with Baby Doc, because the Reigns family put his ass in the hospital! You can't get in touch with Biaggio, because they fucking killed him!"

"What?"

"Do you know what you've done?" Analiza shouted. "You've killed us! You've signed our fucking death warrant!"

"I want my dope!" Chesarae shouted.

"Don't you get it fool!" Analiza shouted. "There is no dope! It's over with! They took Baby Doc's dope! His entire shipment is gone! And now he has the Columbians on his ass wanting their money! He has the Sicilians on his ass wanting their money! He has no dope to give you!"

"Bullshit!"

"Lose my fucking number!" Analiza told him. "Forget you ever talked to me! Forget you even know me! Change your name, get a new identity, get the fuck out of Ohio, and run. If there are any witnesses, anyone who knows what you've done, kill them. Cover your trace, and disappear. That's my advice to you."

"You got me fucked up!" Chesarae shouted. "I ain't going..."

The line went dead before he could finish his sentence.

Analiza paced the floor of her Miami mansion, nervously contemplating her next move. She knew what she had to do, and she had to do it fast. She had to get a hit team together, men who were loyal only to her, and she had to get them to Ohio. She had to hunt down Chesarae, kill him, and erase all traces that they ever knew one another. It was a race against time. If the Reigns family ever got wind of it, even if it was all set up before her deal with Princess, she was a dead woman. She lifted her cellphone to call up her men. They needed to be on a private jet to Columbus, before nightfall.

*****

Texas

Desire walked to her penthouse door and opened it. She found Dante standing in the hallway, with two bodyguards.

"May I come in?" Dante asked.

"Why?" Desire asked.

"We need to talk," Dante told her.

Desire shook her head. "I don't think there is anything left for us to say to one another right now."

"Are you going to make me do this in the hallway?" Dante asked.

Desire looked at the two men with Dante. "Who are they?"

"They're my bodyguards," Dante explained.

"Bodyguards?" Desire asked, lifting an eyebrow.

"Bodyguards, hitmen, soldiers, Sicarios, whatever you want to call them," Dante told her.

The fact that he didn't smile to indicate that he was joking, told Desire that the situation was serious. She opened her door wide and stepped aside for Dante to enter. Dante walked inside.

"Are they coming in as well?" Desire asked.

"No, they are going to guard the door," Dante told her.

Desire closed her penthouse door, and turned to Dante. "What is this about?"

"It's about you, it's about me, it's about us," Dante told her.

"You needed to bring bodyguards slash hitmen to my home?" Desire asked.

"They are always with me," Dante told her. "Everywhere I go."

"Bullshit!" Desire told him. "Dante, what the fuck is going on?"

"Desire, they are *always* with me," Dante told her. "I had it arranged so that you wouldn't notice, but no matter where I go, I'm heavily guarded. And this might seem disturbing to you, but so are you."

"Me?" Desire asked, pressing her hand to her chest.

"Ever since I became serious about you, yes," Dante said nodding. "This building has been guarded, everywhere you go, you're being watched over. It's not to spy on you, but to keep you safe."

"To keep me *safe*?" Desire shouted. "Are you fucking serious? You tell me that my every move has been scrutinized, and that it's all been for my own good? I don't know if you know this, but I managed to take pretty good care of myself for a long time before we met."

"You weren't in any danger, until you became my woman," Dante told her.

"Why would me becoming your woman, put me in danger?" Desire asked. "What am I missing here, Dante?"

"I never thought that I would find someone who I loved as much as I loved Angela. Angela was the love of my life, and when she died, I thought that there would never be another woman who could capture my heart like she had. I was wrong."

"I'm not Angela, Dante," Desire said, shaking her head. "I can never be. You understand that, right?"

"Of course," Dante nodded. "Angela was Angela, and I loved her because of who she was. And now, I love you because of who you are. I have bodyguards,

332

because I am a part of the largest, most violent crime family in American history. I have killed men. Not dozens, not hundreds, but even more than that. My family controls the drug trade in Texas, California, and Florida. My cousin controls Maryland, another cousin controls Virginia, my sister in law controls Louisiana, my future brother in law controls Georgia, and we also control New Jersey, and Philadelphia, and soon all of Pennsylvania again. Because we control the ports in California, Texas, Florida, New Jersey, Virginia, Maryland, Louisiana, Georgia, and through our friend Julian, Mississippi, we pretty much control the majority of the entrance points into the United States. We decided a long time ago that we didn't have to control the entire country, as long as we controlled the distribution and the entrance points, we pretty much controlled the trade. We have made billions importing cocaine into this country. We have killed politicians, policemen, judges, and everyone in between, to secure and maintain our hold."

"Dante, why are you telling me this?" Desire asked. "I'm a reporter!"

"I know," Dante told her. "And I love you. I lost your trust, so I've giving you mine. I'm placing my life, and the lives of my family, in your hands."

"Is there really a such thing as a Distribution Commission, or is that a myth?" Desire asked.

"It is very real," Dante told her.

"And you are a member of this... thing?"

"We are the most powerful family on The Commission."

Desire had to sit down. It was too much for her to take in. She sat down on the sofa and rested her head in her palms.

"Dante why did you tell me this?" Desire said, sobbing. "What do you want from me? What am I supposed to do?"

"Forgive me," Dante said softly. "Love me. Let me love you. I made a mistake. A mistake that I'll never make again. I am a man. I'm man enough to love one woman. Let me show you?"

Dante reached into his suit pocket and pulled out a black felt box from Americus Diamond.

"This where all of my family's rings come from," Dante told her.

Desire spied the box, leaned her head back and wiped away her tears. She held out her hand, and Dante placed the box in her palm. Desire opened the box. The ring was a flawless 6.02 carat colorless round diamond, set atop of platinum band that was filled with large diamonds. It made her gasp and cover her mouth.

Dante took the ring from the box, dropped down to one knee, and took her hand into his.

"Desire, will you..."

"Yes!" Desire said nodding. "Yes! Yes!"

She wrapped her arms around him, and fell into his arms. The two of them found themselves on the floor of her penthouse laughing. Desire kissed Dante's face repeatedly, while lifting her diamond ring into the light and examining it. The rock was big enough to choke a horse, she thought.

"You better..."

"I will," Dante told her.

"What was I going to say?" Desire asked.

"Love you for life," Dante told her. "I will. I will love you for life. I'm ready to take that extended trip that we talked about."

"Around the world?" Desire asked.

"Wherever you want to go," Dante told her.

"We have to plan a wedding," Desire said excitedly. "I have to call my Mom!"

Desire leapt up from the floor and raced to find her cellphone.

"My family is having a get together at the ranch today," Dante told her. "I want you to meet everybody. And we have to break the news to Lucky."

"I love her," Desire sighed. "How do you think she's going to take the news?"

"She loves you," Dante told her. "She's going to be happy."

"I want her to be," Desire said nodding.

"I do have to warn you about my aunts though," Dante smiled. "Be prepared to get questioned down. My aunts are going to dig and dig and dig. Please tell me you can cook."

Desire nodded. "I can cook."

"All my aunts are... well, let's just say that they are all women of a certain class and social standing," Dante told her.

"Dante Reigns!" Desire said, punching his arm. "Are you trying to say I'm ghetto."

"Hell no!" Dante said laughing. "I'm just trying to warn you. They are all very educated, and very accomplished. Except for my Aunt Assata. Assata is educated as fuck, has two Ph.D's, but is as down to Earth as four flat tires. And Assata don't give a fuck, she be reading their asses. Assata is my Momma's sister. Just warning you. My family is wild and crazy, and my uncles are going to be loud and talking shit on the Domino table and about who can barbecue the best. My aunts are going to be talking about people, talking about each other, telling stories about their childhood, and talking shit to each other while playing Spades and Rummy. And then there is the infamous Reigns family football game. If they invite you to play, don't talk about your hair or clothes, or any of that, just play. If you don't, my aunts will never let you live it down. They say you thought you were too good to play football."

Desire leaned forward and kissed Dante. "Quit worrying, I got this. I know how to handle aunts."

"Oh really?" Dante asked, lifting any eyebrow. "How many aunts have you handled before? You been engaged and done met somebody's family before?"

Desire laughed. "Maybe."

"Aw, hell naw!" Dante said sitting up. He pulled her close. "I love you Mrs. Reigns."

"I love you too, Mr. Reigns," Desire said, kissing. She lifted her phone, and dialed up a number. "Hey, Momma! I got some news for you! Guess who's getting married!"

Chapter
Twenty-eight

Peaches paced back and forth in the parlor of her mansion.

"Relax, Peach," Omar told her. "Relax. It's going to be okay."

"Sit down next to me," Vendetta said, patting the sofa cushion next to where she was sitting.

"I can't fucking sit down!" Peaches snapped. "I need to know what happened! I need to find out something, anything! Somebody has to have some information. How the fuck could this happen? Where the fuck were his bodyguards? And what the fuck was he doing over there! He was supposed to stay here and wait until I got back, that was the plan!"

"You think it was Hassan?" Trap asked. "Kharee?"

"Ches?" Chi-Chi asked.

Peaches waved her hand. "Speculation won't do us any good. I need to have facts."

"I got my ears in the street," Omar told her. "Relax, we'll find out soon enough."

"Relax?" Peaches said, lifting an eyebrow. "Do you know what the Reigns family is going to do to me? To *us*? I need to see him. I need to talk to him!"

Peaches tried to go for the door again, but Omar stepped in the way.

"You being on the streets right now, ain't gonna happen," Omar told her. "Especially not knowing what's going on."

"He's right, Peach," Vendetta told her. "You can't be on the streets right now. Not knowing what the play is."

"Besides, my peeps at the hospital say he's still in surgery," Omar told her.

"How is it looking?" Peaches asked nervously.

Omar shook his head. "Not good. He caught eight rounds, including one to the neck, two to the chest, and a couple in his side."

Peaches broke into tears once again. Trap grabbed her, walked her to the couch, and sat her down.

"I need to be at the hospital," she told them. "He shouldn't be there by himself. He shouldn't die in that place alone, with no family, no one knowing who he is. I need to be there."

"There's nothing you can do right now," Trap told her.

"We need to get in touch with his family," Peaches told them. "They need to know. That's not right, they need to know."

"You think that's the right play?" Trap asked.

"I remember thinking about Joaquin after my door got kicked in," Peaches told them. "I would cry thinking that my brother died in some alley alone. It ain't right, V."

Vendetta nodded. "I can call DeMarion."

Peaches nodded.

*****

Reigns Family Ranch

The ranch was packed with Reigns family members. The pool was full of children playing and splashing, picnic tables were full of food, while family members spread throughout the property caught up with one another's lives. Damian walked to where Dante had gathered with several others.

Damian hugged Dante.

"Have you heard the news?" Princess asked.

"What news is that?" Damian asked.

"Say hello to your future sister-in-law," Princess told him, nodding toward Desire.

"Get the fuck out of here!" Damian said laughing.

Dante shook his head. "Serious, bro."

"Congratulations!" Damian said, hugging his brother again. He then embraced Desire. "Welcome to the family."

"I guess I'm the only one who knows about your little surprise too, Damian," Princess said with a smile.

"And what surprise would that be?" Dante asked.

"I'm getting married," Damian laughed.

Dante was taken aback. He shifted his gaze to MiAsia. "Serious?"

Damian nodded.

"Well hell, congratulations to you too!" Dante said, hugging Damian, and then MiAsia. "I can't believe this shit. How? How in the hell, did you get this dude to want to tie the knot?"

"I'll have to tell you when they are no children around," Damian said with a smile.

"Awww shit!" Princess said. "She put that fire in his life. I always knew it. I said once you found somebody who put it on your ass one good time, you was gonna fold and through in your cards."

"Shut up!" Damian said, side eyeing his sister, and causing everyone to laugh.

DeMarion answered his phone, and walked away from the group.

"What?" DeMarion asked. "Tell me you're fucking kidding! Tell me you're fucking kidding! I'm on my way!"

*****

DeFranz lifted his iPhone to his ear. "Hello?"

"Get to Columbus!" DeMarion told him. "Darius' been shot."

"What?"

"You heard me!" DeMarion shouted. "I'm, on my way to the airport right now."

"What the fuck happened?" DeFranz shouted.

"I don't know!" DeMarion said. "I'll find out when I get there! In the meantime, get some soldiers, and get to Columbus. I haven't told anyone but you."

"Why the fuck not!" DeFranz shouted. "You keeping this from Damian? Are you fucking crazy? He finds out his brother was killed, and you kept it from him because you wanted to protect some Ohio pussy, he's going to kill you himself."

"I'm not protecting no fucking pussy!" DeMarion shouted. "I'm a Reigns, through and through, and nobody comes before my family, so you can go fuck yourself! Besides, he ain't dead, he's still in surgery! Look, how fast can you get to the hospital?"

"I'm still over Ohio," DeFranz told him. Hold on. DeFranz rose from his seat and walked to the cabin and opened the door. "We need to go back to Columbus, right now."

"I can't just turn around, I have to file for a new flight plan," the pilot told him.

"Ten thousand bucks, you get my back to Columbus in the next thirty minutes," DeFranz told him.

"Go buckle your seatbelt," the pilot said, nodding toward the back of the cabin.

DeFranz headed back to his seat.

"I'll be on the ground in less the thirty," he told DeMarion. "Should I at least call Brandon?"

"I'll get some soldiers from Philly to meet you at the hospital," DeMarion told him. "How many men you have with you?"

"Thirteen," DeFranz told him. "Don't worry, I'll be good. Hey, did that bitch have something to do with this?"

"I don't know," DeMarion told him. "They are acting like they don't know who, what, or why. But I trust no one at this point. Be on your p's and q's cousin."

"Always," DeFranz told him. "See you when you get here."

"Out."

DeFranz disconnected the call, and peered out the window. He felt like he should have killed that bitch the moment he met her. It was a good thing that he left men in Ohio to help guard her mansion, and to secretly be there in case he ever needed them. That would give him another twenty soldiers, in addition to the ones on the plane with him. That would be enough to do what he need to do if he caught them by surprise. He knew one thing was certain no matter what, and that his family was about to go to war in Ohio. Whether it was against Peaches or someone else it didn't matter, they were definitely going to war.

*****

Wexner Medical Center, Columbus, Ohio

Darius laid in intensive care with tubes and wires all over his body. He was on a ventilator to help him breath, and his body had bandages from his neck down to his knees. He had been shot everywhere.

Peaches sat in a chair next to Darius, clasping his hand, and listening to the steady beep on the heart monitor. Every once in a while, she would rub his hand to warm it, and then rest one of her hands on his chest to feel his breaths. She needed him to breath on his own. She thought if he could win that battle, and get off the breathing machine, then slowly, but surely, he could win each battle one at a time. The doctors told her that the bullets had narrowly missed his heart, but had been close enough to cause stress and swelling in his chest. The bullet in his neck did nick his vertebrae, so there was the potential that his days of walking, or doing anything below the neck for that matter, could be over with. A bullet penetrated his lung, setting up the potential for infection and pneumonia, while another struck his kidney and liver. The bullet that went through his thigh shattered the bone, but walking was something he wasn't going to be doing anytime soon anyway. The bullet that entered his upper arm shatter his collar bone, and exited through his back. He was touch and go.

Peaches kissed Darius' hands, and then suddenly felt a chill run through her body. She felt a present amongst her, and it wasn't spiritual, it was dark. Without turning she could sense that she and Darius were no longer alone.

"Are you a praying woman?"

"Not particularly," Peaches said. "Why?"

"Because the doctors said that my cousin's condition is precarious," DeFranz told her. "That means, your position is precarious. They said that these first hours, are the most critical, and if he makes it through the night, his chances will slowly improve."

"That's good news," Peaches said.

"Pray, Little Peach, that my cousin survives," DeFranz told her. "Because when I finally leave this room, one of two things will happen. I'll either be leaving two live people in the room, or two dead ones. If he dies... If my cousin dies... Then so do you..."

345

CPSIA information can be obtained
at www.ICGtesting.com
Printed in the USA
BVHW071308180719
553799BV00001B/33/P